Famous Texas Folklorists and Their Stories

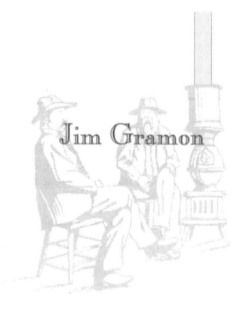

Jim Gramon

REPUBLIC OF TEXAS PRESS

Dallas • Lanham • Boulder • New York • Toronto • Plymouth, UK

Published by Republic of Texas Press
An imprint of The Rowman & Littlefield Publishing Group, Inc.
4501 Forbes Boulevard, Suite 200
Lanham, MD 20706
http://www.rlpgtrade.com

10 Thornbury Road, Plymouth PL6 7PP, United Kingdom

Distributed by NATIONAL BOOK NETWORK

Library of Congress Cataloging-in-Publication Data available

Gramon, Jim.
    Famous Texas folklorists and their stories / Jim Gramon.
        p.   cm.
    Includes index.
    ISBN 13: 978-1-55622-825-2 (pbk.)

    1.Folklore—Texas. 2. Storytellers—Texas.
    3. Tales—Texas. I. Title.
GR110.T5 G7   2000   00-062526
398'.097643—dc21   CIP

⊖™ The paper used in this publication meets the minimum requirements of American National Standard for Information Sciences—Permanence of Paper for Printed Library Materials, ANSI/NISO Z39.48-1992.

Manufactured in the United States of America.

Dedication

To my wonderful family and friends,
I have been blessed.

They all encouraged me to tell the stories,
theirs and mine.

I imagine that the campfire was the world's first theatre. Cavemen hunkering around the warming coals, on which the day's kill is roasting, telling the adventure of the day's and other days' hunts. Jim Gramon has had a good hunt, and now you can sit and enjoy the results. I am more of a folk listener than a folklorist. I am a sound bite compared to those with whom I keep company in Jim's book.

I've sat at the feet of the great Texas triumvirate, Dobie, Webb, and Bedichek. And when joined by Dobie's protege John Henry Faulk as well as Joe Franz, Joe Small, and Mody Boatright, the stories flowed like... well, like Jack Daniels. Folklore run amuck. Dobie's ranch was probably the greatest theatre I've ever visited.

Thank you, Jim Gramon, for putting me in such good company... and for passing the stories on.

Cactus Pryor, author and humorist.

Contents

Contents

Acknowledgments

This book, more than most, would not have been possible without the help of many folks.

Thanks to my entire family who, collectively and individually, told me, "Quit talking about it and write the damn book!"

My mother, Evelyn Gramon, and her family (the Alexander, Bruce, Callan, and Smalley families). They introduced me to the tradition of oral storytelling and oral family histories. Mom, your ideas, encouragement, and help were invaluable.

My father, Jimmy Gramon, who always encouraged me to follow my heart, but to work hard at it. Dad, I wish I could have shared more of these stories with you, to hear your laugh one more time.

My wonderful wife, Sally. (After twenty years I still refer to her as my bride.) You have always been there to encourage me, no matter how incredibly bad the stories got. (Her nose was always my truth detector; it always wrinkles if she doesn't like something, despite the fact that she's telling me, "That's very interesting, Honey.") Thanx Babe.

My son, James, who is a talented artist and writer himself. He contributed several drawings to this book. He has endured the tribulations of having a father who is both a storyteller and a writer! Most teens find their parents mildly embarrassing, you can imagine his anguish. Thanx Bo.

Nicole and Kevin Roark, a wonderful couple (my daughter and son-in-law). Thanks for all of your many helpful suggestions and encouragement.

My uncle and aunt, James and Mamie Callan, who taught me about farming, ranching, living life close to the land, and how to say a lot with very few words.

My subjects (my doesn't that sound royal!), the folks that are the subjects of portions of this book; Liz Carpenter, Allen Damron, Cactus Pryor, and Kinky Friedman. They are all wonderful, generous people. When I called them about this project, they were there for me.

Catherine Gunn, my father's sister, who was at one point book reviewer for the *Fort Worth Star-Telegram*. One day, when I was about ten, I marveled at her small garage filled with books. She told me everyone has a book in them, it just takes work to make it happen. I wonder how she would have reviewed this one.

Dudley Dobie, for taking the time to tell me where to go (let me rephrase that), to point me in the right directions.

Mark Mitchell, author of *The Mustang Professor*, a wonderful book about J. Frank Dobie. Thanks for your insights about Mr. Dobie.

Al Lowman, former president of the Texas Folklore Society, for the use of his incredible library and encyclopedic knowledge of Texas history, folklore, and storytelling.

Caroline Dowell, who gave me the run of her beautiful ranch (actually more like a gigantic petting zoo) outside of Manchaca, Texas. Several of the pictures included here were taken on her ranch. We had to shoot the photos quickly, before the cows came over to join in the fun.

Tim Henderson, songwriter extraordinaire (over 200 of his songs have been recorded), for his counsel, beautiful music, and the use some of his lyrics.

Jimmy Bird at Austin Taxidermist. Jimmy graciously allowed me to shoot some pictures of his mounts for this book.

David and Joella Torres, owners of Texas Hatters, located on I-35 in Buda. David makes my hats and helped me get the answers to all my questions about hat making, then and now.

"Rob" Robinson and the "Gang" at the Hill Country Humidor, located on the square in scenic downtown San Marcos. Their thoughtful comments and thoughtless gestures were a never-ending source of inspiration, and concern. Rob has been the source of many of the cigars that have carried both Kinky and myself through to the completion of several projects, including both of our most recent books.

Clarence Vogel and the "Gang" at the Manchaca Firehall in scenic downtown Manchaca, Texas. They always were there to swap stories with and offer special suggestions. Thanx, guys. (One or two were actually constructive.)

Alfonse "Fonzie" Martinez, his lovely wife Hope, and the "Gang" at Fonzie'z, in scenic downtown Kyle, Texas. Many pages of this book and several of my songs were written while sitting in their booths or at the liar's table. The Gang also provided many good stories and helpful ideas.

Jim Bob McMillan, Sally Baker, and the "Gang" at the Austin Writers League; without their encouragement and advice, this book would have been nothing more than a nagging desire to jot notes down on the back of envelopes and paper towels.

The Gang of storytellers that I meet with on a regular basis. John "Guido" Bohac (my son's godfather), James "Little Guido" Gramon (my son), Rick "The Kid" Pille, Calvin "Cajones" Jones, Jim "The Hat" Bartlett, Ron "Polish" Joseph, Heath "New Mexico Slim" Newburn, John "Wes" Reedy, Jerry "Jersey" Heaney, and Jerry "Two Pair" Gamble. True friends. The stories were great and the company was even better. Thanx guys.

Ginnie Siena Bivona, author and my editor. Without her support and encouragement this manuscript would probably be in a landfill somewhere, near my body.

Bill Erhart, outstanding artist and friend. Get well soon, buddy.

Introduction

I don't like book introductions!

They are normally boring and pretty much a waste of ink and time. I buy a book to read the stories, not to read a boring monologue on something about as exciting as the sex life of an elm tree (my apologies to the rabid arborists out there, both of you).

But, since it's expected of me, here is my token introduction:

Welcome to the humorous world of Texas folklore. This book is chock full of great stories by and about many of the legendary Texas folklorists. Unlike other books on this topic, most of these folks aren't horizontal and pushin' up daisies. Nope, most of these folks are still vertical (except sometimes on Saturday nights).

I am quite fortunate that all of the vertical folk and two of the horizontal ones have been my friends. By the end of this book you will get to know a bit about them and see examples of their work. These legends include:

J. Frank "Pancho" Dobie
John Henry Faulk
Ben King "Doc" Green
Dr. J. Mason Brewer
Mody Boatright
Liz Carpenter
Cactus Pryor
Kinky Friedman
Allen Wayne Damron

This book also includes:
  Webliography (the world's first)
  Bibliography
  Travel Guide and Calendar of Festivals and Events
  How to Learn to Tell Your Own stories
  Where to Find Local Storytellers
  Index (every book should have one, even novels!)

You will be stepping into a time machine of sorts that will be making stops all over the last 150 years. Stories will take you from the Battle of the Alamo to folklore festivals and storytelling events that are going on today.

Having said all of that, I must admit that there is no way one book, or a shelf of books, can begin to cover this topic. I've already started a second book to cover other legends that I couldn't fit into this book.

Texas folklore is as vast and broad as the state. There are hundreds of years of history and thousands of talented individuals who have made contributions. My hope is that my efforts will introduce you to that world and give you the tools to learn more about it.

Texas is a state of mind,
not an accident of birth.
From the snows of Amarillo,
to the sunny Gulf Coast earth,
from the gators, pines and marshes,
to the Big Bend Mountain falls,
you've got to know that where you live
is the greatest state of all.

Song lyrics from
"Here Comes Another I Love Texas Song"
by
Allen Damron, Tom Paxton, and Bob Gibson

Chapter One

What Is Folklore?

F rankly, there is no commonly agreed upon definition of what folklore is. I've always known what folklore was, but I never knew a formal definition. To most folks, folklore consists of stories and songs that represent something out of a distant past.

I've often felt like one of our Supreme Court Justices when he was talking about pornography. His comment went something like this, "I don't know how to define it, but I know it when I see it." Learning how to spot it is much easier than defining what it is.

But if you don't already know what it is, I wanted this book to help you learn. So, I turned to my handy dandy dictionary, which defines folklore as

> (1) traditional customs, tales, sayings, dances, or art forms preserved among a people and (2) legend, myth, mythology, mythos, tradition

When you think on that definition for a bit, it soon becomes apparent that there aren't many things we do in our lives that don't fall into one category or another. Brushing your teeth could be a traditional custom, and some folks even turn it into an art form and a dance.

Not having achieved the clarity of definition I had hoped for, I looked up the definition of a folklorist.

A folklorist is person who deals with the branch of knowledge known as folklore.

Now wasn't that helpful? Sure cleared it right up for me. That was like the dictionary that, under the definition of a LOOP, said SEE DEFINITION OF LOOP.

So, with all that clarification under my belt buckle, I realized a book about folklore can cover quite a number of our endeavors and forms of communication. After cogitatin' on it a bit further, I've come up with a little simpler definition:

Folklore is any form of communication that captures a part of what the lives and the legends were like at a particular point in time, and is generally conveyed in an entertaining manner.

Entertainment, that's the key. Although this book was written to be informative in many areas, first and foremost my goal is to entertain you with the stories that I have laughed at and learned from throughout my life.

What Makes Texas Folklore Unique?

Within this giant state, the diversity is astounding. The deserts of west Texas, the plains of the north, the semi-arid farmland of south Texas, the rich Blacklands region of central Texas, the Coastal Plains bordering the Gulf of Mexico, and then there are the beautiful Piney Woods and Big Thicket of East Texas.

Texans are a hearty combination of hard work and honesty, covered liberally with a desire to have a lot of fun. If you doubt that for a second, take a look at the list of festivals and events. Any group that will hold a festival for shrimp, mosquitoes, 'gators, and black-eyed peas is a group looking for a reason to have a party.

Diversity is part of what has made Texas unique. Few countries in the world have been populated with as many diverse cultures. From all over the world came groups looking for a place where they could express their individuality. Even many of the slaves chose to stay after their emancipation.

Throughout the state are towns that were started by various ethnic groups like Germans, Swedes, and Czechoslovaks (until just recently the town newspaper in West, Texas, was still written in Czech). Each of these groups brings its own centuries of history, but also now has a shared history with all the other cultures.

The cultural influence of Mexico's occupation of Texas can still be seen. (I genuinely doubt that the Fourth of July is as big a holiday in Mexico, as Cinco de Mayo is in Texas). On a daily basis you can see the influence of the many Indian groups of Mexico on the current population of Texas.

The businesses that sprang up in Texas are as diverse as the cultural influences. Some immediately come to mind, like farming, ranching, lumber, and of course, the oil "patch." But there were many others like mining, milling, and fishing.

It is interesting that most of these are high-risk businesses. The rewards are high, but so are the risks. Texans are risk-takers, and that is one of the things that make this state special. If they take a risk and it doesn't pay off, it's not viewed as a failure, just as a delay on the road to success.

All of these diverse cultures and job opportunities have blended in a variety of ways to create some very special towns. The populations vary as much as the landscapes. Many of the towns mentioned in this book are well known, like Dallas, Houston, San Antonio, Austin, and El Paso. But you will also get glimpses of several other towns that you may have never heard of, like Manchaca, San Leanna, Cumby, Terlingua, Luckenbach, Commerce, and Sulphur Springs.

In this book you will meet a variety of wonderful folks who have put their own unique brand on how they convey a good Texas tale. You will meet some who are ink-slingers, some who use their voices and tell the tales through their stories, jokes, or songs.

You will meet many classic, and some legendary, Texas characters who are my friends. Through stories, songs, poems, and pictures they can become your friends too. Unlike most books on this subject, many of the folks I'm writing about are still alive and well. If you keep your eyes open, you can go see them at various events. Then you too can meet some of these living legends.

The men and women who built Texas were special characters, almost without exception. The strength of character to make a living off the land also gave them the strength to speak their minds, whatever the cost, and here is some of what they had to say.

Chapter Two

Folklorists and Storytellers

It is important that we get one question answered right away. What is the difference between a folklorist and a storyteller?

For the purposes of this book, there is not much difference. After checking with several prestigious folklore organizations and distinguished folklorists, it appears that there is not a clear, definitional distinction between the two.

However, within the folklore community there is a significant difference to some individuals. There appear to be three very general groupings of folklorists.

The first group are folklore purists. These folks believe that if a story is not a verifiable, historical fact, then it should not be considered as true folklore. I refer to them as folklore historians.

The second group of folklorists believe that if a story is true to the times and the people, it is still a valuable story, even if all aspects of it are not historically verifiable. I readily confess that many storytellers are not overly concerned with the specific facts of a story as much as they are with the plausibility of it. It's not necessarily that they are liars, it's just that they don't let some of the facts get in the way of improving a good story. Since many of these stories couldn't be verified anyhow, the questions become, "Is this story consistent with the people and places of that time? Is the story in the proper context?"

The third group are pure storytellers who use little or no basis in reality. They specialize in whoppers. They may start with an acorn of truth and from it they grow a giant shade tree of a story. Legendary folks like Paul Bunyon were born in this manner.

Country folk say that these storytellers are bull-slingers and they joke about havin' them come over to your place and fertilize your crops. "Yep, he's sure 'nough doin' his part to keep the county green with all that bullflop he's a throwin' out."

My goal is to entertain you with a lifetime of tales, tall and otherwise and mostly funny. You will learn a great deal about history, because most of the stories were at least based on true events. Only later did they begin to grow (perhaps nourished by a plentiful supply of fertilizer).

What is often missed, when folks hear stories, is that the story itself is sometimes not really the point at all. It's the essence of what the people in the story are about that is the point of telling the story. It's not so much about the cowboy who went out in a winter storm to round up strays, as it is about a cowboy whose sense of responsibility to the welfare of his herd led him to endanger himself in the storm.

Stories change as memories fail and details are lost. But something else can happen when writing about your memories. For example, did you ever go back to your elementary school? Most folks are amazed by how small it is compared with how they remember it. Some of the stories in this book are my youthful memories of some of these folklorists and events. To every extent possible I have tried to make them completely accurate.

Philosopher's Rock at Barton Springs in Austin portrays Roy Bedichek, J. Frank Dobie, and Walter Prescott Webb, the founding fathers of Texas folklore, discussing Texas as they often did at Barton Springs.

This beautiful sculpture is by Glenna Goodacre.

Photo by Jim Gramon

Chapter Three

Becoming a Storyteller

As a folklorist/storyteller/ink slinger, I was a little stumped for an answer when someone asked me how to become a storyteller. It wasn't something I had ever set as a goal and then worked towards. I had not really ever thought about how it had happened. It was just something I had done all of my life.

After some thinking on the subject, I realized that I had learned an appreciation of good stories by being fortunate enough to hear them from some of the best. I believe that can work for you too. By reading and listening to stories, you will learn to appreciate one that is well told and how a good one is put together.

My hope is that these stories will inspire you to learn more about storytelling. Each family, no matter what their background, has stories that can tell not only the family history, but about the character and personalities of the people. Don't let your stories be lost because nobody took the time to jot them down.

Events and Festivals

I've already mentioned the diversity of Texas. And it is plain to see that we Texans will use practically any excuse to throw a party. At most of these events there will be gatherings of storytellers, whether they are formally on the agenda or not.

At the back of this book is a calendar of events, giving a month-by-month schedule of close to a hundred events that I am aware of, and I'm sure there are many more. If you know of one that has some storytelling and is not included here, please let me know (gramon@onr.com), so I can include it in the next book of this series.

Understanding the Habits of Storytellers

In the mornings and evenings folks gather, just like Nature's other creatures. Whether it was the gathering of families to discuss the day, the gathering of the herds of farm animals, the gathering of the thousands of grackles on south IH-35 at Ben White Boulevard, or the ritualistic evening flight of several hundred thousand bats out from under Austin's Congress Avenue bridge. Sunset is a social hour for those who live close to the earth. The next morning they do their visitin' then head out for the day.

Talk around the campfires is so common that some Texans think it's a law, and maybe it oughta be. The campfire tradition is alive and kickin' at the Kerrville Folk Festival. The festival attendees, referred to as Kerrverts, gather in the evenings and have singarounds until the wee hours.

In the mornings, about an hour after sunrise, in thousands of small cafes, diners, and donut shops across Texas, people of the farming and ranching communities gather after performing some of their first chores of the day.

House Concerts

As often as we can, Sal and I go to "house concerts." These mini-concerts are a wonderful way to support live entertainment and get to know the various artists. You get the opportunity to see talent on the way up as well as experienced artists.

The format is simple. You bring your own chair and drinks and sit where you can in the home of the host. They generally ask for a donation of a few bucks, which normally goes to the artist.

After some getting acquainted time, the opening act will come out and do several songs. Then, after a short break for the refilling of glasses, the starring act for the evening will come out and deliver an hour or more of one-on-one music.

Because they are normally at someone's home, most of these house concerts won't have more than about fifty people. These are wonderful events that I've only seen here in Texas.

Check with your local musicians about who to contact, or you can e-mail me at gramon@onr.com and I will try to put you in touch with someone in your locale. Likewise, if you know of house concerts in your area, let me know about them so I can share the info.

Chapter Four

Finding the Local Gathering Places

About 7:00 in the morning, drive by some of the rural eating establishments. Look for a crowd of trucks, many of which will be dirty.

In each of these places, normally in one of the corners, yet near the coffeepot, there is normally a liar's table. Around this oversized table, the locals gather to drink coffee, read the local fish wrap, discuss what's goin' on over at their place, and to swap stories and whoppers.

This table is generally open to all who want to sit in, but you need to understand the rules. Folks come and go all morning long, but there is almost always someone "holdin' down the fort" at the liar's table.

I normally walk on over and say, "Howdy. I'm Jim, mind if I sit in for a bit?" Responses will vary from an unenthusiastic nod towards an empty chair, all the way to a full-blown set of introductions to all the current residents.

Once you are seated, just listen for a bit to get the flow and the topic of conversation. It won't take long before someone will ask you about yourself. Keep it simple and understated. I normally say something like, "I couldn't find a real job, so I became a writer."

This tells them something important. No, what you do is not really significant. What is important is that they know you don't mind poking a little fun at yourself. These folks laugh and tease with each other on a regular basis. They laugh at themselves, but only with those who are willing to do the same. Any hint of being pompous or a blowhard, and you will become the target du' jour.

One other tip, the point of some of their jokes might not be readily discernable, but just wait. At one place I gave a group of folks my, "I couldn't find a real job, so I became a writer" line. To which one guy responded with, "I read a book, once."

While I found the comment mildly amusing, everybody else at the table guffawed and hurrahed him quite a bit. It was only after he left that I found out that he's a well-known author himself.

The "Gang" gathers for coffee and stories every
morning at Fonzie'z Café in Kyle.

Photo by Jim Gramon

Some of these tables even have small plaques dedicating them to some regular.

Sometimes when you sit down you'll notice that the conversation proceeds pretty slowly. That's because there is one sacred, inviolate rule at every liar's table:

The First Liar Always Loses!

Always has and always will. These folks pace themselves and wait the others out. They may tell "a" story to get things going, but they are probably saving their real whoppers for later. So when you tell a story, expect someone to say something like, "Well, that's a mighty fine story, but let me tell you about somethin' that'll make that look like a walk in the park..."

Another thing you will notice is that the language of storytellers is different from their "everyday" conversational language. I realized this in high school, that I had two different vocabularies and styles of speech. When I'm telling stories, my language becomes more "down home." The first thing that normally happens is most of my Gs fall off. Working becomes workin', talking becomes talkin', and so on.

To head you in the right direction, here are a couple of places I go that almost always have storytellers in attendance. When you go in, tell 'em Jim sent you.

Manchaca Firehall

Located on FM 1626, the Manchaca Volunteer Fire Department was formed many years back to help protect this rural community. As the population grew, so did the fire department, and after they built a larger building to house the trucks, they opened a restaurant in what had been the garage.

If you look closely at the walls of the dining area, you will notice that they are actually the oversized garage doors that used to let the fire trucks in. The other walls are covered with a wide variety of neon signs.

Clarence Vogel is there early every weekday morning as the pickup trucks start to gather, the coffee starts to flow, great smells come from the kitchen, and the stories begin. They gather at an oversized round table that even has an oversized lazy Susan in the middle, so things can be easily passed.

Whether you come for breakfast or lunch, the food is great. And on Friday nights they serve some of the best catfish around.

The Manchaca Firehall

Photo by Jim Gramon

Clarence Vogel, manager of the Firehall, and Jim.
Oh, did I mention that they do serve beer if you insist?

Photo by Jim Gramon

Larry Lehman and Clarence Vogel share a story
while sitting at the liar's table.

Photo by Jim Gramon

Fonzie'z

For over seven years Alfonse and Hope Martinez have been serving up delicious food and hot coffee, twelve hours a day, six days a week, in their roadside restaurant located in Kyle, Texas.

True to his generation, Al has used a sixties high school atmosphere. On the wall, in display cases, are high school letter jackets from Kyle and Hays. From the ceiling hang 45 RPM records, and there are even some booths on the back wall.

Over by the coffeepot is an oversized round table with a small brass plaque embedded in the middle of the top. The plaque reads, "Donated by the friends of Roy Brock," who is one of the regulars.

Come in at most anytime of day, and there is usually someone "holding down the fort" at the liar's table. It's a great place to meet folks and hear some good stories.

Fonzie'z Café in scenic downtown Kyle.

Photo by Jim Gramon

Liar's table at Fonzie'z café. Please note the plaque in the middle that says "Donated by the friends of Roy Brock."

Photo by
Jim Gramon

Hope and Alfonse "Fonzie" Martinez, owners of Fonzie'z

Photo by Jim Gramon

Hill Country Humidor

On occasion I do enjoy a good cigar. And when I can I go visit Rob Robinson at his store, located on the north side of the square in scenic downtown San Marcos. This smiling jokester, with the Santa Claus beard and bod, always has some good stories. In addition to stories, Rob keeps Kinky and I in great cigars and coffee.

Walking into the Humidor is like stepping into the past. The building dates somewhere back towards the turn of the century, last century. The heavy wood floors sometimes creak but were made well back then. The chairs and wood bench are worn smooth from a steady stream of visitors who drop by to cuss and discuss cigars and a wide variety of topics.

The Hill Country Humidor
Located on the square in San Marcos.

Photo by Jim Gramon

Oh, and yes, they sometimes even buy some cigars too. The large walk-in humidor is filled to the top with a great selection of cigars. Don't miss a chance to stop by. Tell Rob I said, "Hi" and I bet he'll make you a deal.

Rob Robinson and his staff are hard at work.

Photo by Jim Gramon

Texas Hatters

Located on I-35 in Buda is the legendary Texas Hatters. Most of the folks in this book have a hat made by them. I know I certainly enjoy mine.

David and Joella Torres run this special place that is part hat store and part museum. The space not covered with hats is covered with pictures. Some are decades old, going back to when Manny Gammage founded the business. Several years ago Manny hired David and taught him the secrets of being a hatter. Manny passed away a few years back, and David has made the hats ever since.

Over the years Manny and David made hats for presidents, actors, music stars, and at least one author I know. When movie companies need hats for a frontier or western movie, they often call the Texas Hatters. Their hats have been used in many movies, including *Lonesome Dove* and *The Alamo*.

The Texas Hatters
Located on I-35 in Buda.

Photo by Jim Gramon

The old wood bench and the plowshare stools are rubbed smooth from use by a steady stream of visitors who come to talk hats and whatever else is on their minds. Need a hat or a chat, drop by and see David.

Note: Check the pictures in this book; most of the hats were made by Texas Hatters.

David steams the creases until the hat is just right.

Photo by Jim Gramon

Chapter Five

The Truth About the Truth in Texas

The stories I'm going to tell you are true, to the best of my knowledge, unless otherwise noted. HOWEVER (startin' to sound like a disclaimer, isn't it), I can only vouch for my part of the "truth." Truth sometimes appears to be a rare commodity.

Any student of "truth" will immediately turn the question back on you, asking, "What is truth to you?" You see, your truth may be far different from mine, but that's OK, because it never hurts to have a little extra truth around.

Suffice to say folks don't always agree on the truth, and that's why lawyering, sheriffing, and the prison systems are big-time growth industries. But then we bring in the question of truth in Texas. Now that's a whole 'nother matter.

Texans, except for a coupla badduns, are honest as the day is long, and yet they'll spend a good part of that very same day lyin' to you about it. Of course their "truth" about their lyin' is that they were just "pullin' yer leg," "spinnin' yarns," or "catchin' you a whopper."

"Truth" in Texas is topic sensitive. If you're doing a business deal, a true Texan always stands by his word. There is nothing more sacred to Texans than their word, and they will do anything in their power to meet their obligations.

But when it comes to tellin' stories, the whole truth thing blurs quite a bit. With some of these stories I've been told, the only truth might be that it was a "story" that was told to me. Actually, if you believe all of these stories actually happened as told, I want you to be the guest of honor at a monthly poker game my buddies and I have. These guys would stand by their word to the end, then stand right there, with a straight face, and swear the only reason they came back empty handed from their fishing trip was because they couldn't rent a trailer big enough to bring back that whale of a redfish they caught.

When Texans start talkin' huntin' or fishin', strap on your waders, 'cause it's gonna get deep in a hurry. I gladly plead guilty to enjoying this type of pastime. Your author once convinced a business executive type that the capital of Texas, Austin, is historically four degrees warmer when the Texas legislature is in session. Due, of course, to all the hot air blowin' out from around their pearly whites.

Havin' sold that one to the gent, I proceeded to check out just how gullible he really was. I asked him if he'd ever visited the state capitol building in Austin. He said he hadn't. I told him it was a most remarkable structure. It was built to be higher than any other capitol building, even that one in Washington, D.C. (which is true). But, I also told him the Texans took advantage of the legislature's abundant supply of hot air to sustain much of the roof's weight, as is done in a hot air balloon. That, of course, is why the dome is rounded off on top, just like a balloon.

He nodded thoughtfully and asked how they kept the hot air from leaking out. At that point I knew I had a live one on the line.

Unable to resist, I pushed on farther, beyond the city limits of credibility. "Yep, they originally had the legislature set to meet every four years. But, the dome began to sag about halfway through the recess. So now the legislature meets every two years."

Only then did his lights go on. He starts to laugh and says, "You got me on that one. You're one of those Texas storytellers, aren't you?"

"There you go," I replied.

"You guys in Texas really say that?"

"Say what?"

"There you go."

"I guess we do."

"I thought some silly writer had made that up for the TV shows! I had no idea Texans really talked like that."

"Nope, we really don't 'ceptin' when we're aroun' outsiders. Kind of a code language. When another Texan hears me a talkin' that a way with you, he knows you ain't from aroun' these parts, and he'll be extra careful 'bout what he says. So's as to not let out any of our Texas secrets."

This poor guy nodded thoughtfully, "I see."

"Yep, I'd get whupped good if I taught you the secret handshake."

His eyes brightened considerably, "You did it to me again! Didn't you?"

"Don't ask me 'bout the handshake. I'd hafta hurt you."

By this point he was laughing big time, and I joined in. He was all right, for a yankee city slicker.

True Texas storytellers will never intentionally hurt you with a whopper. But they will carry you through a wide range of emotions. They might even embarrass you (like when they send you to the hardware store to pick up a new framish or a few extra sky-hooks (neither of which exist). Another gotcha is when they tell you that the best way to get over a cold is to rub your face and chest down with a combination of mustard and honey. (It takes a day or two for the jaundiced look to go away.)

But it's harmless fun, aside from a little dent in the victim's ego. Fortunately, I never fell for that one, but many folks did.

Testing someone's sense of humor tells a lot about an individual. A person who can't be teased and can't laugh at himself is probably takin' himself way too seriously. Once that character flaw is spotted, the gang at the domino hall will put in some overtime coming up with ways to make him the butt of some joke.

Now, after all that palaverin', all of these stories were told to me as the gospel truth. However, I'm quite confident that some of these tales are totally truth-free. And that's the truth!

Chapter Six

Cumby, Texas

As the old joke goes, this beautiful little town is so small that both city limits signs are on the same post. Cumby is located in northeast Texas, a half mile north of Interstate Highway 30, in western Hopkins County. My grandparents, aunts, and uncles have lived there all of my life. My father, Jimmy Gramon, is buried in the Cumby Cemetery by my grandparents and a stone's throw from Ben King "Doc" Green's gravesite.

The city was originally settled in 1842 by D. W. (Wash) Cole and was named Black Jack Grove because of its location near a grove of black jack oak trees. The oak grove, just west of the present-day business district, was used as a camp by Texas Rangers during the days of the Republic of Texas.

Freight wagoneers traveling on the Jefferson road to the interior also used the grove as a campground. The Black Jack Grove post office opened in 1848 in the home of the first postmaster, John D. Matthews.

Three years later D. W. Cole bought the grove from Elizabeth M. Wren as part of a 307-acre tract. Cole ran a store, sold town lots, and donated land for a Masonic lodge that was chartered in 1852. In February 1857 the Black Jack post office was renamed Theodocias, and James M. Brown became postmaster. In May 1858 the post office again became Black Jack Grove.

Downtown Cumby and the city water tower.

Photo by Jim Gramon

By 1860 Black Jack Grove was a thriving settlement with physicians, tradesmen, and blacksmiths. The town had also earned a reputation as a tough frontier town, where the worst people in the county congregated and violent fights were common. On Christmas Day 1866 a gun battle over a horse race resulted in the deaths of five men.

The East Line and Red River Railroad reached Black Jack Grove in 1880, and the town gradually began to lose its roughness. In 1886 the railroad and post office, in an attempt to change the town's reputation, suggested that the community be renamed.

Congressman David B. Culberson suggested naming the town after his friend Robert H. Cumby, a Civil War veteran. The Independent Normal College opened in Cumby in 1895 and operated until 1905.

In 1911 the town had two banks, two lumberyards, three gins, a cottonseed oil mill, and a tin shop. The town reached a peak population of 925 in 1929. By 1948 Cumby had twelve stores, six churches, a broom factory, and several other small businesses.

The number of residents gradually declined to a low of 405 in 1970 before increasing to 647 by 1980. In 1985 Cumby had six small businesses and an estimated population of 690. In 1990 the population was 571.

That's what the history books will tell you about Cumby, Texas. During my younger years I spent a great deal of time in and around the town of Cumby, Texas. It's a small dot of a community, but it was a wonderful place to grow up.

Cumby doesn't have a town square. There are just a few buildings straddling FM (Farm-to-Market) 499. Interstate 30 now runs within about a mile of the main street. Heck, there wasn't even a stoplight to slow down the folks on their way to the big city.

For most of the residents, not havin' the city slickers stop is just great. They prefer to keep to their own and "Let the city folk just keep on a rollin'."

Headin' north out of Cumby it's a ten-minute ride, in a good truck, to the small town of Commerce. They do have a town square and it's the home of East Texas State Teacher's College (which then became East Texas State University and is now Texas A&M at Commerce). Commerce is still a pretty small town and not too citified yet.

Thirty minutes to the west of Cumby is the much bigger town of Greenville, which also has a nice square and is home to some pretty big firms. Why, they have folks there who haven't even ridden a horse. Shameful. Ben Green once told me, "They're goin' to have a lot of ketchin' up to do when this car fad dies out."

Another hour's drive, further west, is the city-slicker hangout of Dallas. That's where good, law-abidin' country folk go somewhat regularly to be exposed to the sinful ways of the big city. Where wheeler-dealers are a carryin' on and a doin' too much smilin' and backslappin'!

Around Cumby the country is dotted with dozens of beautiful little farming and ranching communities that even many Texans have never heard of. Towns like Como, Picten, Campbell, and Miller Grove grew up every ten to twenty miles apart, because that's about as far as horse drawn wagons could go in a day and still make it home by dark.

One of the big pluses for Cumby has been that the railroad lines have run through the town, "far back as anybody can remember." In the early years of poor roads, being able to put your produce, cattle, and horses on a train to get it to market was a big plus. Cumby even had a "depot" to aid in loading and unloading.

Now this wasn't a true "train station" by any means. Nope, this "depot" was really more of a large loading dock. As I recollect, it was probably about fifty foot by twenty foot. On each side of the dock was a ramp, which allowed produce to be driven up onto the ramp and deposited, then driven right on off the other side.

The depot was made out of the same heavy wood stock that railroad ties were made from. The whole thing oozed creosote, the dark black, nasty stuff that was used to protect wood from both weather and wood lovin' critters, like termites and wood ants. This was the only thing available to protect lumber before the days of pressure treating.

But creosote had its downside. When you worked with creosote treated lumber you soon had the sticky brownish-black stain on you. And then there was the smell. On a warm day you could pick up that distinctive pungent smell half a mile away.

To this day, when I catch a whiff of creosote covered posts or logs, it takes me back to those days and gives me a warm feeling, like things were being done right. In the days before pressure treating wood was perfected, you knew a place was doin' things right if they used lumber treated with creosote; it would be there for quite a while.

Across from the depot there once stood an "icehouse." This was really nothing more than a fifteen foot by fifteen foot ice chest. Like the depot, the icehouse was built up on a platform, so as to be the same height as the railroad cars. The walls were about two feet thick and filled with cork, which insulated the blocks of ice away from the hot Texas sun. Before the development of refrigerators, folks would go down and pick up a twenty-five-pound block of ice to put into their "icebox," or they could have the ice wagon drop some off to them. The introduction of home refrigerators killed the need for icehouses.

By the time I got to prowlin' around, nobody used ice anymore and the icehouse was in pretty poor shape. But, as a kid, I did have a pretty good time playing with all of that cork insulation. I guarantee you it can make a ten-year-old feel pretty strong when he can pick up an eight-foot section of cork insulation and break it in half.

In Cumby, both the icehouse and the depot are gone now. The depot went up in a spectacular blaze one night in the early sixties. It was a victim of kids playing with matches (not this kid). Someone finally cleaned up the tumbled down old icehouse too.

Though they are gone in Cumby, several small towns still have the remnants of both. In the Texas oil patch, in the scenic little town of Luling, there are still the deserted remains of both an icehouse and a really uptown depot/loading dock. I say it's uptown, because their loading dock is made of concrete, and so the kids there can safely play with matches.

The main highway leading into Cumby.

Photo by Jim Gramon

The railroad was an honored guest in Cumby, making it a real business town. This made the whole area more attractive to folks looking around for a place to settle. The regular train whistles were a twice-daily reminder that things were on schedule (ever once in a while a "special" would come whistling through town and set everyone to wonderin' if their pocket watch was workin' right).

In Hopkins County, the rich reddish-black soil had given rise to crops, cattle, farmers, ranchers, and lots of fine storytellers. In their slow patient way, they told the stories of the land and regularly pulled on each other's leg with whoppers. As a boy I soon learned that when they gathered on the spit-and-whittle wood benches outside the town co-op and lit up their pipes, it was time for some biguns to be spun.

One of the first rules about these gatherings was, if you were silly enough to believe what they told you, you deserved it. As we mentioned earlier, the second rule is the first liar always loses. No matter what story the first one would tell, the others would chime in with, "Aw baloney, that ain't nuthin', let me tell you a REAL story about...."

Obviously folks didn't want to be the first to spin a yarn, which meant that often these gatherings could be quite slow to get started, and pretty raucous by the time they reeled in the last whopper.

The stories I'll tell you about these folk are funny, scary, and Texas true. You see, this land created great people too. Most of the folks I'll be telling you about never signed a contract in their life because they never needed to. Their word was "good as gold." But, as I explained earlier, when it came to storytellin' it could be truth-lite.

Cuttin' Hay

My uncle, James Callan, has farmed and ranched the land outside of Cumby, Texas, for many decades. James and his wife Mamie built up a nice spread while raising my cousins Mary and Vickie. The years of hard work had allowed him to acquire "a bit" of the flat, rich farmland and accumulate "a few head of cattle and some horses."

James and Mamie had several hundred acres of rich reddish-black soil under cultivation. During the summers, when I came to visit, James and I often rode tractors, horses, and wagons from daylight to dark. It was hard, dusty, and dirty work. But by the end of the day, you knew you had earned your keep.

Every year was the same story: If the crops didn't make it, we didn't make it, financially. They say the gamblers are in Las Vegas. But how many of them bet everything they own every single year of their lives? This is true courage, true faith in God or themselves, and one of the purest forms of optimism.

This particular summer day it was as hot as a boiler door, and the humidity was very high. The kind of day that should be spent down on the creek bank, swimming and fishing.

The water level in our well on the back porch was down over three feet. It took another couple of pulls on the rope to get the bucket up. We worried that the well might run dry. And we didn't have the money to dig it deeper. Taking a ladle full of water from the bucket, I always marveled at how cool and sweet it was.

How could something coming out of a deep hole in the ground taste so good? Wasn't deep in the ground where Hell is? Yet this clear liquid from the ground was cool and soothing to a throat coated with red East Texas dust. And it was sweet, not at all musty or earthy in its taste.

It was a sign that we were pretty "uptown" to have an enclosed well in our back porch. Most folks had to walk out to their well and carry the buckets back to the house. Of course the tradeoff was that we had to walk out to the outhouse (and on some cold nights we regretted the choice). But during the winter we kept a bare light bulb burning to keep the "throne room" a little warm.

James is a cowboy-rancher-farmer. A little less than two yards tall, and weighing about two hundred pounds, James is solid. From his tough leather boots (he preferred walking heels and none of those "silly lizard skin" types) up to his sweat-stained western-style straw work hat (he kept his felt Stetson for Sunday-go-to meetin'), it was obvious this man was no stranger to hard work. He was equally at home on a horse, a tractor, or in his decade-old GMC pickup.

If you knew what to look for, his tan told most of the story. His hands and most of his face were a deep reddish tan. But when he rolled up his shirtsleeves or took off his hat, the white skin provided quite a contrast with the tanned areas. Folks living near the land know how harsh the sun can be, and they try to stay covered as much as possible.

One hot summer day, James pulled his truck off FM 273, leaving the highway department asphalt and tar blacktop onto his soft homemade blacktop driveway. The clay-rich red soil of this region possessed a unique ability. When you combined the soil with oil, you produced a pretty good surface for a road if it didn't have to take a lot of traffic.

As he climbed out of the cab of his GMC pickup, it was obvious James wasn't real happy. But in his case, knowing he was upset came not from any loud declarations, stomping, or slamming of the truck door. We read his anger in the way he asked, "How are ya'll?"

"Fine, how 'bout you?"

"OK."

So went most of our conversations with James; they were extremely short and not immediately, obviously on point. He firmly believed that "you should never miss a chance to shut-up." Over the years I had learned that the words would come. Patience was mandatory to talk with most of these men who lived near the earth. Like nature itself, they would wait and watch until the time was right. James would tell his story in his own time.

That time came as we sat on the front porch swing, after we had quietly eaten a lunch of generously salted cold fried chicken and tomatoes from the large garden, over by the barn. We needed the salt to replenish what we had sweated out and was quickly forming white rings on our hats and clothing.

We often lingered around the house after lunch, drinking water, lemonade, or sun tea to give our bodies time to recover from the morning's dehydrating efforts. Air conditioning was several years away, and the porch swing's movement provided the simulation of a slight breeze.

We sat there for what seemed, to a teenager, like an hour. Finally, he spoke, "Willie screwed up." Then he fell silent again.

I knew Willie was a guy that James hired once in a while to do something on the farm. I also knew that if I waited long enough, James would tell me about it. But my patience failed me again. "How did Willie screw up?"

James sat silent for still another, smaller eternity. "He cut the wrong damn field."

"He what?"

"That dummy cut the wrong field! He was supposed to cut the north one!"

"How could that happen?" I foolishly asked.

"'Cause he's dumb as dirt! Never should have trusted him."

James thought for a moment and realized he wasn't quite through with Willie's evaluation. "He never was the sharpest tool in the shed, that's for damn sure. Nope, I never should've trusted him; every time he smiles he shows you all his teeth. Sure sign of a liar! Almost as bad as one of those slickers that come by, mostly runnin' for some cushy office. You know the type, wearin' a vest in the middle of the summer. A man that does that has gotta be a liar, or just plain crazy. Either way, I'm not interested in votin' for him."

Now everyone knew Willie was several bricks shy of a full load. But, this was a new high, in low, even for him. "What are you gonna do?"

"Nuthin' I can do. The hay was too green. He cut it a week too soon. Hafta leave it in the field and pray it don't rain."

Now a scientific fact, known by every farm boy but unknown by most city dwellers, is a phenomenon known as spontaneous combustion. If hay is baled too soon, while still somewhat green and then those green bales are piled into a barn, they will catch fire, on their own, as a result of the heat caused by the fermentation of the fluids in the hay.

(Even when baled at the proper time, hay bales generate plenty of heat. On those days when we stayed in the fields for lunch, sometimes we would crack open a hay bale and put a wrapped roast beef sandwich into the warm center to heat up.)

So, Willie had presented James with a field full of cut green hay, which represented several hundred bales of food his herd would be needing to make it through the winter. Before it could be baled, the hay would have to lay in the field for a few more days. If it didn't rain, there was no problem, it wouldn't be quite as nutritious, but it could then be safely baled.

But if it rained, the whole crop could ruin right there in the field. If you don't have hay, you've got to buy it or sell your herd. James had spent years building his herd up. During an ideal year, he could produce enough hay for his own herd and some to sell for those folks whose hay crop didn't "make."

Willie had put the crop and thus James's financial future for the year at risk. It would be a long week, hoping it wouldn't rain.

As we sat there thinking about this problem, we heard the sound of an even older pickup truck, with a barely functioning muffler, pulling into the winding blacktop drive. The rusty old pickup crunched to a halt, about twenty feet in front of the swing where we sat. We could hear the rattle of the empty whiskey bottles banging against the empty beer bottles in the bed of the truck. Willie had arrived.

He didn't get out. Being down wind from him, we could clearly sniff out the fact that he was wearing his favorite scent, ode de booze, which was drifting out of both the open truck windows. Now Hopkins County was "dry" and always had been. Cumby had only one store (the Co-Op), one gas station/garage, and one blacksmith. But on the religious front, Cumby had three busy churches that didn't look kindly on drinking.

Despite this abundance of religion, getting booze was easier there than in the "wet" areas. Milk was delivered every other day by an overworked, underpaid young man. He supplemented his meager earnings by making a weekly booze run over to Dallas (where sinful drinking went on "pretty nearly round the clock"). On Wednesdays you would leave a note in your empty milk bottle on the porch. Milk, buttermilk, cheese, butter, and booze, er make that medicinal alcohol (many hot toddies were made to "cure what ails ya").

Each Friday the order would be delivered, and the farm families would receive their order of "medicinal" bourbon, rum, gin, or vodka.

Willie looked and smelled like he had taken on quite a bit of the milkman's "medicine."

"Howdy, James, I'm here for my money."

"Ain't gettin' it."

Willie's eyes rolled around a bit, as he tried to focus a few brain cells on absorbing what James had said.

"Sure I am. You're just a joshin' me. I cut that hay field of yours this mornin', and I need to get my money now."

"Won't be no money, Willie. You cut the wrong field!"

"Bullshit! I cut the field you told me to cut. Give me what I've got comin'."

"You're gettin' nuthin. Got nuthin comin'. You cut the wrong field."

"That's crap. I did the work and you'll pay me now, or I'll kick your ass."

Despite the bluster, I noticed that Willie made no attempt to get out of his truck. Even in his condition, Willie was sober enough to realize that, despite his size advantage, even sober he was not nearly tough enough to make James do anything he didn't have a hankerin' to do.

Without saying a word, James slowly rose from the swing. He stepped down from the porch and started walking slowly towards Willie's truck.

Having observed this, Willie proved just how drunk he was. "You're a lying sumbitch, James, and you are going to pay me, now."

James stopped halfway down the sidewalk. He bent over slowly and picked up one of the reddish-orange bricks that lined the small flowerbed in front of the porch. Slowly, through his drunken haze, Willie's eyes began to focus enough to see that James was in the middle of his back swing with the brick.

James launched the brick towards Willie's open driver's side window. Willie jerked his head back just as the brick sailed smoothly through the cab and out the open passenger side window. It had missed Willie's nose by about six inches. The brick proceeded on its course, landing in the yard without touching anything but the yard.

Willie sat there frozen with his red eyes bulging. His stammering eventually evolved into a single stuttering exclamation. "Shit!"

At that point, even Willie was able to correctly conclude that his chances of getting paid were not nearly as good as his chances of getting injured. So, after considerable gear grinding, he pointed his rolling pile of rust back down the blacktop and out onto the farm-to-market road.

James slowly walked out into the yard and picked up the brick that now lay in the mowed weeds that passed for grass in that part of the yard. He carried the brick back and returned it to its original resting place, in the border of the flower bed.

James then walked back up on the porch and sat back down beside me on the swing. In all my years I'd never seen a show of anger of any type from this man. The worst I'd ever gotten from him was a sideways glance. I now sat quietly trying to absorb what I had just seen.

We sat there in silence for a bit. Then James looked over at me and gave me one of his slightly lopsided smiles. "I guess Willie had to go," James said softly.

We never spoke of that event again. That was James's way. Actions were what counted.

That week went by slowly, but Willie got lucky, very lucky. It didn't rain. A week later we baled the hay into eighty-pound round bales, and after a lot more sweat, they were all safely stored in the barn. Yep, that was Willie's lucky day.

Gate entrance to the field Willie should have cut.

Photo by Jim Gramon

A fresh cut field of hay, waiting to be baled.

Photo by Jim Gramon

Chapter Seven

Manchaca, Texas

Manchaca (pronounced man-shack) is an unincorporated area just south of Austin in southwestern Travis County. It was named for nearby Manchaca Springs, where José Antonio Menchaca once camped (please note the difference in the spellings, it will become significant later).

In 1851 a post office known as Manchac House (with a third spelling) opened two miles south of the present townsite, with William Pelham as postmaster. The office was discontinued the next year.

A second office, also called Manchac, was in operation at the present town site between June 1874 and May 1875. After it closed, mail for area residents was sent to nearby Onion Creek.

In 1881 the International-Great Northern Railroad completed its track between Austin and Laredo, giving the small community new life. With the railroad in 1881 came a third post office, now spelled Manchaca.

By 1884 Manchaca had seventy-five residents and served as a shipping point for grain, cotton, posts, and lumber. Manchaca School was founded in the early 1890s, along with a hotel and a Methodist church. The community became the focus of a common school district, which in the 1930s had two grade schools for white students and one grade school for black students.

In 1952 Jimmy and Evelyn Gramon and their skinny kid Jim moved into the Village of San Leanna (more about it in a moment), which lies in the general area called Manchaca.

Manchaca School occupied a two-story, seventy-five-year-old building at the intersection of Manchaca Road and FM 1626. The school building was pretty nice for the times. The wood and brick building always looked pretty good as it gleamed with its coat of white paint.

On the front of the building was a covered but not enclosed stairway, giving the building the appearance of a miniature, low-budget White House. In the fashion of the day, the ceilings were about twelve feet tall. During the warm months, this allowed the hot air to rise away from the students at their small desks, which sat in neat rows attached to runners, each with a hole for an inkwell (by this point we were no longer using them).

During my first couple of years at Manchaca School, the upstairs area was still heated by a pot-bellied stove that sat within a protective guardrail made of heavy, polished brass pipe. The same teacher, Mrs. Stewart, taught three grades at the same time, which sounds like quite a passel of work. However, it wasn't as bad as it sounds, since there were only about twelve students in those three grades combined.

Although Manchaca School was small, it had a cafeteria and a small gymnasium. Upstairs they even had squeezed in a small stage for plays and recitals.

In the early fifties I started attending first grade at Manchaca School. The classes were lightly populated with the children of farmers and ranchers, and a few children of folks who made the daily drive in to their jobs in Austin.

One of the greatest joys of my young life was a wonderful lady named Mrs. Meredith. This special lady was the cook for the school. She prepared incredible food for us every day. One wonderful delicacy was her biscuits. They were huge, light, warm, and wonderful.

In the middle of every morning, we would have a "milk break." During this break we would consume massive quantities of her special biscuits. These were about five inches square and three inches tall.

The addition of a couple of pats of butter, peeled off their little paper squares, was enough for a super start on the day. Adding a glob of homemade preserves and a small carton of milk, you had a meal fit for a king.

Although I was a tall, skinny, wiry kid, I tended to be a pretty hearty eater. In spite of that, just one of Mrs. Meredith's magic biscuits would fill this kid to the top.

That part of my school day was the good stuff, but if you messed up, there was some pretty bad stuff too. First, you got to meet with the "Board" of Education. This was a two-foot-long paddle, made of one-by-six pine. It had been carved with a narrow handle.

When you messed up, the teacher would have you bend over in front of her desk. Then the appropriate number of licks would be administered in front of the class. Of course, back then, the licks were just the start of your troubles. When you got home, then you had to deal with your folks, which often involved even more licks.

If you happened to use some "dirty words," things got really bad. The teacher would take you into the gym area. At the back were two large water fountains. The teacher would walk the student back to the fountain, then wash his mouth out with a bar of soap.

This washing process would go on for several minutes, until there was a nice lather coming out of the transgressing student's mouth. It tasted horrible and, besides being humiliated, most of these folks ended up with a case of the "green apple quick step," also known as "the squirts," from the soap they swallowed.

Nobody ever died from having their mouth washed out with soap, but the offenders talked a little funny for a few days, and you seldom saw repeat offenders. I'm extremely proud to say I missed having this experience.

Manchaca reported a population of 200 in the late 1960s, although accurate figures were impossible since there were no city limits. Most of the estimates were based on the number of post office boxes that were rented at the time of the census.

Another confusion point has to do with the folks who live outside the city limits of Austin on the north or Buda on the south. Some folks who are kind of citified claim Austin as their home, others claim Manchaca. (Personally I always claimed the best of both. Since I was born in Austin, I joke about being one of only three native Austinites.)

During my growing-up years, Manchaca consisted of the school, a post office, three churches, one small store/filling station, and a garage where you could get vehicles of any description repaired.

Earl and Ruth Jones owned the combination store-soda fountain-filling station. I grew up with two of their kids, Woodie and Linda, and one of their cousins, Mark Jones.

The Jones's store stocked the essential food staples while also pumpin' ethyl, regular, and diesel. And of course, there was always plenty of beer and motor oil. They also kept a supply of night crawlers and other fishing supplies for the folks who decided to wet a line in Onion, Bear, or Slaughter Creeks. Some mighty fine bass, catfish, and perch were caught out of those waters.

Jim Jones (I think he was Earl's brother) ran the local garage, and he was a big-time character. I can't really recall ever seeing Jim without a cigar in his mouth. He hardly ever lit it (probably a good idea in a garage full of vehicles with leaking carburetors), but he would work that cigar back and forth till it was a nub.

Jim was a storyteller for sure. Besides tellin' us a bunch of leg-stretchin' whoppers on a regular basis and living on a diet heavily supplemented with cigars, Jim had one other small eccentricity. For the price of a beer, Jim would take out his glass eye for us. He'd pop that rascal out of the socket, roll it around in his mouth a bit (one of the few times he would remove the cigar), then pop it back in the socket.

At the point of this writing, Manchaca has grown considerably. (In 1990 the census estimated 4,700, and we've probably doubled since then.) I always swore that when they put up a stop light in Manchaca, I would be pulling up stakes from Rancho Gramon and movin' further out, where it wasn't gettin' so crowded. Well, I'm behind on that, 'cause we now have two lights.

Manchaca School provided a great education, as far as individual attention went. Trust me, there's no place to hide in a room with only twelve students.

If you are ever drive down Manchaca Road, when you get to Manchaca, you will notice that the school is named Menchaca, not Manchaca. A few years back, the Austin Independent School District, in a demonstration of insensitive power, decided to dump a hundred years of tradition, and they renamed Manchaca School to Menchaca. So, on Manchaca Road, in the area called Manchaca and just a few blocks from the U.S. Manchaca Post Office, is the Menchaca School.

Looking down Twin Creeks Road as it approaches "downtown"
Manchaca. I really like towns where trees cover the roads.

Photo by Jim Gramon

Chapter Eight

San Leanna, Texas

Rancho Gramon, my home, is located in the Village of San Leanna, which began around 1950 as a housing subdivision. It is located just south of Austin, within the general area referred to as Manchaca. San Leanna was the brainchild of Lloyd Arnold, who created the Leanna part of the name by combining the names of his two children, Lee and Anne.

This little chunk of heaven sits quietly astride Farm to Market road 1626 and nestles on the south bank of Slaughter Creek. Besides FM 1626, there are no through streets leading out of the village, so it has remained quite peaceful.

My family moved into the subdivision in 1952. Ours was the third home there. At that time getting to our lot required lowering a gap (an inexpensive, flexible, fencewire "gate" that is stretched between two posts). We had to do this to prevent the cattle and horses that grazed the area from getting out onto the "highway" (FM 1626, which was then a full lane-and-a-half paved road).

By 1957 the village had grown to about twenty homes. Lloyd Arnold had been running the water system, but was having trouble keeping up with the payments. The electric company was going to cut off the electricity, and there would be no water. Late that evening Jimmy Gramon (my dad), O.C. Pool, and Al Ziedler met and were able to purchase the water system from Mr. Arnold.

Lloyd Arnold was about thirty years ahead of his time in his vision for the area. His subdivision plan called for about two hundred homes, some stores, and even a cemetery. It took twenty years before San Leanna had even grown enough to incorporate. Under Texas law, small areas without a large population that are seeking incorporation can do so as a village. And so, in 1970, my parents (Jimmy and Evelyn Gramon) became one of the small group of families that got the village incorporated.

The only commercial enterprise in the village is a cemetery. This kind of sets the pace for this quiet community. Taxes are low, set by the Texas constitution at no more than twenty-five cents per hundred dollars of valuation.

The original rock entrance to San Leanna Estates, which was later incorporated into the Village of San Leanna.

Photo by Jim Gramon

San Leanna reported a population of 200 in 1974; by 1988 the number of residents had increased to 297. In 1990 the population was 325.

The village council oversees two major endeavors: They own the water system, which pumps pure clean water out of the Edwards Aquifer, and they oversee the maintenance of the roads. During one memorable town hall meeting to discuss whether to improve the wells or the roads, one of our citizens uttered the immortal words to live by, "I'd rather drink than drive."

A typical neighborhood street in the Village of San Leanna.

Photo by Jim Gramon

Chapter Nine

Buyin' Mexico

Horse trading was one of the cornerstones of life in the Texas west for many years. Your horse was often all that stood between you being successful in life, or being dead. So you had to choose horses carefully, or you'd end up hurtin'.

My boyhood friend Mark had been looking for a good horse. Now Mark was a little bit crazy, and that's why we got along so well. He didn't just want "a" horse, he wanted one that was "special." One day after school we doubled up on Smokey, a fifteen-hands-tall gray and rode out of Manchaca, to a farm about a mile from where the Onion and Bear Creeks run together. I reigned up along the side of the large corral owned by one of the locals.

Some of this guy's stock was pretty good, while some of it was pretty strange. In addition to runnin' the usual Herefords and Angus cattle, this guy also had some llamas and exotic deer. Probably didn't make any money, but he seemed to have fun with it.

In the corral was a beautiful Appaloosa mare. Her spotted coat glistened in the afternoon sun, as she moved restlessly around the large pen. The owner had told Mark to come on over and try her out. Said her name was Mexico, a cuttin' horse.

Photo by Jim Gramon

Mark climbed the fence and walked over to Mexico, who nervously shied away at first. But she soon was overcome with curiosity and came right up to Mark. Cuttin' horses are a special breed. They are used by cowboys to go into a herd and "cut" individual cows or horses out of a herd. They have to be light on their feet and quick, "able to turn on a dime and give you change." Cuttin' horses are the sports cars of the horse set, and Mark had his hat set on gettin' one that was something special.

Mexico was that and more. Mark swung up onto her bare back and guided her around the corral with a handful of mane. He was hooked. But there was still one more test, was she really saddle-broke? I dropped off my horse Smokey and pulled off her saddle. Mark had brought another bridle and he saddled Mexico up.

She didn't even hold her breath when he tried to tighten up the cinch. Some horses do that. If they did, then when you got into the saddle, the horse would let out its breath and the cinch would be loose. Shortly thereafter you would be lying on the ground because the saddle had slid off.

But Mark was able to cinch up Mexico with no problems. He then rode her around the pen without a problem. Mexico was smooth as silk and really could cut on a dime. I opened the corral gate, and he took her around the open field. She could fly like the wind, and she loved it.

Mark rode her up to the man's house and shook on the deal. When he came back down by the corral, Mark said he made out real good on the deal. Got her at a bargain. We started heading back down the hot, dusty road. I was riding old Smokey and Mark was dancing ahead on Mexico. Next thing I knew he took off down the road in a cloud of dust and was soon gone from sight. This was a bit unusual, but I figured Mark might be testing Mexico's wind.

The next day at school, I expected Mark to be proudly discussing his new horse. But he strangely had absolutely nothing to say.

After considerable proddin', Mark's only comment was, "Damn horse cost me a good 6X hat!" Then he turned on the heel of his boot and walked off.

After school we walked down to the town store. Five minutes of walking hadn't resulted in a single word. Now Mark never was a talker. He threw words around like they were gold nuggets. But now, even that little dribble had dried up.

I was gettin' a little perturbed, 'cause I knew there was probably a pretty good tale waiting to be told. I said, "Well?"

"Well what?"

"You know what!"

He glanced at me, his eyes made it clear he didn't want to tell the story. But, my eyes made it clear I wasn't goin' away.

"Yer just like a damn snappin' turtle, just won't let go. Big pain in the ass!"

"I know I am. It's awful ain't it? So, what happened?"

At that Mark laughed and gave me a resigned shrug. "OK, OK. Remember when I took off on Mexico and left you behind on Twin Creeks Road?"

"Sure do. You were really pickin' 'em up and layin' 'em down pretty good. That Mexico is one fast hunk of horse flesh!"

Mark nodded agreement, "That's for sure. But, I wasn't racin' her off like that. That damn crazy horse was takin' herself out for a run! I was just along for the damn ride! Now I'll grant you, it was a good ride. That hay burner has a good even gait, bit of a lope, but for the most part, she don't pay the rider too much of a never-mind."

"I'm not worried 'bout you Mark. You've had a few surly horses before."

"Yer right there, Jim. But never one quite like Mexico."

A closeup of a mesquite limb. Please note the
needle-like thorns that cover the limbs.

Photo by Jim Gramon

"What's different?"

"Well, I did pretty good with her, till I got past Manchaca School. Then she saw the field down where Chappell Lane meets Manchaca Road. You know that damn mesquite grove? Well, she headed straight for it!"

Now for those of you unfamiliar with mesquite as anything but a flavoring in your barbecue sauce, let me tell about this little charmer. Mesquite trees are, for the most part, a pain to those who live around them. They are generally short, spindly, warped, and possessing little foliage and therefore little shade. Their wood is very solid, but you never get a piece long, or wide, enough to make much with it. For that reason it became the standard wood for making fires and barbecuing.

A dangerous mesquite grove outside of Manchaca, with the type of low hanging limbs that Mexico regularly used to brush riders off.

Photo by Jim Gramon

Mesquites are very hardy and grow well with little water. They tend to gradually take over an area, once they get a foothold. So you'll run into groves of them that may be a mile across.

If that was all there was to it, mesquite would not be the huge problem that it is. However, mesquite trees could also be called hypodermic trees, because whether they are a foot tall or twenty feet tall, their flowering limbs are covered with needle-like thorns that can get several inches long. So for folks living around them, mesquite earns the same disrespect that cactus does. Cowboys wear chaps and heavy leather gloves when they are working in mesquite country.

You can imagine Mark's distress when Mexico started heading straight for the mesquite grove.

"She headed straight for one of the trees that had about a six-foot clearance. I had to swing down to the side, hanging on to the saddle horn for dear life! That damn nag was at a full gallop as we went under the branch. Missed my head by about an inch. Knocked my hat off!"

"Your good 6X Stetson?"

"Damn straight!"

"Why didn't you just stop and pick it up?" I asked. However, no sooner was it out of my mouth, than I knew I had tweaked a pretty raw nerve.

Glaring at me he continued, "Next thing I know, Mexico is weaving back and forth, like she was runnin' barrels, as she ran around the mesquites. It was damn near half a mile before I was able to turn her! Once I got her turned, I kept a tight rein and walked her back. But by then some weasel ridin' down the road had already picked it up. Damn! That was my good Sunday-go-to-meetin hat."

"You're sure right. That hat was a beauty. What are going to do with Mexico?"

Mark glanced up at me, then with a smirk said, "Was thinkin' 'bout the glue factory."

Now I knew that wasn't for real, so I just laughed.

Mark continued, "You know that old sidewinder, Wilcox, who lives over beyond the Marbridge ranch?" (Wilcox is not the sidewinder's real name. I changed his name to protect the guilty!)

"Course I know him. Meanest sumbitch in the county. I always make a special trip by his place at Halloween to leave him a burnin' bag."

In the rural areas where fresh cow plop was readily available, one of the oldest Halloween tricks was to sack up some of the "protein rich fertilizer" in a paper sack. You would then sneak up to the victim's house, set fire to the top of the bag, ring the doorbell, and run like hell. The victim would arrive at the door, see the bag on fire, and proceed to try to stomp the fire out, resulting in a fairly efficient cow plop distribution system.

The second time this happened to a victim, they wouldn't stomp on the bag. The problem with this approach was that in short order, the highly unpleasant odor of cooked cow plop would soon permeate and adhere to everything in the immediate vicinity.

Highly experienced plop victims just kept a flat blade shovel by the door, shoveled the offensive pile up, and put it into their flower beds (the roses just love it).

Mark continued with his story, telling it slowly and savoring each word. "Well yesterday evening I moseyed over to Wilcox's place. Told him I'd picked up the best cuttin' horse in Texas, but couldn't afford to keep her. He thought that was pretty damn funny. I put Mexico through her paces, IN THE CORRAL. Wilcox was real impressed with how good a cuttin' horse she was. Told him I'd paid a bunch for Mexico, but could take a hundred for her."

"Well Jim, you could just see him start to drool. So, of course you know what that old fart did next, he immediately went to dickerin' about the price, and I sold Mexico to him for $90. He's happy as a clam, thinkin' he screwed me, and I made twenty bucks on the deal, which covers the cost of a new hat and a few bucks to boot."

Mark and I had several laughs about that bit of horse tradin'. But that's not where the story ended.

A couple of days later, Wilcox showed up at the Jones's store sportin' a couple of new scraped spots and offerin' "one of the finest cuttin' horses in Texas" for sale. Over the years, we watched Mexico change owners with regularity. As the years have gone by, I've wondered occasionally where Mexico is and how many owners she's had.

Chapter Ten

Ben King "Doc" Green (1912-1974)

Ben King (Doc) Green, storyteller, author, rancher, and veterinarian, was born on March 5, 1912, in Cumby, Texas (about an hour drive east of Dallas, in Hopkins County). Ben was the son of David Hugh and Bird (King) Green.

For most of his life, Ben really had two homes. Cumby, where much of his family still resides today, and Weatherford, where some of his family had moved when Ben was in high school.

Ben was an early bloomer. He started wheelin' and dealin' while just a youngster. He had fallen in love with horses, cattle, and cowboy life, and it was a love that never left him. From early on Ben almost always had a string of critters that he was tradin' or breedin'. These included horses, cattle, mules, donkeys, and anything else that could be rounded up, bred, or traded for.

When he was only twenty-three, Ben ran for a seat in the Texas Legislature. He led the ticket in the primary but lost in the runoff.

Ben loved telling and hearing stories, particularly about livestock and tradin'. Now Ben always told me, "Jim, never tell a story the same way twice, 'cause folks'll get bored." Well it seems that Ben took his own advice when talking about his past. Over the years Ben claimed to have attended many prestigious institutions of higher learning. This list even included the Royal Academy of Veterinary Medicine, in England, even though it didn't even exist.

To the best of my knowledge most of Ben's experience came from a life devoted to raising, caring for, and trading farm animals of every size, shape, and description.

Ben always knew a good opportunity, and so, with the help of some friends, he was grandfathered in when Texas started registering all of its veterinarians. To this day some folks around Cumby still refer to him as Doc Green.

He began writing rather late in life, long after telling me these stories. His writing career was somewhat of a fluke occurrence when Ben met the New York City publisher Alfred Knopf, while riding on a train. Ben got to telling Mr. Knopf all about the critter business in Texas. He must not have done too much harm while bendin' Mr. Knopf's ear, because Knopf loved the stories and published *Horse Tradin'* (1967), *Wild Cow Tales* (1969), *The Village Horse Doctor* (1971), and *Some More Horse Tradin'* (1972).

The books were a breath of fresh air in many literary circles and were even well received by many of the critics. His first book, *Horse Tradin'*, was even referred to as a classic of Western Americana.

In 1973 Ben received the Writers Award for his many contributions to Western literature from the Cowboy Hall of Fame in Oklahoma City. Later he also received a career award from the Texas Institute of Letters for his unique contribution to Texas literature (pretty high cotton for a boy from scenic downtown Cumby).

Now Ben was a classic storyteller, not necessarily a writer. So how did he get a string of best sellers? (Him having a book published was quite a puzzlement to the folks who lived around

Cumby.) Like all of his stories, Ben didn't write them, he talked them. Others typed the stories and organized the books. Ben spent his time talking into his old tape recorder about his earlier adventures as a young man, rancher, trader, and vet.

At one point Ben owned the only registered herd of Devon cattle in Texas and supported it on his "giant" farm in Cumby (actually it was quite conservative by local standards, but he did some pretty fair ranchin' with what he had). For a while Ben was able to make a living raising both Percheron and quarter horses. He was also a regular throughout Texas and the Southwest on the lecture circuit.

In all, Ben published eleven books between 1967 and 1974. Ben was proudest of his last and most controversial book, *The Color of Horses* (1974), which was a combination of Ben's observations and speculations regarding why horses were certain colors.

On October 5, 1974, Ben King Green, renowned Texan, died in northwest Kansas, of heart failure, while sitting in his car in a roadside park. I have often wondered what stories or deal Ben offered Saint Peter at the Golden Gate.

Ben had always said, "I don't never want nobody crowdin' in on me, whether I'm livin' or I'm dead." And so it was that Ben King Green was laid to rest in the same Cumby, Texas, cemetery where my father, Jimmy Gramon, and my grandparents, Kyle and Ludie Alexander, are buried. But bein' standoffish like he was, Ben was buried in a fifty-foot-square, separately fenced area at the very back of the cemetery. (Later in this book you will learn a bit more about Ben's Last Deal, which involved his cemetery plot.)

Meetin' Ben Green

My first recollection of Ben K. Green goes back to the early fifties. I was a tall, skinny youngster, visiting El Paso, Texas, with my mother. We had made the long drive from Austin to El Paso to visit my Aunt Rose. We didn't know exactly where Rose's new place was, so we stopped at a restaurant on the outskirts of town.

Mom was standing in an old wooden phone booth, in the lobby of the hotel, talking with Rose about turning right, turning left, and such. Suddenly a huge arm circled my waist and lifted me up without a hint of effort. I yelped, causing my mom to poke her head out of the phone booth.

As I was being carried off down the hallway, towards the dining room, I heard a deep voice say, "Evelyn, this boy's too damn skinny. I'm gonna go fatten him up a bit."

A shocked, then bemused look came over Mom's face, and she returned to her phone call. Reaching a table, I was turned around to upright and was dropped in front of a chair, into which I plopped. Before me stood what appeared, at the time, to be a giant of a man.

Ben was already full-bodied, and his jacket added to his bulk greatly. The rough-cut, heavy leather jacket had a large, furry sheep's wool collar. The bulky coat extended down past his pants pockets, giving a great deal of protection against the cold, harsh West Texas winds. Atop his rough shorn head sat a well worn, floppy, 3X beaver hat (his old one). His boots were good quality but worked hard and caked with feedlot muck.

"I'm Ben, Ben Green. Your ma and I knowed each other from way back."

"I'm Jim, Jim Gramon. I've known her for a while myself," I said, extending my hand, which soon was engulfed by a huge hand covered with scars as he laughed.

Pleased I had retrieved my hand without having it crushed, I asked Ben, "What do you do, Ben?"

"Oh, this and that. Mostly that," he said with a laugh. "Nah I'm mostly into cowboyin', horse and mule tradin. What do you do for a livin'?"

Well, it's not a question often asked of someone under the age of ten. I thought about it for a bit, then said, "This and that, mostly that."

Ben's rugged, half-shaved face broke into a broad grinning laugh, complete with guffawing and snorting. His big hand slapped me on the shoulder, nearly knocking me out of my chair. He guffawed, "Jim, I think we're goin' to get along just fine!"

That was my first of many visits with Ben Green, story-teller extraordinaire. Over the years I spent many happy hours swapping stories and lies with Ben.

Ben sorta lived around. Ever so often he'd get the urge to move. At first I suspected that much of his traveling had to do with running towards a new payday, or away from the pending arrival of a bill collector. Later on I came to realize it wasn't that as much as it was Ben was a wanderer. Every so often Ben just had to see what was goin' on over the horizon.

When I told Al Lowman, quite a legendary folklorist himself and former president of the Texas Folklore Society, that Ben Green was going to be a part of this book, he said, "I knew Ben Green and found him to be most obstreperous."

Well, as usual, Al was exactly right. Ben certainly was excessively noisy, unruly, and regularly rejected any kind of control. But then Al added another truth about Ben, "He sure could tell a good story."

Ben Green's Li'l Donkey

Every summer and occasionally during Christmas vacation, I would spend several weeks in Cumby. I always looked forward to spending time with Kyle and Ludie Alexander, my maternal grandparents, and my aunt and uncle, James and Mamie Callan.

Main Street runs parallel with the railroad line and about three blocks over. One of the connecting streets is named Depot, because the train depot sits at the intersection of Depot and the railroad tracks.

Now depot is an overstatement. This depot was really just a large, heavy-duty raised platform upon which trucks could be driven with cargo like bales of cotton. Having it raised put the cargo at the same level as the railroad freight cars that would take their products to market or bring their purchases back to Cumby.

One of my favorite Ben Green stories has to do with his return to Cumby, after one of his wheelin' and dealin' trips. Ben had been doin' some tradin' in Fort Worth—a few horses, a few mules, and a scraggly little donkey.

Well, when all the jawin' was finished in Cow Town, Ben had done real well and had sold everything but the little donkey. Ben rode the freight train back to Cumby, feelin' pretty good about his tradin'. He later told me, "Jim, I gotta tell ya, that was a good day's work. Got top dollar for ever damn horse and mule. But, fer the life of me, I couldn't give that little donkey away. Folks in Cow Town weren't in a donkey mood."

Now when Ben arrived, I happened to be at one of my favorite hangouts, in front of the general store. It was on this portion of elevated sidewalk that I could sit with the spit-n-whittle crowd, listen to their stories, and daydream about bein' in bigger towns and exotic places that I'd only heard about at that time, like Amarillo, Beaumont, or Brownsville.

Now, as I explained, Ben was feelin' pretty good when he arrived back in town with his little donkey. So, in an ill-planned show of exuberance, he decided to just hop on this little donkey to ride the half mile to his place.

Now this was no problem for the donkey. They are some bit sturdy and routinely carry heavier loads than Ben. No, the misfortune of this trip was that Ben's path took him right up Depot Street and in front of the general store, where we all were sittin'.

A donkey similar to the one Ben was riding in this story.

Photo by Jim Gramon

Here is a current picture of downtown Cumby. The store where we were sitting is on the right and Ben was coming straight up Depot Street, which intersects on the left, where the white car is starting to pull out.

Photo by Jim Gramon

So here comes Ben a ridin' the little donkey up the street, not really realizing what a humorous sight he made. You see, Ben was a biggun, pushin' six foot and quite a few biscuits past two hundred pounds. His mud-caked boots were nearly draggin' the ground, and he was a smilin' and a wavin' to everyone.

And everyone in turn smiled and waved back at him, then started to laugh. Each one had the same thought. Here comes old wheeler-dealer Ben, purveyor of the best horseflesh in the county. Boy howdy, somebody really got to him on this deal.

By the time Ben turned the corner by the general store, he realized he would have been much better off to have led the little donkey through town, rather than riding. But by this point that boat had already sailed. All he could do was try to urge the little donkey into a little faster gait, to get the embarrassment over with as quickly as possible.

Well, the little donkey took to steppin' a little faster, but it was an awkward gait for the rider. Ben's stomach and chest took to bouncin' as the donkey was a joggin'. For those of us watchin', we couldn't hardly believe that the sight had even gotten funnier than before.

Nobody said anything as Ben jiggled and bounced on his little donkey, whilst tryin' to get through town as quick as possible.

Amidst the howls of laughter, I've no doubt that Ben would have had a pretty pointed reply. But we'll never know for sure, 'cause just as Ben turned his head to look at us, the little donkey proceeded to do a little hop-skip-and-jump rabbit step, which caused Ben's 3X beaver horse tradin' hat to drop down over his eyes.

The donkey then took a mind to turn up the alley that ran past the general store, back towards the cotton gin. Ben rounded the corner, out of sight, trying to hang on to his hat and maintain his seat on the donkey.

For some time after that, Ben didn't get down to the store very often. And the few times he did, the kindly folks would all inquire as to the health and wellbeing of that "beautiful donkey you traded for in Fort Worth." If Ben responded at all, it was nothing more than a disgusted snort.

In all our later talks, I damn sure wasn't ever goin' to bring up that donkey incident with Ben. But he did once, about a year later. It was late in the day, kind of fallish and cool as I recall. Ben and I were sittin' in front of the store sippin' Cokes (I suspect his also contained some "cough medicine" to "cure what ails ya").

As he was given to do at times, Ben had waxed a little philosophical. He told me, "Jim, you're a good kid, you'll have a good life if you follow my advice; just stick with soft women and hard liquor. Oh, and never, I say never, ever ride a donkey to town!"

The Last Trail Drive Through Dallas (The Short Version)

by Ben Green, as told to Jim Gramon

It was one of them egg-cookin-on-the-sidewalk days. Dust devils danced across the road as I headed up from Manning's Filling Station to the Cumby General Store to get somethin' cool to wet my whistle. Rocked back on an old wooden Coke carton sat Ben Green. He was whittlin' and whistlin' as I scurried up.

I was steppin' out right-smart, because, as usual for a twelve-year-old I was barefoot, and that blacktop tar road was mighty toasty. Ben happened to be sittin' in the closest shady spot after I hot-footed it across the road. So I slid to a stop by Ben, whilst doin' a little jig, trying to cool down my feet, much to his amusement.

He laughed at my high-steppin' and asked, "Howdy, Jim. You sure was movin' along there with a lot of quick. Somethin' wrong?"

"Heck no, Ben, I was just in a hurry to get over here to visit with you. Why it actually felt real good. Here, let me help you off with those little bitty butt-ugly boots you're a wearin', so's you can get out there and enjoy it too." (I don't rightly know their size, but he did have some smallish feet.)

Ben rocked back with his big laugh, which was a whole lot bigger than his feet. As one friend of the Green family said, "They're good folk, but a noisy bunch. You never had to look up to know if one's around."

As he continued to laugh, Ben said, "Evelyn done all right raisin' you (referring to my mother Evelyn Alexander Gramon). Tell you what I'm gonna do...."

Now this phrase "Tell you what I'm gonna do" was a warning sign for the locals that Ben was getting into his wheeler-dealer mode.

"Tell you what, Jim, you go into the store and buy us both a sodey water, and I'll tell you a story."

"Forget it, Ben. I can hear lots of stories for free. So I'll just mosey in and buy myself a drink, then come back and drink it here and tell you exactly how cool it is and how good it tastes."

"Damn, Jim, you are some bit contrary. Puts me in mind of a horse I once had...."

I interrupted him, "See, I told you I wouldn't have to pay for no story."

Ben laughed again. "OK, you caught me. But, for a drink, I'm gonna tell you a really special story."

"Right! You mean the one about how you beat me out of a Coke today?"

"Damn, Jim, you damn near hurt my feelings, not trustin' me and all. Jim, this one's for serious. I'll tell you the whole story about me a drivin' the last herd of horses into Dallas over land, over curbs, and over cars."

"Did ya get in trouble? I always like the stories where you get in trouble."

"Boy, you for sure are a caution. Go get me a Coke and I'll tell you the whole story."

Ten cents and two Cokes later, I sat down and Ben began his story.

Over the years Ben told me this story about three times, and each time it was a little different. It was also in his wonderful book *A Little More Horse Tradin*, published by the University of Oklahoma Press. I mention this because Ben always said, "Don't ever, ever tell a story the same way twice, 'cause people won't be interested if there is nothing different."

What I'm recounting here is a composite of all of the various times he told me the story. Obviously, after all these years,

I can't recall his stories word for word, but I do remember the details of the story itself. So as you enjoy this story, please realize that though some of the dialogue is mine, the story is all Ben's.

To set the scene, Ben was a teen-aged horse trader. He heard that a West Texas ranch in Paint Rock was selling fine horses for less than ten dollars each. The horse market was dead and so was the hay crop that year. But in East Texas, the hay was good and he could sell the horses for about fifty dollars apiece, once they were saddle broke.

After finally convincing the ranch foreman that he wasn't just a kid looking to only buy one horse, Ben got to look at the herd. They cussed and discussed for a bit, and Ben haggled him down to about seven dollars each for 120 horses, most of which were unbroken broncs.

Ben knew he was going to need some help with a herd that large. So, in Paint Rock, Ben found a chuck wagon cook from Mexico, named Frijole. Frijole knew of an Indian cowboy who went by the name Choctaw.

The first portion of the drive went well. The grass was green and the horses were pretty manageable. A friendly gentleman allowed them to camp on his property just outside of Dallas. The next morning he came by and had some of Frijole's fine breakfast cookin'. We pick up the story as the man questions the wisdom of Ben leading the herd into Dallas. Ben takes up the dialogue from here.

I looked at the man and said, "Hell, partner, for a friendly country wager, I'll bet you I could drive a few head of horses into the elevator on the first floor of the Jefferson Hotel in downtown Dallas."

With this wagon full of my braggin', the nice man backed off and didn't say anything more about us havin' trouble with horses. But the look in his eyes showed a fair bit of concern about our ability to drive them half through Dallas without any trouble.

I went to settle up with the man for the use of his field for the night. But he just said to forget it. He'd enjoyed the conversation and the wonderful breakfast. (Frijole started to showin' a whole bunch of teeth when he heard that.)

When he got in his car and drove off, he said, "I sure wish you luck on gettin' through town, but if I were you I would wait a little while till all these people going to work get out of the way."

I waved at him and hollered "Much obliged" as he drove off. Choc turned to me and said, "That feller thinks me and you are green hands at drivin' horses, don't he?"

I said, "I guess so, but this ain't a big enough bunch of horses to get away from me and you in a town no bigger 'n Dallas."

We put the herd in the middle of Davis Street and headed east. Right off it got a little boogery. We was wranglin' horses and cars all over the road. More than a few of them cars would go a divin' for the ditch when they saw the herd headin' their way.

The cars that were goin' the same way we were goin' were tryin' to work their way through the herd. It wasn't really causing us no never-mind, but it did appear to give some of them rushy type drivers a bad case of the reds.

We passed the park on Zangs Boulevard and headed straight as a flamin' arrow for the mile-long Oak Cliff Viaduct that crossed the Trinity River bottom. The concrete sides of the viaduct would make for easy herdin' if we could get them into it before they got too spooky.

Gettin' them into the viaduct was the problem. This big old concrete ditch had embankments very high on each side. We got them to headin' out pretty smart, until some old geezer in a Model T drove by with a big white tarp flappin' in the breeze.

This spooked them into stoppin', and they tried to turn back on us. It took a but of horsemanship, but me and Choc got 'em turned back right again.

Lookin' back at the traffic jam behind us, I could just barely make out Frijole in the camp wagon, stuck in between a whole passel of cars. I could distinctly hear the bawling and hee-hawin' of those snorty West Texas mules. They was feelin' pretty crowded up and spooky, but there wasn't a chance for them to run away because there was no place for them to go.

By this point we had the traffic stopped dead, and these horses were millin' and a snortin' in the middle of the bridge. Not helpin' one damn bit was this bunch of cityfied folks who were a honkin' and a hollerin' at us from behind the safety of their vehicles. You'd have thought they had never seen a herd of horses before. Any damn fool knows you don't get a horse to cooperatin' by a honkin' at 'em.

We was about to the middle of the bridge, and things was kind of settlin' down a bit, when here comes a bunch of motor-cycle police comin' from several different directions.

One of 'em rode up kind of close to me and went to hollerin', askin' where the man was that owned these horses. Between fightin' horses and wavin' and hollerin', I told him he was talkin' to him. He said, "Kid, you don't own much more than the shirt on your back. Where's the man that owns these horses? Is he back there in that wagon?"

I was pretty busy and didn't have no more time to be a jabberin' with this fool, so I said, "OK, have it your way. Go talk to the man in the wagon back there." I thought that would be a way to get at least one of these motorcycles out of the way.

He rode back to the wagon, and by the time he got there Frijole was so scared he couldn't speak a word of English. After a passel of flappin' and fussin', Frijole had made enough signs that the cop turned around and headed back towards me.

When the officer got back to me, I was still a ridin' and wranglin' pretty hard to get the herd across the bridge. At that point the officer set about to explain to me the traffic laws regardin' blockin' traffic.

Between the cowboyin', folks hollerin', horses whinnying, cars honkin', and motorcycles a rumblin', I couldn't really make out a word the officer said, but I nodded friendly-like a lot. I don't think it really helped much, 'cause this particular guy was turnin' a couple of different shades of red.

I finally heard him say that I better get them horses off the bridge. I really had to wonder what he thought we was a tryin' to do. Anyhow, I suggested to him that the job would be a whole bunch easier if he'd get all them damn cars off the bridge.

I can't really say that this set too well with him, seein' as how he had now turned a whole 'nother shade of red. It also appeared to me that he had acquired a stutter that I hadn't noticed before.

The cars was beginning to stack up to the west, all the way out of sight down Zangs Boulevard. Back to the east they was stacked up too, all the way down past the train depot.

Well, just when I thought things couldn't get any worse, I heard a train whistle. Amazingly, with all the other noise, we hadn't heard the train approaching on the tracks that ran under the very same bridge we just happened to be crossing at that very time.

Now this bunch of West Texas ranch horses was plenty spooky, but they didn't have any clue what that noise was, or where it came from. See, like most of us, they weren't used to havin' sound come from underneath their feet.

And the steam coming up from around the sides of the bridge didn't help none neither. One thing was for sure, if these horses could have jumped straight up in the air, they sure would have done it in a heartbeat.

The concrete banister on the viaduct wasn't very high, and when that train whistle blew a second time, one of them wild, bald-faced, chestnut horses came out of the milling herd and cleared that bridge railing with a pretty fair country jump. I stood up as high as I could in my stirrups and looked over the banister.

The chestnut made quite a sight as she plunged downward. She was fallin' so fast that her mane and tail was stickin' straight up. Quick as a cat, I moved to block off the other horses from headin' in the same direction to follow the chestnut in her high divin' act.

Beauty, one of my favorite horses, and I headed them off and in the process got a couple of them up on the sidewalk beside the banister. Well, as they are prone to do, they just queued themselves up, one behind the other, and then the others began to line up. Choc and I just laughed and shook our heads. I took the lead, while Choc herded the rest of the herd onto the sidewalk.

A motorcycle cop was comin' towards them, head-on, and I hollered at him to get off the walk and turn off his loud rumblin' motorcycle. He didn't have the time, or space, to turn the noisy thing around, and he just barely got it out of the way before a hundred head of horses came a stompin' by him.

There was a park about a block east of the depot and just south of the Jefferson Hotel. Choc and I herded the rest of the group towards the park to try to settle them down a bit.

When horses that are used to being around one another get separated from one another, they start to whinnying and nickering trying to locate the others. When the horses got strung out, single-file, across the bridge, this separated them from one another. Because of this they had set to millin' and bawlin' big time whilst a searchin' for their runnin' pals.

Seems as though the bald-faced chestnut had hit the river just right, hittin' the deep water and not getting' hurt at all.

Havin' climbed out on our side of the river, she now heard the squalin' and bawlin' and came chargin' up the embankment to join the rest of the herd.

The chestnut was some bit of a mess. She was covered from head to foot with mud and dripping mud. As she pulled up towards the rest of the herd, the red-face motorcycle officer decided to do his bit towards helpin' us herd the horses along. He pulled up near the soggy chestnut and revved up his motor a bit.

This unexpected noise, from right behind the horses, made them bolt forward. As she did, the chestnut whipped her mud-covered tail, hittin' the officer up side of his head. His cap went a flyin' off into the air, and the rest of him followed right behind it.

His motorcycle, without a rider, ran wild into the horses before it fell over on its side. The cop lay there with a dazed look on his face. As I rode past it, I hollered back, "That's all right, Mr. Officer. I don't think you hurt any of 'em."

He started to speak, then just lay back on the ground.

When we got them all across, we headed them east towards the shortest way out of town. By this point the whole herd was pretty boogered and were movin' along at a fast lope.

Now, being a country boy, I didn't know anything much about citified stock. I don't know if they know what to do when they are approachin' a traffic light or a stop sign. But I'll guarantee you, none of these West Texas horses had any idea what to do.

Since they didn't know what to do, they just kept on running, right over the cars and curbs. People were tryin' to cross the street, and cars were comin' and goin', and we had a few head of human stock mixed up in the drive once in a while. Far as I could tell, most of them managed not to get hurt.

I didn't know exactly what was happening with the rest of the traffic at the stop lights because that bunch of ranch horses didn't seem to know the signals, and they just kept goin' at a pretty high lope.

The herd started to split up when I saw a man that was a friend of my daddy's. I stood in my stirrups and hollered loud enough to rattle some of the windows, "Mr. Carpenter, please head them damn horses off and don't let them go down that street!"

This was in the days before air conditioning, and all the windows in the buildings above me were open. All of the honkin' and catterwallin' had heads poppin' out of damn near every single one of them, staring down on the action in the street.

I wondered to myself if any of them realized that they was a watchin' the last trail drive through the streets of downtown Dallas.

Responding to my request, old man Carpenter grabbed off his 7X Stetson and set to wavin' it in wide arcs in front of the horses that had the misfortune to head in his direction. He had gone back to his childhood cowboyin' days, as he squalled and hollered at them horses. The way he was working at it, you would have thought they were his own.

As I passed him I hollered, "Much obliged! You would've made a good hand if you'd stayed in the country."

He beamed at this compliment. And while his pearly whites was a beamin', several of his friends was a backslappin' and congratulating him on the job well done.

The horses were pretty lathered up and draggin' by the time we got to Gaston Avenue. At that time Gaston was lined with a bunch of mighty fine homes. Choc and I were able to pretty much keep the herd on one side of the street and out of the pretty petunias that lined many of the sidewalks.

For the most part we were able to keep the cars and horses away from one another. Since the herd had slowed, the cars were able to do a better job of gettin' out of the way of the horses. But, once in a while I would hear a fender thump or the breakin' of a few headlights, but I never slowed down to worry about little details like that.

Now that things had slowed, I began to wonder what had happened to Frijole. It had been a long time since I had seen my little Mexican friend. Hell, I figured he might have just made a right turn and hauled butt back to Mexico. For sure, he had done some serious worryin' about the police, the traffic, the herd, and his two tired little mules. All I could do was to hope he could follow our trail. Sure enough, a couple of hours later a very frazzled Firjole showed up.

Soon we came upon a nice big open spot on the south side of the street. Some of the horses drifted over on it a little bit, and here come a bunch of grown men wearin' kids' knickerbocker britches and caps and wavin' clubs in the air.

I guess that was the first time I realized that golf players were one of the most excitable breeds of people. So while Choc rode point, I winged them on the side and got them off that golfin' ground without causin' too many new holes in that pasture land with all them cute flags.

'Bout middle of the afternoon, we watered our horses at the spillway of White Rock Dam. Since we was kind of in the country, we held them up and let them shade and rest a little while. There was a hamburger joint across and back from the road a little piece, and it took a batch of 'em to fill up me and Choc after that morning's drive.

As they watered and grazed, I had a few minutes to think about our experience. That old man at the cement plant had sure enough called it. We could have been in some pretty deep cow flop if we hadn't been some pretty good cowboys.

Ben, Choc, and Frijole continued their journey eastward across Texas. They sold off the last of the horses in Bossier City, Louisiana. As the train was arriving to take him back to Cumby, Ben auctioned off his last horse and made it home with a full poke.

The cemetery in Cumby, Texas

Photo by Jim Gramon

Ben Green's Final Deal

By this point, you must realize that nothing thrilled Ben Green more than pulling off a good deal. The only thing that could make it better was if the victim of his deal didn't even realize he had been had for quite a while. Now I don't know for sure that Ben had it planned out this way, but I'm sure he would appreciate the irony of it.

In Cumby they have a quiet little cemetery. My father, grandparents, and several other family members are buried there. To give you an idea of the age of the cemetery, my Uncle James Callan said it is his understanding that some Indians are buried there. They were killed as they raided the community about 150 years ago.

Shortly before his death, Ben offered to leave a couple of acres of land in his will to the owners of the cemetery in Cumby. This particular patch of land was right adjacent to the current cemetery grounds, so the cemetery association was delighted by the bequest.

Ben did have a couple of strings though. One, they wouldn't get the land till he died, and two, they would agree to perpetually maintain his gravesite, which was to be a separately fenced off area, at the back of the cemetery grounds. He had often said, "I don't let nobody crowd me when I'm alive, and I sure ain't gonna let 'em do it when I'm dead."

Well sir, the cemetery folk thought this was right fair of him and accepted his offer. And just as promised, when Ben passed, his will left the land to the Cemetery Association. An area at the back was fenced off, and Ben was properly laid to rest therein.

Things went well for a couple of months after the funeral, then a bill arrived from the original owner of the land. It seems the land that Ben so generously donated was actually not entirely his to give. Apparently he still owed a good bit more on the land.

After much cussin' and discussin' it was finally decided by the Cemetery Association that they needed the land and that they would be better off paying off the remaining loan balance on the land.

So if you're ever cruisin' through Cumby and you turn into the Cumby Cemetery, drive all the way to the back corner. There you will find Ben's gravesite in a fenced-off section of land, about fifty foot square. I might add that the area is very well cared for.

I don't know if this was Ben's plan, but as I stood looking on Ben's grave, I would have sworn I could hear old Ben laughing at how it had turned out.

Uncle James looks at Ben Green's gravesite. Ben's last deal.

Photo by Jim Gramon

Chapter Eleven

John Henry Faulk (1913-1990)

Portrait of a Patriot

One of the greatest characters, patriots, and storytellers to have ever walked the Texas earth was John Henry Faulk. I was just a boy when I first met John Henry. He would occasionally come through Cumby to visit with Ben Green. Later in life I also made the acquaintance of John Henry's brother-in-law, Ken Koock, who had married John Henry's sister, Mary.

The Koock family still runs the elegant Green Pastures restaurant in south Austin. The restaurant was originally the Faulk family home, where John Henry and Mary grew up. If you are ever in Austin, don't miss the chance to enjoy their wonderfully old southern-style dining, in a home to match.

At the time I didn't really know what all was goin' on in John Henry's life, that he would ever so often end up on the front steps of the general store or in the Cumby domino hall. But it never took more than a few minutes before he'd be all settled in and folks would take to spinnin' yarns.

John Henry Faulk was one of the greatest humorists and authors that Texas ever produced. When I knew John Henry he was in the middle of the fight of his professional life. He was in court fighting the McCarthyism that led this patriot to be black-listed and prevented him from being employed for many years.

John Henry Faulk as a young man

Sketch by James Gramon

In the late fifties he was in the heat of the fight. And I remember him speaking fervently of the Constitution and the Bill of Rights, which he loved so much. And his emotional love of our country inspired me to become much more interested in my, our, government.

Amazingly, considering what he was going through, what I remember most about Johnny was his incredible sense of humor. And frankly, being a youngster, that's what attracted me to him more than his burning patriotism. He made me laugh, even when he was making the joke at my expense.

It was much later in my life that I learned the facts of Johnny's life and had the occasion to meet some of the other members of his family. Here is a thumbnail biography of an exceedingly complex man.

Johnny was the fourth of five children of Henry and Martha (Downs) Faulk; he was born in Austin, Texas, on August 21, 1913. His parents were pillars of the business and religious community. They were also independent thinkers who taught him to reject racism in any form.

Johnny entered the University of Texas in 1932. Once there he had the incredible good fortune to get guidance from four folklore legends: J. Frank Dobie, Walter Prescott Webb, J. Mason Brewer, and Roy Bedichek. It was here that the seeds of his interest in folklore, writing, and storytelling in its many forms took root.

For his master's degree thesis, John Henry recorded and analyzed ten African-American sermons from churches in Travis and Bexar Counties. His research convinced him that members of minorities were being systematically denied their civil rights. Between 1940 and 1942 he taught English I at the University of Texas. It was then that he began to fully develop his skill at storytelling to demonstrate the things that made Texas and Texans unique.

His unflinching look at society often made his contemporaries uncomfortable. Fellow faculty members tended to view him as a bemusing and sometimes annoying rustic, who regularly told a blend of incredible yarns and bawdy jokes. What few of his faculty contemporaries realized at the time was that they were witnessing the birth of his entertainment and literary career.

When World War II broke out, Johnny tried to join the army, but they refused to admit him because of a bad eye. So in 1942 he joined the United States Merchant Marine. He served a year of trans-Atlantic duty, then spent a year with the Red Cross in Cairo, Egypt.

As the war proceeded, the number of enlistees was decreasing. In 1944 the army had relaxed their standards enough to allow Johnny to join. He served limited duty as a medic, then finished the war stationed at Camp Swift, Texas.

Johnny's friend Alan Lomax worked at the CBS network in New York. Through Alan, Johnny became acquainted with radio industry leaders. Christmas 1945 was good for John Henry. Alan hosted several parties to showcase Faulk's tale-spinning abilities. The New Yorkers were fascinated with the wit and wisdom of this rural yarn spinner. Their interest resulted in CBS giving him his own show, "Johnny's Front Porch," as soon as he was discharged from the army in the spring of 1946.

"Johnny's Front Porch" lasted for a year. It was the first in a series of shows from New York and New Jersey radio stations between 1946 and 1950. These included "Hi-Neighbor," "Keep 'em Smiling," and "North New Jersey Datebook." On December 17, 1951, the "John Henry Faulk Show" debuted on WCBS Radio. The program was quite progressive for the times. In addition to John Henry's political satire and humor, it also featured music and listener participation. This predecessor of talk show radio ran for six years.

In 1957 the United States entered a horrible period of political repression. Wisconsin Senator Joseph McCarthy, fueled with cold war paranoia, started blacklisting anyone who disagreed with him or his cronies, by labeling them as communist sympathizers.

He was able to pull this off by working in conjunction with AWARE, Incorporated. This New York based group provided background checks on people for the radio and television media and advertising industries. McCarthy, through his senate committee, would pressure people to implicate others to keep from being blacklisted themselves. Then, for a fee, AWARE would investigate the backgrounds of entertainers for signs of communist sympathy or affiliation.

In 1955 John Henry was concerned with how AFTRA (the American Federation of Television and Radio Artists union) was being administered. He helped organize the Middle-of-the-Road slate, which overthrew the existing power structure, many of whom were McCarthy supporters.

Predictably, John Henry was soon the focus of McCarthy's and AWARE's attention. Soon AWARE branded him a communist, primarily based on the fact that Johnny had argued that our constitution provided freedom of speech to everyone, even communists. Soon thereafter sponsors began to withdraw under pressure and, despite his consistently high ratings, his show was cancelled.

Even then Johnny did not realize the hornet's nest he had stirred up. It was only after several potential jobs vaporized, that he discovered the AWARE staff and their continued circulation of the specious bulletin were preventing radio stations from hiring him.

Typical for a wronged Texas boy, John Henry took on the whole group by filing a libel suit against AWARE and several individuals. A few prominent radio, TV, stage, and movie artists of the time put their own careers at risk by testifying and even financially supporting him during his six-year battle. These brave folks included newsmen Edward R. Murrow and Walter Cronkite, actor Tony Randall, and actresses Myrna Loy and Kim Hunter.

Their financial and emotional help allowed Johnny to hire heavy hitter attorney Louis Nizer. The attorneys for AWARE included McCarthy-committee counsel Roy Cohn, who managed to stall the suit from 1957 to 1962.

During much of this time, Johnny had returned to his south Austin home and continued to try to make a living any way he could. With the help of old friend and fabled storyteller Cactus Pryor, Johnny was able to get some radio work at the local radio station. But it was spotty.

The timing of this drama in Johnny's life, while unfortunate for him, was most fortuitous for me, since it allowed me the opportunity to make the acquaintance of this great man. I don't know how John Henry came to know Ben King Green, but they were cut from the same cloth in many ways. Ben once told me, "My friend Johnny has been over at ET (East Texas State Teachers College, now Texas A&M at Commerce), jawin' with some of those educated idiots over there." This, and other comments, left me with the distinct impression that he had been lecturing to one of the classes.

When the trial finally concluded in a New York courtroom, the jury had determined that John Henry should receive more compensation than he sought in his original petition. In June 1962 the jury awarded him the largest libel judgment in history to that date—$3.5 million. An appeals court subsequently reduced the amount to $500,000.

When all the barristers had collected their fees and all the debts he had accumulated had been paid off, John Henry didn't get anything out of his long ordeal but the satisfaction that he had taken on one of the strongest political forces this nation had ever seen and whupped 'em good.

Despite his vindication, CBS would not rehire Faulk. Many years passed before he was able to work again as an entertainer. In 1963 he wrote one of the most moving books I have ever read, *Fear on Trial*, about his experiences. It is one of my favorite books, and it should be required reading for every government class, from high school through college. It demonstrates how our political system can be abused.

Johnny returned to south Austin in 1968. From 1975 to 1980 he appeared as a homespun character on the television program "Hee-Haw."

During the 1980s he wrote and produced two one-man plays. In both *Deep in the Heart* (1986) and *Pear Orchard, Texas* he portrayed characters imbued with the best of human instincts and the worst of cultural prejudices.

In 1974 CBS, the network that had fired Johnny and had refused to hire him back, broadcast their movie version of *Fear on Trial*. Also in 1974 he was finally able to read the dossier that the FBI had maintained on his activities since the 1940s. It was filled with rumors and half-truths.

Disillusioned and desirous of a return to the country, Faulk moved to Madisonville, Texas. He returned to Austin in 1981. In 1983 he campaigned for the congressional seat abdicated by Democrat-turned-Republican Phil Gramm. Although he lost the three-way race, John Henry was pleased that he "gave the voters some clear options."

During the 1980s he traveled the nation, lecturing to anyone who would listen that they must be ever vigilant of their constitutional rights and to take advantage of the freedoms guaranteed by the First Amendment. The Center for American History at the University of Texas at Austin sponsors the annual John Henry Faulk Conference on the First Amendment.

John Henry's personal life was almost as tumultuous as his professional one. In 1940 he wed Hally Wood and they had a daughter. But the marriage didn't last.

John Henry married Lynne Smith, whom he met at a New York City rally for presidential candidate Henry Wallace in the spring of 1948. They had two daughters and a son. But eventually that marriage also ended in divorce

In 1965 John Henry married Elizabeth Peake. They had one son.

John Henry Faulk died in Austin of cancer on April 9, 1990. The city of Austin named the downtown branch of the public library in his honor.

John Henry Faulk, left, as I knew him, with J. Frank Dobie.

Photo courtesy of Austin History Center, Austin Public Library

Meetin' Johnny Faulk

My first recollection of the fabled storyteller and super patriot John Henry Faulk took place on the front steps of the general store in the northeast Texas town of Cumby. John Henry moseyed up with Ben Green, a longtime storyteller who was indigenous to the Cumby, Weatherford, and Dallas areas.

Now, Ben was a notorious storyteller and raconteur. And my grandfather, Kyle Alexander, had been known to spin out some Moby Dick sized whoppers. So, I watched patiently to see if this new guy was going to be chewed up and spit out by the old hands.

It was another hot summer day, and the conversation focused on the fact that we were in a drought that had gone on for almost two months. John Henry listened for several minutes, then said, "Hell, boys, that ain't nuthin'. We had a drought down around Austin, it went so long, it never did rain again!"

As we all laughed and nodded our heads, I knew that this was a man fully prepared to deal with the locals and not give an inch. You see, he knew "the first liar always loses." John Henry had out-waited two of the best in the west. Then he went in for the kill with a punch line that had all of us on the ground.

Seems as though John Henry was visitin' in our neck of the woods, as he put it, "a talkin' to some of those educated idiots at the college down the road in Commerce." I would find out later that John Henry had always had a love-hate relationship with all sorts of educational organizations. Much of this distrust grew out of his horribly unjust treatment at the hands of the McCarthy Committee, which caused him to go from one of America's best known entertainers to a cab driver.

Upon learning that I did some of my growing up south of Austin, just like he did, John Henry said "It's the prettiest spot this side of Heaven." He paused for a moment, took another draw on his pipe, and said, "Hell, maybe we all have done died, and this is Heaven." He paused again, then said, "You know, I'm probably wrong about that. Oh, we may be dead alright, but it's too damn hot for Heaven!"

John Henry asked me where I was going to be going to high school. I told him I was attending Porter Junior High and would then go to Travis High, which is about half a mile from his family home. I added that I would like to go to the University of Texas. He rocked back on the wooden soft drink carton, upon which he was seated, and stared at me.

I began to get nervous. I fully expected him to say something to imply that I might not have what it takes to get through the "big" university. But that was not at all what he had to offer.

In his slow, twangy, somewhat nasal drawl he said, "Well, I guess that could be all right. But I sure do wonder 'bout some of the folks that run that joint. I think if they had built the UT tower in proportion to the intellect of the board of regents, it would have been an underground structure!"

As I recovered from my full-blown attack of guffaws, it was the first time I realized I was truly in the presence of greatness.

Ben Green seldom sat back and relinquished the floor for long. But he too rocked back and sucked on a horrible smelling, greenish-black, cigar. Getting down wind on his smoke, I said, "Ben how can you suck on that thing? It smells like somethin' the cat dragged in!"

Ben thought that was hilarious and proceeded to puff harder, sending off enough smoke signals to be seen five miles away. Having noticed my implied criticism, and the fact that I had sidled around to the upwind side of the gathering, Ben turned and offered me the mate to the cigar he was sucking on.

Well, to my way of thinking, this was a huge step towards manhood. To actually get to sit there, kinda like the grown-ups, with a cigar was something mighty special. Then again, I started to think about why I had moved to the other side of the group, 'cause that cigar did put out a mighty powerful stink.

I'm pretty sure my face went blank and my eyes might have rolled around a bit, as I tried to get my mind wrapped around this puzzlement. I say that because all three of these fine gentlemen began to chuckle and look at me funny like.

Not wanting to appear to be a tenderfoot, I wanted to accept that cigar. Now, for neither the first time nor the last, I was using some pretty lame logic (or stinkin' thinkin'). The way I had it figured, these were grown-ups that wouldn't offer me anything that wouldn't be all right for me. (You bet!)

So I accepted the cigar. John Henry said, "Here, let me light that stogie up for you." I was trying to act like this was just an everyday thing for me, which everybody, including the old hound asleep in the shade on the sidewalk, knew was not the case. I actually think I heard that mutt chuckle to himself, since I didn't even realize I needed to clip off the tip, before lighting up.

After getting the tip clipped, John Henry leaned forward, holding out a nice shiny Zippo lighter, trying to put the flame on the very tip of the cigar. I was nervous enough he had to work at chasing the tip of the cigar around for a bit. But eventually his persistence paid off. For him, but not for me.

I did know enough not to rear back and really take a big draw on it. I figured I'd just sorta puff at it a bit and then stub it out. Then I'd tell them it was to "save the rest for later."

I don't know where they get the gases for gas warfare from, but I could suggest one damn fine source. The smoke from that nasty devil went through my sinuses and lungs like Sherman's Civil War march to the sea. Just as in Sherman's march, I felt there were some critical areas of my being that were on fire, and in ruins.

I ended my stay with them that day by coughing out a thank you to Ben for the "great" cigar, after which I stumbled off down the street towards my grandparents' house. I thought that would be the appropriate place for me to die, since I was sure that was soon to happen. I could hear them laughin' for a full block.

That night my grandmother called me for supper. To say that eating wasn't something I wanted to do was an understatement. But I made a stab at it, with very limited success. Every so often I'd look up and catch my grandfather glancing over at me with a sly smile.

After eating only a few bites, I asked to be excused, and my grandmother said that would be OK. As I was gimping back to my room, I heard her say, "That boy eats just like a dog, one meal he eats everything in sight. The next meal he doesn't eat diddly."

I heard Kyle just chuckle, then say, "Yep it's a mystery, sure enough," then chuckle again.

You know I do enjoy a good cigar every now and again. But in all these years I have never encountered anything as nasty as those cigars Ben had. Thinkin' about it today, if Ben hadn't passed a few years back, I would have him arrested for assault with a deadly weapon!

The last time I was in Cumby, I went to the Cumby Cemetery to visit the graves of my father, Kyle and Ludie, and Ben. I walked to the back where Ben has a kind of a corral around his marker, and I lit up a cigar and recalled that story. I'm sure I heard Ben and Kyle a laughin'.

Sometime after the cigar fiasco, Ben had told me a bit about how John Henry had been a "big-time radio feller. Why he was even on television pretty regular. You know, Jim, I frankly don't hold with furniture that talks to you. It just don't seem natural."

That afternoon John Henry had completed, as he put it, his "jawin' at that institution of higher learnin'." We had settled in again on the front porch of the general store and were sippin' on some sodas. Ben asked John Henry, "How'd you ever get so crosswise with that McCarthy feller that he put you on that blacklist?"

John Henry sat quietly for several minutes. He finally said, "There are lots of people who will trample all over other people to achieve power. Fortunately, it's very rare when someone achieves the power to trample all over the constitutional freedoms that our forefathers so wisely laid out. We have the best political system in the world. And even it went terribly wrong because of fear of the unknown [communism]. It was really no different than the Salem witch trials. McCarthy didn't really know anything about me 'cept that I wasn't 'bout to cowtow to all that blarney he was a spewin'."

John Henry talked for nearly an hour solid, about our country, our constitution, our laws, our political process, about patriotism, and about some of the weasels we've elected over the years. It was one of the most stirring events of my life. Before then all of those things were ideals that were to be believed in, but were not active, living, parts of my everyday life. Before that day, history and government were just names for incredibly boring classes in school. Only then did they begin to come to life.

But that day, hearing that man talk about the country he still so deeply loved, despite the fact it was that same government that had destroyed his life, I developed a much deeper appreciation of just how fragile this way of life we take for granted really is. I've never looked at the government, the constitution, government service, or the privilege of voting in the same way again. Before me sat the man who all holders of public trust should be required to study.

No, John Henry and I didn't always agree on everything politically. But I never, never doubted that his objectives were the same as mine, to create a better government for the people of this nation.

Barbara Jordan was a neighbor of mine for a few years. I did get to meet her a couple of times, but much to my regret, I never had the opportunity to really sit down and chat. She was the only other person I've ever heard speak with the same fervor and overwhelming love of country that John Henry did. I don't know if those two super patriots ever had the opportunity to discuss their views. But I would have given anything to be a fly on the wall. It would have been the equivalent of sitting in on Washington, Jefferson, and Franklin swapping thoughts in a backroom in 1776.

The Fight

by John Henry Faulk

It was in the late fall, and I was in Cumby for a few days. It had been dry for several weeks, as one blue norther after another swept across the state, dropping the temperature and the humidity. The usual culprits had gathered on the sunny front porch of the general store to commiserate on the weather and swap some tales. John Henry was up from Austin again and hangin' out with Ben Green.

As they strode up, Ben was clenched onto another ugly cigar, and John Henry was clenched onto his pipe. They had somehow gotten onto the subject of folks getting into disagreements. Ben commented on the number of times he'd seen "full growed men a rollin' around in the cow plop tryin' to negotiate a better deal."

As was his way, John Henry listened attentively, nodding at the appropriate times. It was only after Ben had wound down a bit that John Henry started his story about two ranchers who shared a mile of fence that separated their two ranches. Now, truth be told, they were both about as tight as a tick when it came to money. And they both tried to put as little work and money into their joint fence as possible. (It was, and still is, the custom to share the costs of a fence and its maintenance if both parties are running livestock.)

So John Henry explained that about once a month the cattle from one or the other would get through the fence and upset the rancher on the other side. Often it was never really known whose cattle knocked down a section of fence, because by the time it was discovered, all the cows would have decided the grass was greener in the other field, and they would have just traded fields.

Well one day it happened again, and for rancher John, that was the final straw. Now, he knew rancher Bill was in town, and he set out to straighten it out once and for all. Well, when rancher John arrived at the co-op, rancher Bill was loading some of the small square hay bales onto his trailer. Small is a very relative term, most of these "small" square bales run from forty to a hundred pounds apiece.

Bill and John set to jawin'. Then they set to pushin'. Then they set to punchin'. And finally they both grabbed hay hooks. For those of you unfamiliar with a hay hook, it is one very nasty little device. The hook part is similar to the nasty-looking device that Captain Hook used in *Peter Pan*.

With one in each hand, you then stick the hooks into the opposite ends of the bale of hay and lift it up by the handle, which fits into your hand like the pull handle used to start small gasoline engines. These handles allow you to maintain a solid grip and lift quite a bit of weight.

John Henry laughed as he described how these two took to a dancin' and a swingin'. Neither one was going to back down, but neither one wanted to really kill the other. They only wanted to hurt each other, a lot.

Now, you might ask, why didn't some of the passersby jump in the middle and break them up. Which just proves that you've never seen a hay hook up close. Nobody wanted to take a chance on gettin' their gizzard sliced open by these two fools. Besides, "sooner or later they wuz gonna have to have a come-to-Jesus meetin.'"

Bill drew first blood, hookin' John a bit in the upper arm. Bill was a prayin' that John would give it up. "When hell freezes over" was his comment as they set back after each other. John decided that he needed an advantage, so he hopped up on the stack of hay bales. Bill scurried right up there with him. So there they stood, dancin' like a pair of banty roosters, ten foot up on top of these hay bales.

By this point, a pretty good sized crowd had gathered, and there was even some "speculatin' on the outcome" (you see, gamblin' is a sin, but there is nothin' in the Good Book about not speculatin').

At that point, here come the two wives, who had been shopping together, because they were each other's nearest neighbors and best friends. They come a strollin' around the corner and realize who the two fools are that are dancin' about on top of the hay bales.

One of the wives screams as the two ranchers are makin' another move at each other. Well, hearin' the scream, they both turn and look, just in time to totally miss each other and fall off the bales of hay and into a heap on the ground, both of 'em a moanin' and a groanin' from some mementos they picked up from their fall.

Bill's wife, Judy, asked the rhetorical question, "My God in Heaven, Bill, what on earth has possessed you to get out there like that and go actin' the fool?"

Bill mumbled that he thought he'd broken his arm. To which Judy sent back an unsympathetic harrumph.

John's wife, Ann, stood there over her fallen husband, with her hands on her hips. She shook her head in disgust and a mumblin', "damn fool."

John, tryin' for some sympathy, said, "I think I broke my ankle, and my ribs aren't feelin' too good either."

"Good," she replied. Turning to Judy she said, "My mother told me not to marry this jackass."

"I didn't do one bit better myself," replied Judy.

The ladies asked what they were fighting about, and they mumbled something about the other not taking care of their part of the fence they shared. The ladies looked at each other and shook their heads in disbelief.

The wounded warriors sat there in total shock as their spouses agreed to add two more strands of wire to the existing fence and to have a "healthy" neighbor come over and put in a few new posts.

The ladies then told the guys, "We're takin' one car, you two share the other car to get over to the doctor and then come on home." And the ladies walked off together.

By this point all of the spectators were chuckling and settlin' up on their "speculatin'" that they might have won.

As they limped over to the car they would be sharing on the ride to the doctor's office, the two could be heard arguing about who had won the fight.

We all waited to hear what John Henry had to say to wrap up his story, since he normally had a moral at the end of the trail. Well, he leaned back and said, "You know, I think those two guys were pretty damn smart."

We looked at him confused, and I asked him why in the world he thought those two yahoos were smart.

"'Cause they both realized they were better off a fightin' with each other, than tryin' to fight with those women!"

Chapter Twelve

Richard "Kinky" Friedman

Legendary Author, Entertainer, Storyteller, and Character

Kinky is not typical; this is a truism of all the levels of our existence. While some march to a different drummer, Kinky marches to a different band. Knowing this, it will come as no surprise that his approach to folklore and storytelling is very, very different.

If you have never read his books, you should. They are not classic folklore fare. Through his books he entertains and also sneaks in some education about Texas too. Do you know how Pipe Creek got its name?

Most of the folklorists cited in this book came to my acquaintance by some fluke of timing and proximity. Most of these folks were encountered, and I then realized how special they were and sought to learn more about, and from, them.

Richard "Kinky" Friedman is another story completely (folks have been sayin' that about him most of his life). I first heard of Kinky in the sixties. I saw in the local paper that a group named Kinky Friedman and the Texas Jewboys was appearing in Austin. I figured that someone willing to run with that moniker had to be somethin' special.

At that time I was singing with a couple of different bands and was always interested in all the other groups on the scene. That was no small task in Austin at the time; it seemed like everyone who had a garage had a band practicing in it. It took me many years to realize that this was not the case in every other town in America.

One of my favorite spots to sing was the Chequered Flag, located on the corner of Fifteenth and Lavaca. The "Flag" had become the waterin' hole for a whole passel of talented folks. Allen Damron and Rod Kennedy had created a forum for the sixties' new wave of artists. If you cared about the music and tried to do it well, Allen would let you "run it up and see if anyone will salute."

On this particular Friday night, I was sittin' at one of the back tables with one of the neatest folks it's ever been my pleasure to meet, Bill Moss. At slightly over six foot tall and well over two hundred pounds, Bill was an imposing specimen. He wore a dark knit watch cap most of the time, giving him the appearance of a longshoreman. His voice was full and rich, with an often-used laugh that filled the room.

All of these things were impressive about Bill, but what immediately caught my eye was his incredible talent at playing the guitar. Bill would sit on a stool, smoke a cigarette, and tell jokes. Nothin' special 'bout that, except that the whole time, he would be playing his own background music on his guitar with one hand! He did this by "downing" the strings on the neck of the guitar with his left hand. Trust me on this one, that takes a truckload of talent, not to mention some damn strong fingers.

I later learned that Bill had attended the Julliard School of Music. As we talked on, Bill answered a question that it had never occurred to me to ask, "I've been black most my life."

"Do tell."

"Yep, had this beautiful built-in tan most of my life. I know it's the type of tan you skinny white boys would kill for. That's why the news networks are always hiring me as a stringer for things going on in Austin. I'm their 'color' man!" Then came that beautiful basso profundo laugh again.

"You know anything 'bout this Kinky guy?" I asked.

"You don't know the Kinkster?" More basso profundo laughing. "Jim, you are in for a real trip."

Now, at that point in our culture, a "trip" could cover a wide range of things, from good to bad and back again. At that point, out walked what appeared to be a five-and-a-half-foot-tall cross between a cowboy and a rabbi. His well-worn boots were in desperate need of attention; they perfectly matched with the rest of his outfit. His cowboy cut shirt, vest, and hat were pretty standard fare for the "hat" acts of the time.

The only thing that looked like it had been purchased in the last decade was a beat-up, old, butt-ugly cigar that protruded from his clenched teeth.

It was from the shoulders up that things got very interesting. Kinky had earned his moniker fair and square. The top of his head was covered with hair that seemed to be desperately trying to escape his scalp in every possible direction. I felt certain that there had to have been an electrical accident involved. (He refers to it as his Lyle Lovett starter kit.)

Atop this full head of springs, precariously sat a large black hat (about a 4X beaver I would guess from the droop in the brim). Now I didn't see any way his lid was going to stay atop his bobbing head for long. (Much to my amazement that hat rode through the whole evening performance without moving an inch. Only later did I discover the Kinkster's secret. His hat was stuffed full to the top with even more hair. You couldn't have knocked his hat off with a cannonball!)

Kinky Friedman with his cat Cuddles.

Photo by Stefanie Kong

Peeking out beneath the floppy black hat brim were two dark eyes that didn't miss a single thing in the room. These eyes were perched above a nose that strongly indicated some distinctly Yiddish ancestry. Beneath that was a full, black, bristly mustache that threatened to grow over the smallish mouth below.

However, no matter how much the mustache tried, there was no way it would ever overgrow that ever present, huge cigar that seemed anchored between clenched teeth. It seemed at times to serve an additional purpose, as a battering ram, such as those found on the front of icebreakers in the Arctic regions.

Kinky walked with Allen up to the table where Bill and I were seated.

"Howdy, Bill."

"Hey there, Kinky, this is Jim; he does some singin' here now and again," said Allen.

"So?"

"So, say hello."

"Maybe later." Kinky turned and walked towards the stage.

I turned to Bill and asked, "Is he always that friendly?"

"Nope. You caught him on a good night."

"Damn. I'm lucky I don't need some bandages."

"Like I said, ya caught him on a good night. Just stay tuned."

After the performance, Kinky said his howdys as he worked his way through the crowd, back to where we were sitting. Then, as if there had been no break in the conversation, he says, "So Jim, what kind of singin' do you do? And, why the hell would you hang out with losers like Allen and Bill? You got no taste at all?"

"Nope, I lost it all bettin' on the ponies."

"You know, Jim, horse sense is what keeps horses from bettin' on people."

"I'll bet you're right."

This exchange was vintage Kinky. He is highly intelligent, extremely articulate, and has a very quick wit. He's a former honors program student from the University of Texas. (In a strange twist of fate, one of Kinky's roommates during part of this time was Charles Whitman, who sometime later climbed to the top of the tower with a small arsenal and killed sixteen people.)

For those around him, Kinky's wit can be a double-edged sword. Like most of the folklorists I know, he doesn't abide fools, AT ALL. He likes ya, or he doesn't. And even if he likes you, some days it takes a pretty keen eye to tell.

People continuously ask me, "What it's like to be a friend of Kinky's?"

"'Bout like bein' one of his enemies," is my standard reply.

A mutual friend describes it this way, "Bein' around Kinky is a lot like makin' love with a porcupine. Oh, it can be wonderful, but you will always pick up your share of the barbs."

Kinky is one of the kindest individuals I know. His list of charities is lengthy. Oh, he can be cantankerous, but I've never known him to be mean to anyone. At times folks might think Kinky is picking on them, but that's just part of his nature. If you hold yourself out to be anything special, you might as well paint a bulls-eye on yourself, because Kinky will put you in his sights.

If Kinky was ever Politically Correct, I am sure it was totally by accident. The term has never entered his vocabulary except as an object of derision. Amazingly, songs like "Keep Your Biscuits in the Oven and Your Buns in the Bed" failed to win over many converts from the libbers crowd. (Kinky says "Biscuits" won the "highly coveted" Male Chauvinist Pig of the Year award from the National Organization of Women.)

After he did the same thing for rednecks, with "Asshole From El Paso," folks began to realize that he was poking fun at the world around him. Kinky targets his pointed humor at everybody. Liberal, conservative, young, old, rich, poor, black, brown, or white. If you're in his world, you're fair game.

To all he has the same comment, "To hell with 'em if they can't take a joke!" And that's why it works! If you put the same words in anybody else's mouth, they would be roasted on an open fire. But Kinky keeps right on truckin', because he targets everybody. There is no discrimination when everyone is treated the same.

To steal a quote from an acquaintance, Texas State Comptroller Bob Bullock, the lifelong Democrat had once been asked why he hung out with so many Republicans and Independents. Bob looked at the questioner and said, "If you've got two people with the same opinion, one of 'em is not needed!"

Kinky's that way. He seeks the challenges of life, studies them, and then faces them down.

A couple of years ago Kinky was doing a benefit for the Austin Writer's League at Esther's Follies, on east Sixth Street in Austin. My wife Sally, son James, and I had volunteered to help out where needed. Kinky had arrived with a lovely young lady. He introduced her to me and said, "Jim, while I'm on, you be sure and keep her away from the *other* dirty old men."

When he returned after his show, I told him, "Kinky this lady is young, bright, and beautiful. What the hell does she see in you?"

Kinky stopped, peeked out from under his hat brim, and switched his stogie to the other side of his mouth. He then kicked his hat back a bit and said, "Damn if I know. What the hell are you doin' here? Couldn't find a payin' gig?"

"This is a payin' gig. I'm makin' a fortune sellin' rotten fruit and vegetables to your audience."

"Damn, Jim, you're mean as ever."

"Ditto."

We talked on for about an hour about writing, singing, and other interesting topics. That's Kinky and that's why we get along so well.

Kinky Friedman's contributions to Texas storytelling have come through several forms. Originally it was his songwriting and performing. Now he doesn't perform as much, but has become very well known as an author. He has published four-teen novels about a politically incorrect private detective, named Kinky Friedman, who lives on a ranch south of Kerrville and also has an apartment in the Greenwich Village area of New York City. All of which is true for Kinky.

It is through his novels that I believe Kinky has made a sig-nificant contribution to the world of Texas folklore. At first glance his books seem too amusing and quirky.

But on closer examination you realize he has introduced you to Texas and what it's like to be a Texan. His love of Texas and its history pops up throughout the stories. He teaches the history of the towns and traditions.

Biography of Kinky "Big Dick" Friedman

The Making of a Jewish Sex Symbol

Kinky was born at an early age and spent most of his growin' up years tryin' to grow up on his family's Echo Hill Ranch, which is a camp for kids. Even now Kinky fits right in.

He graduated from a highly selective University of Texas Honors program (in which Kinky says most participants were recognized by characteristic facial tics). He joined the Peace Corps and served from 1966 to 1968 in the Borneo jungles.

Returning from the jungles of Borneo, he attacked the jun-gles of the music world, by forming his now infamous band, Kinky Friedman and the Texas Jewboys. Kinky describes them as "a country band with a social message," which he later con-ceded was a ludicrous notion.

The Jewboys produced country hits, such as "Get Your Bis-cuits in the Oven and Your Buns in the Bed" and "They Ain't Makin' Jews Like Jesus Anymore." They toured with Bob Dylan and played the Grand Ole Opry. However, their career lasted only as long as that of Hank Williams, one of Kinky's inspirations.

Kinky then moved to Greenwich Village in New York City, where he became close friends with radio talk host Don Imus and a group of colorful Greenwich Village people who later became characters in his books. He also became a regular performer at New York's famous Lone Star Café and appeared in several movies.

One evening in the mid-1980s, Kinky was walking back to his loft from The Monkey's Paw, where he'd eaten dinner, when he saw a woman being robbed. He quickly subdued the criminal and saved the woman from the crazed robber. Newspapers screamed, "Country Singer Plucks Victim from Mugger."

Thus began the Kinkster's career as a crime fighter. This event inspired him to write his first book, about a private detective living in Texas and New York and coincidentally named Kinky Friedman. Real friends have been merged into his novels.

Greenwich Killing Time, Kinky's first mystery novel, was published in 1986, and it was a huge success. After thirty years of writing, Kinky was an overnight success. Since then the Kinkster has published over a dozen additional novels, each selling well and adding new praise for his talents as an author.

High praise came from old friend Willie Nelson when he said, "Kinky Friedman is the best whodunit writer to come along since Dashiell what's-his-name."

In the series of books, Kinky Friedman the detective has encountered lions, armadillos, drug dealers, Nazi SS troopers, crazed music promoters, pretty women, and the FBI. And throughout it all, Kinky tells the stories of being a true son of Texas.

Like Kinky, his books are totally unique. His mysteries are characterized by their clever, twisting plots that hold the reader in suspense to the very last page. Yet every page is filled with his unique humor. One-liners are scattered throughout his books, and any regular readers will find themselves quoting him.

I love Kinky's books. To me they have an old-time private detective Sam Spade or Mike Hammer quality about them. And yet the humor, unique characters, and plot twists make them so much more.

In his usual, self-deprecating way, Kinky says, "One of the joys I get out of writing is that people seem to be getting a lot more out of my books than I put into them."

It's certainly true that a lot of people do get a lot out of his books. His fans are as unique as he is. This spectrum of admirers include Nelson Mandela, Bob Dylan, Steve Allen, Dave Berry, President Clinton, George Bush, Waylon Jennings, and Willie Nelson; literary figures include Joseph Heller and Larry McMurtry.

Kinky's novels are now published in fifteen different countries and in so many different languages even he can't read two of them.

Although it wasn't his first book, I would recommend you start his series with his 1998 book, *Blast from the Past*. This book is a prequel to the other books and will answer a lot of questions about how Kinky became involved with many of the cast of characters, referred to as the Village Irregulars.

You'll meet Steve Rambam when he was a rabbinical student, Mort Cooperman when he was a street cop on the parking-ticket detail, and Ratso when he was, well, Ratso. *Blast from the Past* also marks the first appearance of the girl in the peach-colored dress, an already spunky and flirtatious six-year-old, the unusually perspicacious and drop-dead-gorgeous Stephanie DuPont.

Kinky's other books include;
Greenwich Killing Time
A Case of Lone Star
When the Cat's Away
Musical Chairs
The Kinky Friedman Crime Club (a compilation)
Road Kill
The Love Song of J. Edgar Hoover
God Bless John Wayne
Three Complete Mysteries (a compilation)
Armadillos & Old Lace
Frequent Flyer
More Kinky Friedman (a compilation)
Elvis, Jesus and Coca-Cola
Spanking Watson
The Mile High Club (due out Fall 2000)
Meanwhile, Back at the Ranch (due out in 2001)

As Kinky tells it, he now lives a rather monastic life with two cats, five dogs, a pet armadillo, a much-used Smith-Corona typewriter, and a small truck load of Montecristo #2 cigar butts on a ranch in the Texas hill country near Kerrville, Texas. He says he's the only non-land-owning, cigar-smoking, mystery-writing, cat-loving, Irish whiskey-swigging, country musician and Jewish sex symbol from Palestine (Texas, that is).

Kinky seldom performs except "at bar mitzvahs, whore-houses, and book signings." This is only half true, because Kinky is a very generous person, and he performs regularly for a wide variety of charities. You'll be in for a treat to catch his act at any one of these places or at a rare public venue.

Now, about his name (you thought I had forgotten, didn't you?) Kinky often gives his full name as Kinky "Big Dick" Friedman. That's even the message on his answering machine. I thought it was amusing and thought nothing more about it.

Then a few months back, Sal and I were planning a trip to the coast, and Kinky asked us to stop by the ranch on our way. I

Jim and Kinky enjoy a good cigar together.

Photo by Sally Gramon

knew he was working around the clock to meet a book deadline, so I asked him if I could pick up anything for him. Knowing I smoke a cigar once in a while, he asked me to pick up a box of cigars from our friend Rob Robinson, who runs the Hill Country Humidor in San Marcos.

We got to the ranch, did our howdys, dropped off the cigars, and he gave me a check for them. Now Sal is an accountant, so I just handed the check over to her to deposit the next time she got by the bank. We did our good-byes and wished him well on completing the book and left Echo Hill in our rearview mirror.

A bit further down the road, Sal was high diving into her purse to find something (it's big and it devours things like car keys and cell phones). Anyhow, she holds up the check and asks if I had read it. I told her no and asked if Kinky had misplaced a decimal. She said the amount was right, it was the name that was a surprise. There it was, bigger than Dallas, the name on the check was Kinky "Big Dick" Friedman.

Here is an example of vintage Kinkster. It was recently announced on his web site that, "much to the dismay of Kinky's many female fans, he will not, as was rumored, be signing a contract as an exclusive model for Speedo swimwear. He is however considering modeling American Latex Products and demonstrating the merits of the Sealy Mattress Company's products."

That's the public Kinky. But let me tell you a little bit about my friend Kinky. Regularly, over the years, Kinky has put on benefits for friends and organizations that need help. He is a regular supporter of many worthwhile organizations, including the Austin Writers League.

Kinky helped found the Utopia Animal Rescue Ranch, located in Utopia, Texas (northwest of San Antonio). This wonderful organization provides homes and care for deserted and neglected animals (www.utopiarescue.com). Each year Kinky heads an ever-growing list of celebrities that put on an annual "Bonefit" to raise money to help cover the expense of caring for these critters. One of my favorite Kinky quotes is "Money can buy you a dog, but only love can make him wag his tail."

Kinky writes just like he talks. He is always irreverent and unpredictable. And when he talks, Kinky brings out the soul and spirit of Texas. Here are a few examples:

"If someone is late to meet you in New York, it is a cause for major stress and consternation. Texas, on the other hand, is close enough to Mexico to have absorbed the cultural common sense of mañana. Tomorrow will be just fine."

"I've found that my normal lifestyle is not healthy for green plants or children. I never really was a role model for either one. But I always figured if kids were going to screw up their lives, they should figure out their own ways to do it, not learn it from their elders."

He often checks to see if there are kids in his audience. It never hurts to check out who is in your audience when one of your hit songs is "Asshole From El Paso."

Commenting on some of his New York friends, he says, "They just don't have many folks like them in Texas, and we'd kinda like to keep it that way."

In one of his early books, *Armadillos & Old Lace*, published by Simon & Schuster in 1994, he described his drive from the San Antonio airport to his Echo Hill ranch south of Kerrville after spending some time in New York. Notice how skillfully he blends the story, humor, and Texas history.

He describes the small towns they pass through including Pipe Creek, so named after an Indian raid a hundred years ago. During the raid one of the settlers ran back into his burning cabin to retrieve his favorite pipe.

"Farther down Highway 16, we took a left and rolled in a cloud of dust across a cattle guard, and into the sunset toward Echo Hill. The ranch was set back about two and a half miles from the scenic little highway, but ever since we passed Pipe Creek we'd been in a world that most New Yorkers never got to see. They believed the deer, the jackrabbits, the raccoons, the sun setting the sky on fire in the west, and the Cypress trees along the creek only really existed in Disney movies."

Many Texans, Kinky and I included, love a good cigar. To give you an example of his skill at making something simple fun to read about, here is how Kinky described to me the simple task of lighting up a cigar: "Jim, the first thing you do is pick a good cigar. I prefer the Montecristo #2s. Next you begin the prenuptial preparations. Having acquired an intimate knowledge of the subject, you are now ready to light up. I always use a kitchen match, always keeping the tip well above the flame."

Kinky's description of his friend Ben Stroud: "Ben was not tall, but he was large and loud. In Texas you have to be large and loud, even if you are an autistic midget. Especially if you are an autistic midget!"

Echo Hill is one of Kinky's deepest passions. Every time we walk outside his cabin he comments on its beauty. "Over all these decades I've lived here, the outside world has always stopped at the cattle guard. That's the reason very few folks visit. The people at Echo Hill are special, because everybody is somebody here. Of the longtime residents and campers, everybody got to first base at least once in their lives. They may never get any farther, but at least they'd had a chance."

On describing his personal charm: "When I want to be, I have a certain superficial charm that lasts for about three minutes."

On chicken-fried steak, Kinky had some fightin' words: "It's an over ordered dish in Texas, and most of the time it's really nothing you'd want to write home about."

For many years Kinky had a pet armadillo named Dilly, who would often come by late at night and scratch on the door, looking for a snack from the always obliging Kinkster. He has often commented on how ironic it is that the extremely shy armadillo has been fated to share this great state of Texas with some of nature's very loudest creatures, human beings.

Kinky once observed that his cats would not only come up and sit on the papers he was trying to read, but somehow always knew exactly what portion of the document was important and then place some part of their anatomy over it, close their eyes, and smugly purr. To make use of this talent, he speculated that police, lawyers, and all other folks who must study large volumes of documents and pictures should just spread them out, then sit back, smoke a cigar, and see where the cat came to rest. Then just study the material under the cat, since that's obviously the only portion of importance.

It should be no surprise to you that Kinky has his own vocabulary and expressions:

You don't talk on the phone, you talk on the blower.

When we meet for lunch, we meet at Gary Cooper time, high noon.

You don't meet at midnight, you meet when Cinderella meets the guy with the foot fetish.

He often says, "If you have the choice of being humble or cocky, go cocky, there will always be time to be humble after you screw up. But after you screw up, it will be too late to try to be cocky."

And one final Texas Kinkyism: "Whether your destination is heaven or hell, you always have to change planes in Dallas."

Be sure to read one of Kinky's books. I guarantee it will be a one-of-a-kind experience. And if you read the whole series, I guarantee you will learn a great deal about Texans and the great state of Texas.

Chapter Thirteen

Liz Carpenter

It is said that the true measure of a person is what you do in the face of adversity. Liz Carpenter has spent her life facing huge obstacles and overcoming them. Her accomplishments are substantial, yet they pale in comparison with her monumental spirit and an incredible sense of humor.

After observing Liz Carpenter for many years, I think it would be more appropriate to measure her enthusiasm for life with a Richter Scale, because she is truly a force of nature. Erma Bombeck once observed, "No one remains the same person after meeting Liz; she makes Auntie Mame look like a shut-in."

At seventy-nine years of age, Liz Carpenter hasn't slowed a bit and maintains that life gets better all the time. Each day she works her way through a long list of phone calls and projects for her friends and charities.

Being a native Austinite, I had known who Liz Carpenter was many years before I had the privilege of meeting her. I became aware of who she was during the late 1950s, when she began handling the press releases on behalf of Lyndon Johnson and his family.

Our first meeting occurred at a benefit sponsored by the Austin Writers League. This wonderful organization has provided tremendous support to the local writing community in general and myself in particular. (In the webliography, at the back of this book, there is information on how to contact them.)

The benefit was being held at a super little Sixth Street club named Esther's Follies. This club provides a wide variety of very talented comedy, musical, and magic acts. It is a great place to spend an evening.

Our mutual friend Kinky Friedman was the evening's headliner. This particular evening was special for many reasons. My wife Sally, our son James, and I were having a wonderful time helping out as volunteers. And it was the first time in several years that Kinky and I had been able to visit. Between shows we were able to catch up on old times.

Following the last show, I had the privilege of meeting Ms. Carpenter as she came by to congratulate Kinky on another great show. I was immediately impressed by her, but not just by her lengthy list of accomplishments. No, what impressed me was Liz Carpenter, the down-home friendly person, and her obvious, boundless enthusiasm for life.

Her home is located near the top of a hill in West Lake Hills, just across the Colorado River from Austin. Nestled into the side of the hill, her Texas limestone home is totally surrounded by oaks, elms, mountain laurels, and a host of other native plants. It is so surrounded you can't even tell the home is there until you see the driveway.

As I walked through her lovely, orderly home, she led me into a beautiful, fully windowed room that looked out over the rolling hills of West Lake Hills and a skyline view of Austin. This was obviously her writing room, but the organization of it made it clear this was also her command center.

Beneath the windows, all the way across the far wall, extended a desk high countertop. Covering this workspace were telephones, computers, printouts, sticky notes, and, of course, her Rolodexes.

In the middle of the room sat her chair. Everything she needed to take care of business was within an arm's length. Phone calls came in a steady stream. Questions for her to handle. Like Van Cliburn on the keyboard, her fingers danced from notes to Rolodexes to the computer keyboard, retrieving the information the caller needed quickly. She still possesses her legendary capability to get things done.

Liz and Jim discuss writing, storytelling, and Texas in the middle of her "command center" in her beautiful home in West Lake Hills.

Photo by Jim Gramon

I marveled at the amount of activity and asked how she maintained the pace, despite being near eighty. She told me her secret energy source is "activist DNA." It is true that her Texas roots go back to a time before there was a Texas (I know this is most difficult for most Texans to envision, but there really was a time BT.)

Liz was born in the historic Texas town of Salado, Texas. Salado had once been a stopover on the early cattle trail that originated in San Antonio and led to the meat markets as far north as Chicago and Denver. In that age before motels, their home had a travelers' room in the house. This room did not open into the rest of the house, but was there to provide travelers with a place to stay for the night. (Now it's hard to imagine that folks did that sort of thing for total strangers. Most of the homes didn't even have locks for many years.)

A precocious child, Liz was brought up in a family interested in the world of education. She learned to never be inhibited about trying to achieve her goals. Her maternal grandfather, E. Sterling Robertson, was one of the founding fathers of Salado. In 1853 he had built the home now known as the Robertson house. It is the oldest home in Texas to be occupied by the same family.

Primarily interested in education, Robertson started Salado College, an institution that offered a classical education. Later, as a member of the Constitutional Convention of 1875, Robertson helped write the article providing free public education for children.

Also in 1875, Liz's great aunt Luella, then only eighteen years old, risked speaking out in public. She stood on Salado Hill and spoke to the college alumni and townspeople on: "The Mental Capabilities of Woman and a Plea for Her Higher Education." She said, "A young lady's mind should be garnered so well with seed for future usefulness, that even in the desert of life, she can find enjoyment and companionship in her books, her truest friends.... No inferiority on account of sex is observed in childhood...That [women] shall not be educated in common with man is a disgrace to the age in which we live." Succeeding years would prove that this educational and activist legacy was not wasted on Liz Carpenter.

When she was seven, her mother moved to Austin to be near the University so her children could get a college education. While attending Austin High School, Liz was the editor of the school paper, the *Austin Maroon*. As soon as she graduated from Austin High, Liz dove into activities at the University of Texas. She majored in journalism. Also she was already showing signs of an interest in politics. In her junior year she became the first female vice president of the student body.

After graduation in 1942, Liz headed for Washington. She married her college sweetheart, Leslie Carpenter, and they set up housekeeping. Liz took a job as a reporter with UPI (United Press International).

Franklin Roosevelt was president when she attended her first press conference. He was also the first president with whom she shook hands. But he was certainly not to be the last.

President Roosevelt's wife, Eleanor, also impressed Liz with her stand on the social equality of women. Liz was to remember Eleanor's crusade in years to come.

Liz and Les Carpenter organized the Carpenter News Bureau in Washington. They provided reporting on political activities in Washington for a string of southwestern newspapers.

Her perspective on the news changed considerably when Liz became the first woman to serve as an executive assistant to a vice president of the United States, a man with whom she would be associated with for the rest of his life, Lyndon B. Johnson. She was no longer reporting the news. Liz had become a part of the news.

The demands on her time during this period were tremendous. Her job required nearly round-the-clock dedication, and she juggled that along with her role as wife to Les and mother of Chris and Scott. A person without boundless energy could not have done it.

Then, in an instant, a life that she thought could not be more hectic, became just that. Liz was riding in the motorcade with President John F. Kennedy when he was assassinated, November 22, 1963.

In a few horrible hours her boss became president of the United States. One of the first things Lyndon did was ask Liz to join him and Lady Bird Johnson as a member of the White House staff.

Not only did they ask Liz to join them, the Johnsons paid her the high compliment of asking her what position she wanted. After brief contemplation Liz told Mrs. Johnson that she wanted to be her press secretary.

Life changed from that moment on. The busy life she had known before quickly became "the good old days, when things moved at a slower pace." Liz was now at the center of the lives of two of the most influential people in the world and at the center of many of the activities of the most powerful nation in the world.

Unfortunately, the job comes with no manual of instructions. Everything was learned on the fly, and, as she puts it, "some things flew better than others." But, like most of life's endeavors, Liz learned new things at every step of the way. And soon the young lady from Salado became adept at taking care of whatever came up in Washington.

Commenting on Liz's appointment, Lewis Gould later said, "Her appointment represented a key development in the institutional history of the position of the first lady. No previous presidential wife had appointed a professional journalist to serve as her press secretary."

Liz wasn't intimidated by the task of being a press secretary for the president and first lady, which made her an instant "spokesperson" at the White House. No, this Texas girl was invigorated by the whole opportunity. She once told me that one of the things that makes Texans unique is that they don't really see a setback as anything more than a delay in achieving a goal. They learn from the experience and move on.

Liz was soon the spokesperson to the world for not only President and Missus Johnson, but also the two daughters,

Lynda and Luci. She loved the action. Liz always said, "Show me the eye of a bureaucratic storm and I head right into it."

You see, Liz Carpenter is a force of nature, and as such, not only is her body in constant motion, she also sets all of those around her in motion. By the use of her art of persuasion and her famous (or infamous) row of Rolodexes, she can find the people she needs to mobilize for whatever the task at hand may be. Many of my friends are shocked to find out she never was a lobbyist.

It's not hard to see why Lyndon Johnson decided to make her an invaluable member of his administration and his family circle. Liz believes she has twisted more arms and cajoled more people than any politician, lobbyist, or journalist she knows. And the Johnsons were not the only ones who noticed that Liz can get things done. She has served in the administrations of three U.S. presidents.

And throughout all of that activity, her Rolodex kept growing and growing and growing...As she has often said, "What you need is a mission, a long-time Rolodex, and a lot of gall. I'm always looking for the people with fresh ideas, energy, stimulating dialogue, and inspiration."

The Liz Sutherland Carpenter Distinguished Visiting Lectureship in the Humanities and Sciences was established by the University of Texas System regents using funds raised at a benefit honoring Carpenter in 1983. Every year the lectureship brings together panels of notables to discuss humor and politics, and humorous politics.

These panels have included notable Texans like Molly Ivins, Cactus Pryor, and Governor Ann Richards. Liz has also brought speakers to the University of Texas such as former President Gerald Ford, First Lady Hillary Clinton, poet Maya Angelou, screenwriter and columnist Liz Smith, and actress Carol Channing.

Liz is a Distinguished Alumnus of the University of Texas at Austin and the author of three books. Her most recent book, *Unplanned Parenthood: The Confessions of a Seventy Something Surrogate Mother,* is the story of three teen-age nieces and nephews who became her wards when she was seventy-one years young.

It is true that her Texas roots go back to a time before there was a Texas. Her family's contributions to Texas began before there was a Texas. One of Liz's great-uncles died at the Alamo, at the age of only seventeen. Two of her great-grandfathers fought at the Battle of San Jacinto.

Years later her great-aunts worked for women's right to vote. "One [great-aunt], wearing a white dress and carrying a white parasol, worked behind the scenes sweet-talking the senators; another became so disgusted with Woodrow Wilson that she joined a group that threw eggs at the White House," said Carpenter.

Liz has often mused, "I've often wondered which aunt I would have gone with. I would have been torn."

"My mother instilled in each of us the belief that we could do anything. So, we learned to dream big and strive to realize those dreams," said Carpenter, who was one of the founders of the National Women's Political Caucus, worked for the Equal Rights Amendment, and more recently was asked by President Clinton to serve on the White House Conference on Aging.

The late author James Michener once said of Liz that "Texas never had a truer daughter. Her combination of wit and wisdom is infectious, encouraging and enlightening. Her zest for life is an example to us all."

Good news: Liz has just completed her third book, and the title says it all: *Start with a Laugh: An Insider's Guide to Roasts, Toasts, Eulogies and Other Speeches.*

Liz is an excellent writer. But she is also an excellent speaker. The following speech was delivered to a women's group meeting in San Antonio a couple of years ago.

One of my favorite pictures of the ever young Liz Carpenter

Photo by Jim Gramon

Texas Pioneer Women and The Alamo
A speech given by Liz Carpenter

If you are looking for PIONEER women of the West, you need look no farther. In this room are many of them—whether they are in prairie skirts or mini skirts. The dogged, gutsy,

DNAs we have inherited from our mothers and grand-mothers—women within our memories are in us.

Like many of you, I grew up with a very personal feeling about the dramatic story of the Alamo. My mother and father were history lovers. Both families had come to Texas before 1830. Ours was a house with boxes and trunks of letters written in early Texas times. If you were in Texas that early, you were likely to be part of the events that shaped it. So we children were swept up with the exciting drama of the Texas Revolution and knew exactly why there are three hallowed dates we now celebrate: March 2, March 6, and April 21.

Author's Note: For you non-historians:
1) March 2, 1836, Texas declares its independence from Mexico. 2) March 6, 1836, the Alamo fell after a thirteen-day siege. 3) April 21, 1836, the Texas army defeated Santa Anna at the Battle of San Jacinto.

The Alamo stirred my blood from the time I first heard of an ancestor, William Sutherland. He was only seventeen...this kinsman who fought here with Travis and died. Born in Alabama, he came with his family, fresh from a small college, settled in Jackson County, and attended the Navidad-Lavaca meeting in July of 1835.

There, he was fired up by the sense of betrayal which farmers and planters felt toward the Mexican government. In 1835 he rode into San Antonio and lived the next few months with the Jose Navarro family to study Spanish and ultimately medicine, in hopes of practicing here.

By January the tension and reports of Santa Anna's invasion grew. Colonel Travis called for volunteers to join the army, and William was there, in the square of this city, to sign up.

His story made Texas history come alive for us. We grew up knowing by heart William Barret Travis's stirring letter, summoning help, carried by couriers to Goliad and Gonzales. But we also had our own Alamo letter, written in the aftermath by my great-great-grandmother, Frances Menefee Sutherland, the mother of that seventeen-year-old boy, to her sister back in Alabama.

Like a prairie fire, news of the Alamo spread across Texas— we read in the accounts—routing the terrified settlements into retreating before the oncoming army of Santa Anna. Texans rallied behind Sam Houston, whole families moving with his army. One witness described the mood of those traveling along, "Tight-lipped women, prayerful mothers, squalling children, frightened slaves, the aged and infirm, all fleeing by ox cart, sled, two-wheeling jig."

Every able-bodied man in Texas was trying to reach Houston's army. They retreated toward the American army in Louisiana, followed by families and what belongings they could carry, moving from river to river until they reached San Jacinto, and here, on April 21, they stood their ground and attacked the unwary Mexican army as it slept.

There, in the swamps of San Jacinto, 600 stood with Sam Houston and won that eighteen-minute battle that turned the tide of history. There were no trumpets or drums. No band, but a Polish boy and his lone flute playing a plaintive love song—"Won't You Come to the Bower?"—for the march into battle. The Texans won.

Frances Menefee Sutherland wrote in June of 1836:

> Dear Sister, I received your kind letter in March but never had it been my power to answer till now, and now what I must say (Oh God support me). I will try to compose my mind while I give you a short history of a few months back.

My poor William is gone, yes, sister, gone from me. The sixth day of March, in the morning he was slain in the Alamo. Then his poor body committed to the flames. He was there, a volunteer when the Mexican army came there. At the approach of thousands of enemies they had to retreat into the Alamo where they were quickly surrounded by the enemy. Poor fellows!

The Mexican army kept nearly continual firing on them for thirteen days. They scaled the walls and killed every man in the fort but two black men...dear sister, Pray for me that I may have the grace to help in these great times of trouble.

Frances Menefee Sutherland's account of all this, written in anguish in the June that followed, is a valuable account of the runaway scrape those families that followed Houston's army a few miles ahead of the invading Santa Anna endured. We still read it in pride at our Sutherland family reunion—reunions that have been going on for sixty-seven years and indeed, I believe, these ties of Texas history bond us together more tightly.

What are the lessons of the Alamo for us today? Courage, of course, the courage to take a stand for freedom. That was the common valor of the fiery Travis, twenty-seven years old at the time, and others who were there including the oldest, men in their fifties like Davy Crockett, and Jim Bowie much older and ill who, when the line was drawn in the sand for those who were willing to stay, had his cot moved over.

"Braver men were never assembled in a fighting band," historians have said. For me, the living message of the Alamo offers lessons for us today: rallying cries for support do bring recruits. We see it in our pioneer mothers and aunts, and we see it in the liberated women of today.

Travis sent out his call:

To the people of Texas and all Americans in the World: I am besieged by a thousand or more of the Mexicans under Santa Anna. I have sustained a continued bombardment and cannonade for 24 hours and have not lost a man. The enemy has demanded a surrender at discretion, otherwise the garrison are to be put to the sword, if the fort is taken. I have answered the demand with a cannon shot, and our flag still waves proudly from the walls. I shall never surrender or retreat. Then, I call on you in the name of Liberty, of patriotism and everything dear to the American character to come to our aid, with all dispatch. The enemy is receiving rein-forcements daily and will no doubt increase to three or four thousand in four or five days. If this call is neglected, I am determined to sustain myself as long as possible and to die like a soldier what is due to his own honor and that of his country.

Victory or Death,

William Barret Travis, Lt. Col. and Commander

P.S. The Lord is on our side—when the enemy appeared in sight we had not three bushels of corn. We have since found in deserted houses 80 or 90 bushels and got into the walls 20 or 30 head of Beeves.

Travis relied upon the character of the early settlers and knew that aid would come, and it did—thirty-two brave men leaving a town of wailing children and certain widows in Gonza-les...too few to save the Alamo but enough to become the stuff of which legends are made.

A handful of committed people still create legends in peace as well as war in the nineties. You and I have known many of them. The great movements of the sixties for justice, for women's equality, for the environment didn't begin in Washington but in a church in Selma, in the noisy women's caucuses of Austin and Houston, in the shrinking wilderness, in the crowded city streets. A few brave souls, often dismissed as cra-zies and zealots, drew their own line in the dust and rallied others to their cause.

In my time of seventy-seven years, I have heard the rallying voice of Franklin Roosevelt, telling a generation that it "has a rendezvous with destiny"; Dwight D. Eisenhower's warning "to guard against the unwarranted influence of the military-industrial complex"; the pledge of Martin Luther King, "We shall overcome"; the familiar challenge of John F. Kennedy "Ask not what your country can do for you. . . . Ask what you can do for your country"; and the commitment of the president I knew best—Lyndon Johnson, "I want a great society where every boy and girl in America can have all the education he or she can absorb."

But other voices haunt us as women. . . Abigail Adams, to her husband writing the constitution of the new country, "to remember the ladies," voices from 1848 in Seneca Falls—Sojourner Truth—"Ain't I a woman," and on across the continent as their descendants moved west. The advance guard of civilization.

Still we come. In the 1900s it was women of the West who were first to be counted for suffrage—Wyoming and Nellie Tayloe Ross here in Texas. It was the remarkable Minnie Fisher Cunningham who spearheaded the drive for women's vote. I am so glad I knew her and learned her lesson on how to get things done: "Address the envelope first and stamp it, then write it and mail it. It was Sarah T. Hughes, the first woman in the legislature and ultimately the judge who came that dreadful day in Dallas in 1963 to Air Force I to swear in the presidency of LBJ. I thrill to the story of Sarah Weddington, the teacher's assistant at the University of Texas, who at age twenty-seven, found Jane Roe, drove a beat-up car to Washington, argued and won the Roe vs. Wade case before the U.S. Supreme Court—her first case in court. That will be twenty-five years ago this January from the time the decision was handed down in 1973.

On and on with so many more who took on risks and made a difference—our first woman senator Kay Bailey Hutchinson, Barbara Jordan, Lady Bird Johnson.

And so many unknown women who are in the footsteps of their ancestors. Their stories need to be told, and you are the front line of writers who can do it.

Today we have our own Alamos of poverty and ignorance and disease. There are caring people out there ready to "ride from Gonzales" and throw themselves against the enemies of the human family. It takes just a few idea-driven people to make the difference for a civilized society. Thank God for the strong and gutsy women of the West who showed strength, gave strength, and made the history that deserves our admiration, our pens, our typewriters, our word processors.

Go for it!

A Cactus Pryor Story

by Liz Carpenter

When Lyndon Johnson was president, Liz had arranged for the first lady and a group of dignitaries to do some river rafting. At the end of the first day the group would pull ashore, set up campfires, and spend the evening on the banks of the river.

To add some zest to the day's activities, Liz had made arrangements for Cactus Pryor to portray an old-time prospector who just "accidentally" stumbles in on their camp that night. As he always does, Cactus fully prepared himself for his role, complete with tattered clothes, fake beard, old boots, floppy hat, and an old shotgun.

Well things were going according to plan. Liz and the first lady were chatting with their guests around the campfire about their journey. Meanwhile Cactus was making his way cross-country to their campsite. But as he rounded a corner, he found himself staring down the barrel of a pistol being carried by a very serious looking gentleman who told him, "Drop the gun!"

The gun was dropped very quickly. Then Cactus was frisked, and a whole passel of questions were being thrown his way.

You see, there had been one small oopsy in the planning. Seems as though the Secret Service team guarding the first lady was never notified that Cactus was going to be wandering in out of the dark to put in an appearance! The "surprise" for the rafting tour, had turned into a much bigger surprise for Cactus.

After some very tense moments, they got verification that he was expected, and Cactus was allowed to proceed into camp. There he completed his interrupted impersonation of a prospector, much to the enjoyment of everyone.

Chapter Fourteen

Allen Wayne Damron

Allen Damron is a consummate entertainer. When you attend one of his concerts, he will reach you. That's what this Renaissance man does so well, reach his audiences with a charming combination of music, humor, and stories. The songs he performs will take you through a full range of emotions.

Allen is so skilled at this, that he is the man top performers go to when they want to learn how to perform better. But don't take it from just me.

A little-known fact is that Allen was the first person to record Jerry Jeff Walker's wonderful song "Mr. Bojangles." Jerry Jeff had this evaluation of Allen: "As a song stylist and interpreter, Allen Damron is the best there is. I like my songs done his way." There is no higher praise an entertainer can get from a writer.

Allen takes the stage like he approaches life. He charges on, because he loves it and is determined to enjoy every minute. This love of life is both obvious and contagious.

Allen Wayne Damron, entertainer, songwriter,
musician, race car driver, marksman, educator, and
good friend.

Photo by Brenda Ladd

Honors

In recognition of his many contributions in the areas of Texas music and storytelling, the Texas Legislature designated Allen as a Goodwill Ambassador from the State of Texas. Only nine performers have ever been honored in this way. In that capacity his duties have included a series of performances from New York to California, showing those poor unfortunate non-Texans what they have been missing.

Allen is a Four Star performer with the USO, a Knight of the Cross of Jerusalem Franciscan Order, a retired colonel in the Confederate Air Force, and a lieutenant in the Royal Bavarian Gondoliers. Having never been sure exactly how to address him, I've always called him Allen, which just seems to fit his laid-back manner.

Musician

Allen plays the six-sting guitar, twelve-string guitar, banjo, autoharp, and both the five- and six-hole Indian flutes. He has over fourteen albums and CDs. The diversity of the titles will give you an idea of Allen's wide range of interests; they include *Heroes and Sheroes and Other Life Stories*, *All You Can Eat Texas Music Café*, *Texican*, and *Songs for Kids (of All Ages)*.

Allen was a co-founder of the Kerrville Folk Festival, along with Rod and Nancylee Kennedy. His contributions to the festival over the years have been substantial. Twice he saved the festival from closing by putting up his own land to help raise the money to keep the festival going.

Allen managed and/or owned several of the most famous music clubs in Texas, including the Rubiyat in Dallas, the

Eleventh Door and the Chequered Flag in Austin. He also owns his own recording company, Quahadi Productions.

Actor

Allen's movie credits include, Michener's *Texas, In Broad Daylight, Two For Texas,* and *Alamo, The Price of Freedom*, which still plays at the Imax Theatre near the Alamo in San Antonio.

During the filming of *Alamo, The Price of Freedom*, Allen played about seven different characters. One day they would be shooting scenes where he was dressed as a Texan firing at the charging Mexican soldiers. The next day he would be dressed as a Mexican soldier, charging into the Alamo. Well, through the magic of moviemaking, in the final movie you can see Allen the Texan, shoot down Allen the Mexican soldier!

He performed the title role in *Hondo Crouch, Mayor of Luckenbach*, a play that ran at many theatres and universities throughout the southwest, including the Chamizal National Theatre.

Songwriter & Poet

Allen has written and co-written hundreds of songs (some of these lyrics appear later). His CDs and albums always include stories and perhaps a poem or two. His cultural diversity shows up in his writings. Some of the songs are pure down-home country, others are written in Spanish, and still others hark back to Irish and Scottish folksongs.

On his CD *Allen Wayne Damron, 35 Years, More of Not the Same*, some of the songs he includes are "San Antonio Rose," "Nancy Whiskey" (an Irish folksong), "Maria Consuela

Arroyo," "Rivers of Texas," "Jalisco," "Finnegan's Wake" and "Boy from the Country" by Michael Murphey. Oh, and he also performs "Beethoven's Ninth" "a la banjo."

And then, when you think you have an understanding of the man, he does something like "Not Me." This is one of my favorites and is for children and their parents.

Storyteller, Folklorist, and Historian

If you spend an evening at one of Allen's concerts, you will come away knowing much more about the world around you and its history. His interest in history is contagious.

But this isn't history like you were probably taught. His music brings the stories to life, and you often feel the experience. That's what good folklore and good folklorists do, they make you feel some of what it was like to be there.

Other

Allen has raced formula cars with the Sports Car Club of America. He was a hunting guide in the Trans-Pecos and a fishing guide along the Laguna Madre.

As a professional diver he worked guiding and diving off of South Padre Island, and on the dredging operations in Lake Austin. In 1955 he recovered coins from the Spanish galleon *Santa Maria de YClar*, which was lost in a hurricane in 1554. Among the coins he found were Spanish quatro reale, which were the first and largest ever struck from the mints in Mexico City, where they had melted down the silver idols and other treasures looted from the Aztecs. Allen kept a few coins and donated the rest to the University of Texas for historical preservation.

Allen is a world-class rifle shot and teaches firearms classes. He is also experienced with black powder and other types of historical firearms.

Oh, and if that wasn't enough to fill up a life, he's also worked as a cowboy, a roughneck on the oilrigs, and a dog sledder.

Are you beginning to see why I've had a rough time capturing who and what Allen Damron is in just a few lines?

The problem is that this multitalented man has made significant achievements in numerous arenas. Unlike most legends in this area, Allen's contributions to Texas folklore come in several different ways. His work as an entertainer, actor, educator,

Sal shares a laugh with Allen and Marie Damron while on a visit to Caroline Dowell's ranch. Sal and Marie wear hats Allen wore in the movie Alamo, The Price of Freedom.

Photo by Jim Gramon

storyteller, and songwriter have all told the stories of Texas. In each his contributions have been significant, and perhaps a greater contribution has been in helping so many folks in these same diverse areas.

Allen's Biography

Allen was born on a ranch near Raymondville in 1939. He grew up working on the ranch doing a variety of jobs. He was a good student and did well in school and was a Silver Arrow Eagle Scout. He had the opportunity to attend several colleges on athletic scholarships, including an appointment to West Point. But Allen decided to accept an academic scholarship in drama at Lon Morris College where he received multiple awards for both his Shakespearean and comedy performances.

After completing his Associates Degree with Honors at Lon Morris, Allen went to the University of Texas at Austin. He majored in Psychology, with a minor in Sociology.

Since then Allen has devoted most of his life to the entertainment industry as an entertainer, actor, songwriter, and club manager.

Allen subscribes to Johan Sebastian Bach's statement, "As an entertainer, once you've got their feet tapping, you've got 'em."

He often says, "Encourage the talented folks that are out there. Always help the folks that are coming along."

And one final funny anecdote about one of Allen's performances. He was performing on an outdoor stage for a while and was doing one of my favorites, "Is There a Heaven for Balloons?" This is a fun sing-a-long song about balloons that float away into the sky.

Things were going well, the audience was enthusiastic, and there was good eye contact. Then, without explanation, they were no longer focused. They were talking and laughing and even more enthusiastic than before, but the eye contact was gone.

They seemed to not be focusing on him. They seemed to be looking through him. In all the years of performing and reading audiences, he had never had one behave in this manner. Finally he reached a point where he was playing a guitar bridge and could turn away from the audience. And there, where there had been blue Texas sky before, was the Goodyear Blimp!

Meeting Allen Damron

In the late sixties Austin was awash with a wide variety of musical talent. Swimming in this sea of talent allowed me the opportunity to meet many colorful characters including, Janis Joplin, Jerry Jeff Walker, Allen Damron, Rusty Wier, Willie Nelson, Roy Head, Alvin Crow, Johnny Cash, Kinky Friedman, Bill Moss, and so many more. It was a wonderful time.

As a performer, I did a bit of singing at some of the nonstop fraternity and sorority parties at the University of Texas and at Southwest Texas State. Regularly I sang at four different spots. In the daylight, most of those places would scare you to death and make you want to make sure your shot record was up to date.

One exception to that was a beautiful little club called the Chequered Flag, which was located on the corner of Fifteenth and Lavaca, about five blocks from the University of Texas campus. The "Flag," gone now, was owned by singer, songwriter, folklorist, and friend Allen Damron, and Rod Kennedy. They named the club in honor of their mutual interest in driving racing cars.

The Flag was a center for all sorts of balladeers and folksingers. The music was eclectic and always fresh and, most of the time, musically solid. There was a lot of country and rock and even some soul. As the war in Vietnam progressed, there were also many classic folksingers.

There were few places that were open to almost every performer, whatever their style, like the Flag. But it was in those open clubs where the "Austin sound" was born. Performers and patrons alike found that they could enjoy the best of several styles, while creating a new and exciting music style.

In a society that was becoming more and more polarized by the Vietnam war, the Flag was one of the few places where both sides could, and would, have a good time together. Some evenings it had that coffeehouse feel, sometimes it was more like a blues club, and other evenings there was a definite country twang. But the magic was that Allen made sure they all felt welcome.

On the first night I was in the Flag, Allen sang a song that really touched me and my country roots. The way he sang "Texas in His Ways," with such emotion, I was sure he had written it. When songwriters perform their own work, there is often more emotion and feeling in the delivery.

I was wrong. "Texas in His Ways" was written by an incredible songwriter, Tim Henderson. I was shocked when Allen said Tim had written it. I told him of my surprise, because his delivery was so strong. Allen smiled, "That is a very special song to me. You see, Tim Henderson wrote it about my father, Jack Damron." Here is Tim's wonderful song:

Texas in His Ways

by Tim Henderson

You can't tell him from the countryside,
he's dusty as the land,
And he's all crow's feet and wrinkles,
like the back of Granny's hand,
He ain't never had much learnin'
but he still turned out O.K.
He's got a lot of Texas in his ways.

His old bluejeans have faded to the
color of his eyes,
And his hair is like the whispey clouds
that mock a summer day,
Hell, he's never had much money
but he'll make it through O.K.
He's more than a little Texas in his ways.

And on Friday night the Texan drives
his pickup truck to town,
Drops his woman at the church
and goes to drink a couple down,
He's a listenin' to the jukebox
while his woman kneels and prays,
"God, forgive him for the Texas in his ways."

He's the fabric of this land,
and he's respected in his town,
He plays dominos on Sat'day
while his woman shops around,
Shoots straight and tells the truth,
and any debt he owes he pays,
There's more than a little Texas in his ways.

*And on Sunday night the Texan
drives his pickup truck to town,
Drops his woman at the church
and goes to drink a couple down,
He's a listenin' to the jukebox
while his woman kneels and prays,
"God, forgive him for the Texas in his ways."*

Clockwise, Tim Henderson, legendary songwriter; Dyanne Fry
Cortez, author of Hot Jams & Cold Showers; Dyanne's husband
Javier; Jim's bride Sally; Kathleen McGraw, minister and Internet
entrepreneur; and Shug Mauldin, writer, singer, and record
company owner.

Photo by Jim Gramon

I learned a lot from Allen Damron—how to sing and perform better, technically. But I also learned that it wasn't necessary to go along with the "tried and true" formulae that the recording companies tried to make the performers follow. Allen followed his heart and the music wherever they led him.

Allen says he's an entertainer, and he is truly one of the consummate professionals in an industry where many performers barely show up, much less put on a great show. An example of Allen's dedication took place at a recent show. There were seven performers scheduled to appear on an outdoor stage. The temperature had soared to 108 degrees. Four of the scheduled acts refused to go on because of the heat.

Allen not only went on, but he did a much longer set than usual. Despite the heat he delivered another outstanding performance. The audience never realized that Allen was still recovering from being seriously ill. Because he is a true professional.

But Allen is truly at his greatest at being a friend to the folks that he crosses paths with. Allen's friendships are the stuff of legends in the music scene. Many folks got an early break when Allen helped them get work: Janis Joplin, Jerry Jeff Walker, Kinky Friedman, Rusty Weir, Steve Fromholtz, Townes Van Zandt, and many, many more.

These are all things that Allen is rightfully proud of, but he is just as proud of a high school student he helped many years ago, when he was a high school teacher. The boy had a quick mind but was making poor grades. After working with him, Allen realized that the boy was having trouble reading. Months of extra time paid off. Allen beams as he closes the story by explaining that the boy is now a doctor.

That's Allen. Don't ever miss the opportunity to see him perform.

A Texan In New York

by Allen Damron

Here is a short story that shows Allen's ability to see Texas and Texans for all that they are, and aren't.

The story goes that this Texan is walking down the streets of New York. A woman walking by says, "Hello there, Tex."

"Now how did you know I'm from Texas?"

"Because your tonsils are getting sunburned from looking up at all of our big tall buildings."

The Texan laughed, "Well they're mighty nice buildings for sure, but we've got bigger and better'uns back home in Texas. Everybody knows that everything is bigger and better in Texas."

"What about that bridge right there, the Brooklyn Bridge, you got anything like that in Texas?"

"Oh heck yes, lady, we've got a bridge across the Pecos River that is at least twice as long as the Brooklyn Bridge."

"OK Tex, what about subways? You got any subways in Texas?"

The Texan lowered his eyes, and speaking slowly he said, "No ma'am, we haven't got any subways in Texas. The ground is too oily!"

She shot him a nasty look and tried again, "Well, what about Long Island? You got anything like Long Island in Texas?"

"Lady, we've got an island down off the Texas coast, called Padre Island, that must be a thousand miles long. Well, maybe it's not that long, I've never been to both ends in the same day, but it's for sure a lot longer than Long Island."

"OK Tex, what about that building right there, the Empire State Building, at one time it was the tallest building in the world. You got anything like that in Texas?"

"Oh hell, lady, we've got outhouses bigger than that."

To which she replied, "Brother, y'all need 'em!"

Allen Damron's music appeals to a diverse audience.

Photo by Jim Gramon

Twin Sisters

Song lyrics by Allen Damron and Bill Ward

Thisstory is based on the true story of a pair of cannon that were donated to Texas as they fought for their independence from Mexico. Reading the lyrics, you will see how skillfully Allen and Bill blend music, rhyme, and history.

Came the word from Texas,
Goliad and Alamo,
Travis, Bowie, Crockett
and the fight with Mexico.

There was shock and there was sympathy
from our neighbors to the north.
They read the bloody headlines,
as the story issued forth.

And from the folks in Cincinnati
came a thousand pounds of steel.
A pair of 4-pound cannon,
to help in the ordeal.

It took eighteen minutes to avenge
the fallen Texan's blood,
as the caissons of the Twin Sisters
advanced through the Texas mud.

Chorus:
When those sisters roared in unison
there was nothing left to say.
Soldados were a fallin'
half a mile away.
And the men of Santa Anna

were no match for the campaign
of a handful of Texas soldiers
and a couple of feisty dames.

But the story did not end there
on the San Jacinto fields.
The Yankees stole the Ladies
to melt them in their mills.

And as they lay there silent
in the boxcars on the tracks,
from the railroad yards in Houston,
Texans stole them back.

They are buried now in secrecy
'neath well-defended soil,
silenced now their fiery breath
and stilled their great recoil.

But if you've a mind to mess with Texas,
I'd think twice about it friend.
'Cause if those girls are ever needed,
we can dig 'em up again.

Chorus

Here Comes Another
I Love Texas Song

lyrics by Allen Damron,
Tom Paxton, and Bob Gibson

This song expresses many of the sentiments that most Texans feel about their home, while poking fun at all the songs that talk about how much the author loves Texas.

I can sing you songs of love.
Songs of hearts so true.
Songs that make you want to dance.
Songs when you feel blue.
I'll sing you songs of glory
and songs to see you through.
But the bestest song I'll ever sing
is the song I'll sing for you.

Chorus:
Here comes another I love Texas song.
It seems to me if you love Texas,
you can't do no wrong.
If you've been away for just one day,
you've been away too long.
Here comes another I love Texas song.

And Billy-Bob out in the backwoods
tired of life on the run.
Tradin' shots with the sheriff
and dodgin' the deputies' guns.
He's low on ammunition.
Knowin' that he'll hang.
As an act of sweet contrition,
he rocked back on his heels and sang

Chorus

I squired sweet Susan to the square dance.
We danced the dosado.
Allemande left to the corner
we sashayed round the floor.
I said, "Come out in the moonlight,
there's a question in my heart."
Then she throwed her arms around me
and said, Before we start

Chorus

Texas has its twisters.
Texas has its droughts.
When hard times come to Texas,
there's folks who'll help you out.
Seldom is heard a discouragin' word
from a real true Texan's mouth.
So everyone who's a loyal son,
lift up your voice and shout.

Chorus

Texas is a state of mind,
not an accident of birth.
From the snows of Amarillo,
to the sunny Gulf Coast earth.
From the gators, pines, and marshes,
to the Big Bend Mountain falls,
You've got to know that where you live
is the greatest state of all

Chorus

The Gringo Pistolero

by Allen Damron and Tim Henderson

When the bandit Chico Cana crossed the river at Boquillas,
Stole the young bride of the rancher Juan Otero,
Juan caught up his fastest mare and north to Marathon he rode,
To hire himself a gringo pistolero.
Spread the word along the river, tell it through the borderland,
That the hound of death is howling after Chico Cana's band.
Juan will seal their fate as surely as the rising of the sun,
With the guns of the Gringo Pistolero.

The round hat of a trooper cast a shadow 'crost his eyes,
As he listened to the tale of Juan Otero.
At the name of Chico Cana there could be no talk of price,
Just the Gringo's vow of vengeance, "Yo arrero."
Oiled the big Colt automatics and with daylight he was gone.
With the coming cold and darkness, he rode into Castollon.
And a drunken bandit caught there read the message,
"Talk or die!"
In the eyes of the Gringo Pistolero.

Where the Canyon Colorado twists its way among the rocks
And the ribbon of the sky is long and narrow,
In a jacal of adobe, bruised and tied up on the floor,
Wept the young wife of the rancher Juan Otero.
Bandit mirrors on the cliff-tops flashed the message,
"Now he comes."
Ask the number of his followers, the number of their guns.
And the Aviso flashed to Chico like the falling of a stone,
"He comes alone, the Gringo Pistolero."

Hidden high above the canyon where the falcon rides the wind,
Chico's best hawk-eyed Aviso, Juan Romero,
Put his mirror in his shirt and gazed with worry toward the rocks,
Where he last had seen the Gringo Pistolero.

"Put your sights up to eight hundred, hold a yard left for the wind,
And there's one By God Aviso that will never flash again."
Weeping red tears from a third eye that's a gift he cannot feel,
From the Springfield of the Gringo Pistolero.
"Chico Cana you have stole your last damn U.S. dollar bill.
I have come for you and all your Companeros.
You can fight and do your damnedest, or just send the lady out,"
Came the challenge of the Gringo Pistolero.
Bandit rifles down the canyon to the left and to the right,
Fearful eyes that watched and waited till the falling of the night,
Angry cut-throats that ignored the weeping lady on the floor,
And through the back door came the Gringo Pistolero.

Big Colt autos spitting thunder-death at everything that moved,
Flashing lightning in the jacal, long and narrow,
Ending hate and greed and cruelty with final flying truth,
From the sure hand of the Gringo Pistolero.
When one hot and smoking pistol dropped down empty in the dirt
Then another sprang like magic from inside the gringo's shirt.
And the lead-storm never stopped till there was no one left unhurt,
But the lady and the Gringo Pistolero.

Word has spread to Ojinaga, where the Conchos tumble down,
And a man's death can come swifter than an arrow,
That although the law be empty words, still justice can be found,
For no border stops the Gringo Pistolero.
And the old wives tell how Juan's wife came back,
beautiful and fair,
And lived happily through children and the years of silver hair.
But the young girls say Otero did not treat her well, back there,
So she left him for the Gringo Pistolero.

Chapter Fifteen

Richard "Cactus" Pryor

Cactus Pryor is a Texas original. He doesn't fit neatly into any of the standard molds that storytellers come from. No, Cactus took his own path. He is well known as an emcee, toastmaster, broadcaster, after-dinner speaker, actor, and writer (and I should also include world famous impersonator of Danish Admirals).

This native Austinite is a very funny man. He analyzes life in Texas with a finely tuned funny bone. He then turns those observations into humor that keeps you laughing. He can also see the serious side of where we are headed, and he regularly has commentary on serious topics like the environment.

As an emcee he has presented programs and humor for some of the world's most famous people. He has entertained Presidents Ford, Carter, Reagan, and Johnson. He was a favorite emcee of Lyndon B. Johnson for many years. As such, he entertained such notables as President Ayub Kahn of Pakistan, Chancellors Adenauer and Erhard of Germany, President Diaz Ordaz of Mexico, the ambassadors to the United Nations, and many more.

He has appeared as emcee of stage appearances with such stars as James Stewart, John Wayne, Charlton Heston, Fred MacMurray, George Peppard, Raquel Welch, Dean Martin,

Sonny and Cher, James Cagney, Doris Day, Lucille Ball, James Arness, Helen Hayes, Carol Burnett, Ann Miller, Eva Marie Saint, and many more. He appeared with Bob Hope and Joey Heatherton in a nostalgic revival of vaudeville. Cactus has appeared on the *Merv Griffin Show*, the *Tom Snyder Show*, *20/20*, and the *Today Show*. He also has appeared with Johnny Carson. He was co-host of the *Darrell Royal TV Show*.

As an after-dinner speaker, he is in constant demand throughout the nation. In this arena, Cactus often appears in the role of a foreign visitor giving his hilarious impressions of life in the United States as viewed from another nation. He writes a daily column that is syndicated.

Cactus has appeared in a number of motion pictures including *The Green Berets* and *Hellfighters* with John Wayne. He also appeared at various theaters as J. Frank Dobie in a play he wrote about the famous late folklorist-professor.

Cactus was a voice and drama major at the University of Texas. He has been in Austin radio and television for many years. He is Senior Vice President of Radio for the LBJ Company. He presents a daily commentary and interview show on station KLBJ in Austin.

In his often humorous commentaries, Cactus possesses the ability to see how special Texas and Texans are. He focuses an unflinching eye on the humor and the ugliness of where Texas was and where we are headed.

Among his many accomplishments Cactus has authored two books: *Cactus Pryor: Inside Texas* (Shoal Creek Publishing, 1982) and *Playback* (University of Texas Press, 1995). Both are humorous and introspective looks at Texas and Texans.

Cactus is just finishing his third book, a collection of stories about his favorite pastime, golf. The working title is *Fore Play*.

Cactus Pryor, emcee, humorist, storyteller, and one of the pioneers
in the radio and television industry

Photo by Jim Gramon

Meeting Cactus Pryor

It was the fall of 1952 and my family had made a giant step into
the "modern age." We brought home a TV set. It was a gigantic
box (by today's standards), possessing a very small black-and-
white screen, and overall it was pretty ugly. But back then we
thought it was beautiful and believed that basking in its pale
blue glow would be a big step towards enlightenment.

When we got the huge thing lugged into the house, we hooked it up and turned it on. Just like our old Crosley radio, the tubes started to glow, and crackling sounds came out of the back. Then a miracle, a small dot of light, in the middle of the screen, began to glow and grow.

After trying the rabbit ears out in thirty bizarre positions, fuzzy images began to appear, and finally there was a man standing there doing a live commercial. Based on years of listening to that old Crosley radio, we immediately knew the owner of the rich resonant voice was Cactus Pryor. This was my first visual introduction to Richard "Cactus" Pryor. He has been a staple in our lives and Austin TV and radio ever since.

Over the years Cactus offered us many wonderful moments, often at his own expense, compliments of live TV commercials. It was many years before videotape came along, and all the commercial breaks were done live. So if there was a problem, that went out live too.

One Cactus classic occurred while he was doing a commercial for a furniture company. The man was fighting with a couch that supposedly had a bed hidden within it. He was trying to demonstrate how "easy" it was to open. The couch was winning.

Standing behind the couch, Cactus was reaching over to the front of the seat cushions and pulling on a cord that would magically make the bed pop up and start to unfold. He pulled so hard that he lost his footing and fell over the back and onto the cushions, trying to look graceful while falling. He actually rolled into sitting position and smiled while saying, "And now back to our show."

It was one of the very few times we were anxious for the next commercial, because everyone knew that the story of the couch wasn't over. When the next commercial came on, Cactus informed us that the problem had been that a tie-down strap had not been removed. He then smoothly demonstrated how the bed worked. It was classic live TV.

Cactus possesses a sharp wit and keen eye for the world around him. As a storyteller, humorist, emcee, and author, he has been a treasured asset of the Austin community for over sixty years.

Cactus and I share a love of the Texas coast in general and Port Aransas in specific. On almost every pilgrimage my family makes to Port Aransas, I run into Cactus. Whether it's down at the beach, one of the bait shops, or perhaps over at Yankee and Betty's, we cross paths.

When I told Cactus that I wanted to include him in my book, he was sitting out some rainy weather at his place in Port Aransas. But he assured me that, as we all know, a bad day in Port A is still a great day.

As I described my goals, I could hear the skepticism creep into his voice. Not about my goals, but about whether he should be included among the likes of J. Frank Dobie and John Henry Faulk, despite the fact they were both close friends of his.

Now it's not that Cactus isn't a bit of a ham. But he was still skeptical about his status as a storyteller. However, following some discussion about my definition of what a Texas storyteller is, he conceded that he met all the criteria and then some.

A week later I received a letter from Cactus. In it were two stories. This first one exemplifies the self-deprecating humor Cactus possesses, and I truly believe his tongue may be firmly fixed in his cheek. See what you think.

Southern Notables

by Richard "Cactus" Pryor

I received a letter recently, informing me that I had been chosen as one of the "South's Notables." As such, I was to be honored by having a one-paragraph biography of my life published in a book that would include other such notables. Immediately I was suspicious. I didn't want to have my name printed alongside a bunch of other people who were comparable to me. Not even misery wants that kind of company.

I became more suspicious when the letter asked me if I knew any other southern notables worthy of being included in such a publication. If they're notable, how come these people have to be notified of their notability? And all of my reservations were confirmed by the last paragraph of the letter, where for only twenty-five dollars I could purchase a beautifully leather-bound volume of this book listing all us notable folks. In response to their offer, I composed the following reply:

> Gentlemen:
>
> Thank you for the honor that you have bestowed upon me and for having the foresight to recognize the qualities in me that no one else has had the good judgment to perceive. I accept your designation of being a southern notable with great humility.
>
> I have included the one-paragraph biography of my accomplishments that you requested. I'm sorry that it's such a long paragraph, but three single-spaced pages were the best I could do. If you must delete any of it, you might cut the part about the chicken pox, mumps, and dislike for liver and okra. If this still doesn't meet your space requirements, you might prune down the hilarious part about the time I was caught skinny-dipping in the University fountain, but everyone I tell that story to really gets a kick out of it.

As to other notables I might recommend for your book, I have enclosed a five-page list. I'm especially anxious that you contact names number five and number seventy-eight. Number five is the math teacher who failed me in algebra four straight times. I'm sure this lady is notable among all those who studied under her.

Number seventy-eight is the former owner of the most heavily attended pit bulldog fight arena and rooster fighting ring that the state of Texas ever boasted. You can write to him in care of the Ellis Unit, Huntsville, Texas.

You might notice that I have suggested the names of dozens of other residents of this same address. All of them are notable for one reason or another. I have included in my list the entire roster of the Texas Legislature. They are all aware of their notability and take great pride in it. Therefore, I feel sure that you will find them anxious to be included in your publication.

I have included the names of Billie Sol Estes and Ben Jack Cage. However, this is probably redundant since I am sure you already have them listed in your publication.

You will find the list of twenty-five very popular young ladies who certainly should be included in a listing of southern notables. However, they may be a bit difficult to locate since the Chicken Ranch has long been closed now.

Incidentally, I have decided not to accept your generous offer to purchase a leather-bound volume for only twenty-five dollars. I appreciate it deeply. However, when the world becomes aware of my notability, as it undoubtedly will after your book is published, I'm sure I will be deluged with numerous copies of it from adoring fans.

Humbly yours,
Cactus Pryor, Southern Notable

I never heard another word from them.

The Rape

by Richard "Cactus" Pryor

Well, we've done it. We've soiled our nest. We've contaminated our sacred waters. To many of us the water of Barton Springs is sacred. Many of us were baptized into the true church of God when we plunged into that icy cold, pristine body of spring water. And now that pool is contaminated with bacteria. This is an insult to the memories of Barton Springs addicts like J. Frank Dobie, Roy Bedichek, Bob Morrison, and my dad, Skinny Pryor.

I heard it thunder the other night and I thought, "That's Mr. Dobie reacting to the news that Barton Springs has been closed due to a high bacteria count in the water."

It would be fun if he were here. He would unleash the anger that made him sit out a traffic citation in jail rather than pay the fine that he thought was unjustified.

I can hear him now:

"Barton Springs contaminated? It's like blaspheming your own mother. It's like stabbing yourself in your own heart. These waters that have been gushing forth from the limestone rocks of the Edwards aquifer for eons are the lifeblood of this community. This is what our life here is all about. We have chosen a place to live where we can live in harmony with nature, not in opposition to it.

"Just as the Indians had the good sense to make their campgrounds around those springs of pure water, we've had the good sense to make our homes in this Texas oasis. Barton Springs is much more than a swimming pool, it is an attitude, it's a statement for quality of life.

"There's been more philosophy taught sitting in the sun next to those magical waters than in the entire forty acres that make up the University of Texas. There have been more sound political decisions made at the feet of those majestic ancient pecan trees guarding the pool than in all the smoke-filled rooms of the houses of state.

"There's been more poetry inspired and romances begun at Barton Springs than anyplace I know. It is our rebuttal to those who say: 'One must devote one's life to the pursuit of the almighty dollar no matter where the venture may take you, no matter what the personal sacrifices, no matter what the cost.'

"This pool of water is sanity and now it is suffering from the insanity of man. Barton Springs is a microcosm of the world in which we now live, with its disregard for traditions, for the natural, for the precious. This is what we have come to—fecal bacteria infecting our very lifeblood. It's the end of the world that we have known. Damn, damn, damn."

I don't think I'm presumptuous in speaking for the late Mr. Dobie. I only hope I'm not speaking about the late Barton Springs. We'll see.

I Am You

by Richard "Cactus" Pryor

My dear late friend, humorist, and civil-rightist John Henry Faulk planted the seed in my mind. We were walking on Austin's beautiful hike and bike trail during the latter days of his life. It was one of those mornings that make you want to hold onto life forever.

John Henry said, "You know, Cactus, I am part of all this. I am at one with those bass making circles out there in the lake and those ducks coming in for a landing. I am at one with my Chinese brothers, my German brothers, with people of all races and colors, and with that moon sinking below Mount Bonnell over there. I am at one with the universe."

A few years later, I recalled Johnny's words during that incredible time when the world seemed to change overnight.

The Berlin Wall came down. The Soviet Union surrendered communism and unshackled millions of people. The Free World bonded together to deal with corrupt dictators who stole food from starving masses. It was a return to that which inspired this nation...a sense of dignity for the individual. A recognition of the specialness, the uniqueness of each and every one of us. And yet, despite our universal distinctiveness, we are all the same.

We are all passengers on this incredible spaceship called Earth. We are all riders on Walt Whitman's Brooklyn Ferry: "Just as any of you is one of a living crowd, I was one of a crowd."

I delivered the following commentary for my Christmas broadcast:

I am you and you are me.

I cry, you cry.

I laugh, you laugh.

I hunger, you hunger.

The wind that brought the bogeyman outside my rattling window brought him outside your flapping desert tent or your shaking palm leaf hut.

We all run to mother when we are hurt.

We come back to where we began...to that wonderful, familiar, soft safety.

And we all look to father to protect us and feed us, even though sometimes mother is father, also.

And sometimes father is mother, also.

And when they are no longer here for us to run to, we become the haven for our children to run to.

We all seek another...for love...for comfort...for the sweetness of sharing. And if we don't have that, we hurt for not having it, especially if we had it and have lost it.

We look at the stars, and we wonder...how far? How many? And who put it all there? And will we go there? Anywhere? And why? Why us? Why here? Why now?

And when will we leave? And will I be afraid? Will it be peaceful?

And what will you do when I am there, and you are here? Or you are there, and I am here?

Sometimes I smell the flowers; sometimes I can't.

Sometimes I like you.

Sometimes I don't.

Sometimes I am sad and don't know why.

Sometimes I am happy and don't know why.

Sometimes I lose me and wonder if I will ever find me.

Sometimes I am full of me...sick of me...tired of me...joyous of me...proud of me...ashamed of me.

Sometimes I even like me.

I soar, I fall. I sing, I cry. I succeed, I fail.

But I am not alone...for I am you and you are me.

So are we all.

And we are all special, for we are here.

If we were not, we would never have been here...

This wonderful, painful, glorious, sorrowful, magnificent here.

Cactus Pryor is standing beside a radio that once belonged to
legendary folklorist J. Frank Dobie.

Photo by Jim Gramon

J. Frank Dobie

by Richard "Cactus" Pryor

The old man and I were friends before we knew each other. He was "old" simply because I was so young. I would often walk from our home on Speedway Street to Eastwood Park where Waller Creek had dug out my favorite fishing hole in the limestone rock bottom. I was always armed with a cane pole, earthworms dug from our backyard worm bed, a brown bag full of mother's "world's best fried pies," and the conviction of a young boy that the fish would be big and hungry.

Eastwood Park was a place of magic. The tall stand of trees provided haven not only for the squirrels and birds but also for Daniel Boone, Robin Hood, and, on certain magical days, Geronimo. I caught more dreams than fish in that special fishing hole by the cedar bridge—stringers full of them.

I sometimes shared this catch with the old man. I'd look up and find him standing there on the bridge, leaning on the handrail on his elbows, smoking that curved pipe and watching me. When I'd wave, he'd speak. "I didn't want to get in the way of your thoughts," he'd sometimes say. "A feller catches some real important thoughts when he's fishing."

Sometimes he'd come down and accept my offer to enjoy some of Ma's fried pies. Other times he'd just lean there on the bridge and watch. We didn't talk that much except about fishing and fried pies and squirrels. We didn't even know each other's names. We never asked. We just accepted each other as fishin' hole friends. He'd stay until his pipe ran down. Then I knew that he'd soon be heading up to his pretty, two-story white house a short distance away for a refill.

Age got in the way of that fishing hole, as I exchanged it for others. It was years later when I again encountered my old friend. I was invited to the ranch of J. Frank Dobie, an opportunity to sit at the feet of the gods, the Texas triumvirate of

Dobie, Walter Prescott Webb, and Roy Bedichek. When these three unique, earthy intellectuals got together with nature and Jack Daniel, those who were within earshot were blessed for life. As I was introduced to my host I learned, for the first time, the name of my old fishing hole friend. Mr. Dobie didn't recognize me. The kid with the cane pole had grown up. But he was kind enough to remember when I recalled the days.

There were a few other visits to the Dobie Ranch during these delicious twilight years of the three magnificent conversationalists. I learned more about the world and about the dignity of the individual in those warm bluebonnet afternoons and cedar fire evenings than in all my days of schooling. It was a crash course in bird watching; Shakespeare; vocabulary; city, state, national, and international politics; bean cooking; horse breaking; and corporation damning. The conversation ebbed and flowed like fine blue smoke from a well-seasoned pipe. This was what learning is supposed to be like.

I conducted the last interview J. Frank Dobie ever granted a member of the media. I told him that he had made that little fellow with the cane pole the luckiest fisherman in the world.

Cactus Pryor IS ALIVE AND WELL !!!

In the spring of Y2K, Cactus and I were chatting about the people and places we both knew. I told him he was looking great. He laughed and said, "Spread the word."

"What do you mean."

"Well a couple of weeks back I was doing one of my disguises. This particular day I was in Houston, impersonating an admiral in the Danish navy, Hans Kristopherson. I love that bit. There's a whole flock of folks in New York that still think I'm an admiral." And he laughed his trademark soft low chuckle.

"You're kidding! They really don't know who you are, even now?"

"Nope. I even get invitations to parties as Admiral Hans."

"That's amazing!"

"It gets better. I was portraying the admiral at an event being held at one of the Houston golf courses. Things had gone well, and as we were saying our good-byes, they asked where I'm headed next. I tell them that I'm headed for Austin, to do an interview."

One guy says, "Oh, if you're going to Austin, you're probably going to be interviewed by Cactus Pryor. He's a great guy. He's an old friend of mine. I've known Cactus for years."

Cactus laughed, "Jim, I don't think I've ever met the guy before in my life."

I was laughing at the scene he had painted, when he said, "But, it gets worse, or better."

"How?"

"Well Jim, the second guy standing there pipes up and says," Nope you won't be interviewing with Cactus. I knew him too, and I know that he died two years ago. A real loss."

"Well Jim, you can imagine how amazed and disappointed I was to find out that I was dead!"

"Cactus, you really do look damn good for a dead guy. I knew that you had died on stage a time or two, but you are really looking great for an escapee from the cemetery."

"Jim, that may explain why I haven't gotten quite as many emceeing gigs. I guess they are looking for the un-dead. Please do me a favor, get the word out that I'm doing just fine and, to quote Mark Twain, 'rumors of my death were greatly exaggerated!'"

Take my word for it friends:

Cactus is alive and doing well!!!

Chapter Sixteen

J. Frank "Pancho" Dobie

J. Frank Dobie had an influence on Texas that will probably never end. Every person in this book will tell you straight up that they were influenced by Mr. Dobie's work.

With a combination of wit and down-home horse sense, he earned the respect of friends and foes alike. Nobody had a better friend or more discerning foe than Mr. Dobie.

Pancho, as his friends called him, was an observer. And, as such, almost everything fell under his scrutiny. He is another example of the truism that you can take the boy off the farm, but you can't take the farm out of the boy. Obviously, this fact struck a big chord with me.

One of my biggest regrets is that I never had a chance to meet Mr. Dobie. I felt like I grew up with him. All of my life my acquaintances have told me stories about Mr. Dobie.

I first heard of him one July day when I was walking down the sidewalk in Cumby. Well walking was not exactly true. As usual I was barefooted and also as usual the concrete and asphalt were hot enough to cook on. So I was really hot footin' it from one shady spot to another.

I spotted Ben Green and John Henry Faulk all leaned back in front of the store, chuckling at my predicament. Once I had finished my high steppin' across the road, they returned to their conversation, which was about somebody that Mr. Faulk referred to as Pancho sometimes and Mr. Dobie on others.

I could tell from the way they both spoke about him that they thought a lot of this man. There was almost a reverence in how they spoke of him.

I was young and, as the young are prone to do, never wanted to admit that I really didn't know who they were talking about. So, for a while, I smiled and nodded along, just like I had a clue. But finally I could take it no longer and had to ask who this Pancho Dobie person was.

Ben and John Henry glanced at each other in a bemused fashion. Then Ben said, "Johnny, he was your teacher, so you fill Jim in on who Mr. Dobie is."

J. Frank Dobie, legendary Texas folklorist and storyteller

Sketch by James Gramon

John Henry leaned back and relit his pipe. "That's a mighty big question, Jim. You see Mr. Dobie is the premier Texas storyteller and historian on the Southwest."

"How did he come to get that title?" I asked sincerely. The question seemed to crack them both up. Between chuckles John Henry continued with his story about Mr. Dobie.

"Well no, Jim, it wasn't a title any particular group gave him. Nope it happened after he became the person that everyone came to for information on almost everything Texas. You pick it—cattle, snakes, Indians, horses, settlers, treasure hunting, cactus, Texans—stories and storytelling, and so on were Mr. Dobie's specialty.

"Mr. Dobie's been a teacher most of his life. Now he's a professor at the University of Texas at Austin. He's also put out several books."

J. Frank Dobie was born on a South Texas ranch in the brush country of Live Oak County on September 18, 1888. Growing up in this part of the country, he learned to love it and he discovered that he loved collecting stories from everyone and everywhere.

His parents encouraged all the kids to read everything they could get their hands on. Eventually they sent Frank and his sister Fanny to live with grandparents in the town of Alice, Texas. They wanted the kids to get some formal education so they all could go to college.

At this time Alice, Texas, was a boomtown. Hundreds of thousands of head of cattle were herded into town, to be either shipped by rail up north or back east. Thousands of others were processed right there in Alice. One story tells of a giant pile of bones overlooking the stockyards. They were left there to bleach and were then ground up for fertilizer.

Frank was fascinated with it all. He became familiar with the cowboys, vaqueros, ranchers, trail cooks, and all the other

folks that were involved in the business. He also became familiar with many of their stories.

Frank's maternal grandfather was a real western character,
as well as Alice's justice of the peace. Grandpa Dubose had
fought in the Civil War, herded everything that could be herded,
and had even driven a stagecoach. Needless to say he had
plenty of stories to share with Frank.

Frank attended Southwestern University in Georgetown,
Texas. One of his English professors got him interested in the
romantic poets. And he also discovered another poetry lover,
Bertha McKee. Soon they fell in love, and Bertha became his
bride and lifelong companion.

In 1920 Frank received his B.A. degree and started teaching high school in Alpine, Texas. During the summers be began
his writing career by working as a reporter for the local
newspaper.

Frank decided he wanted to teach at a higher level than
high school, so he went to Columbia University to get his Masters degree. Returning to Texas, degree in hand, he started to
teach in the English Department of the University of Texas at
Austin.

His first year there, Frank shared an office with Stith
Thompson. Professor Thompson introduced him to the Texas
Folklore Society, and it was a match made in heaven.

Unfortunately, World War I started, and soon Frank was
called from the classroom and was sent overseas. Fortunately
he was only in Europe briefly before the armistice was
declared.

The war and the time he had spent in the army in Europe
had greatly expanded the scope of Frank's horizons. However,
this enlightenment raised many more questions and provided
him with very few answers.

So when Frank returned to the University of Texas after his
discharge from the army, he was even further away from

knowing where he wanted to go with his life than he was before the war started.

The only thing Frank was sure of was his love for Bertha. In 1920 he left the University of Texas to go run his Uncle Jim's ranch in South Texas. He thought that returning to his roots might give him the sense of direction he lacked.

He was wrong. It just didn't work, so he returned to teaching, writing Bertha, "in the university I am a wild man; in the wilds I am a scholar and a poet."

While working on the ranch, Frank had enjoyed hearing the stories of Santos Cortez, one of his Uncle Jim's vaqueros. Santos told Frank stories about the old vaqueros who had been used to guard buried Mexican treasure in various spots around the southern part of Texas and northern Mexico.

He loved these stories, but he was also hit with something else, a strong sense of loss. This way of life was gradually disappearing. It was then that Frank realized what his calling was. "It came to me that I would collect and tell the legendary tales of Texas as Lomax had collected the old-time songs and ballads of Texas and the frontier. I thought that the stories of the range were as interesting as the songs. I considered that if they could be put down so as to show the background out of which they have come, they might have high value."

Realizing what he wanted to focus his life on, he plunged into every aspect of identifying and tracking down the folk legends of the southwest. He became the editor of the Texas Folklore Society in 1921.

Having found his passion, Frank was not shy in his pursuit of anything that he thought might help to preserve the folklore, stories, and artifacts of the Southwest in general, and Texas in specific. Frank took over the helm of the Texas Folklore Society, which had been previously founded as a branch of the American Folklore Society.

But soon there was trouble. The Texas Folklore Society under Dobie broke from the practices of the American Folklore Society. The American Folklore Society wanted to examine each statement and story from a purely historical, objective, and scholarly viewpoint. In their opinion, if a story could not be verified by unimpeachable sources, then it was not really folklore.

Anything that could not withstand this scientific scrutiny was considered to be just a story, not folklore. Frank and his followers believed in collecting and presenting "folklore" as an ongoing process that was their lives during that time and place.

He believed that if stories were within the context of the people and the times, then it should be preserved. His position on this matter set in motion the independent direction of the Texas Folklore Society, which still follows the standards he set, today.

From the Introduction to his wonderful book *The Mustangs*, here are Frank's very pointed comments on this dispute. In addition to the salient parts of his arguments, you will also observe his keen intellect and rapier wit that delighted friends and tormented his adversaries.

> The historian must have the perspective of imagination in order to arrive at truth, he cannot, like the novelist, discard those facts that "fail to comply with the logic of the character"...I do not mean that my ambition was ever to write "pure history." Pure history is a naked collection of documented facts; if the facts are patterned into pictures or directed into conclusions, purity is defiled. Yet I am more appreciative of pure historians than I once was. Most of them are teachers, and while they may not open windows, they do not shrink intellects, like political school superintendents and academic flunkies of material power. They seek truth and discipline minds, and the pure histories they write are profitable to consultants. Nevertheless, excellence in

historical writing comes only when interpretive power, just evaluation, controlled imagination and craftsmanship are added to mastery of the facts.

Author's Note: The dispute between the folklore historians and the folklore storytellers is still going on today in the folklore community. Historians point to things like Ben Green's oft repeated comment to me to "never tell a story the same way twice, or folks'll get plum tired of hearin' it." To a historian it is obvious that there is only one way to tell a story, the way it actually happened. There is only one truth. So, interpretive variations on a story are not acceptable.

Although the essence of the story may remain the same, the historical aspects are often compromised in stories that have been handed down over time. Memories fade. Things may be embellished or shortened. I personally believe that, although passed down from one person to another and probably altered along the way, the story can still be of significant folklore value as a representative depiction of the way things were in that time and place. The essence of the story can take you there, despite changes in some of the wording.

In 1924 the Dobie-led Texas Folklore Society published its first book, *The Legends of Texas*. It was a labor of love, mostly written and researched by Frank.

In 1930 he introduced his course *Life and Literature of the Southwest*. He had to fight to get it included into the curriculum. The faculty chairman had said, "There is no literature of the Southwest."

To which Frank replied, "Well there is plenty of life. I'll teach that!"

Life and Literature of the Southwest became the most popular course ever taught at the University of Texas. Only Frank Dobie ever taught it. Students regularly crowded into the classroom to hear Frank bring to life the stories about things like trail drives, ranching, indian raids, buried treasure, and learning how to live in the desert by eating cactus pears.

Many eyes were opened by Frank Dobie, and many students hung around him to learn everything they could. One of these students was a bright, free thinking young man by the name of John Henry Faulk.

John Henry Faulk and J. Frank Dobie

Photo courtesy of Austin History Center, Austin Public Library

The University of Texas was beginning to become a sort of Mecca for talented writers. Frank's history teacher friend Walter Prescott Webb wrote *The Texas Rangers*. It was an immediate success, and Webb started to work on a book about the joys, trials, and tribulations of pioneer life.

Then an English professor, Mody Boatright, produced a book of collected tales about the East Texas oil fields and the roughnecks that worked them. This book also sold well and brought even more widespread attention to the University and the Texas Folklore Society.

Not to be left behind, Dobie produced his second book, *Coronado's Children*, which received national attention and broadened his celebrity far beyond the Texas borders.

Buoyed by this success, Frank sent his creative energies flying in many different directions. He wrote more books, more articles, and in 1932 Dobie even had a radio program "Longhorn Luke and his Cowboys."

Frank regularly traveled in search of material for his books. He would spend weeks traveling through Indian villages in northern Mexico, often on horseback. Sure, he would have been delighted to find one of the treasures that were purportedly hidden there. But more importantly he returned from each trip with dozens of new stories.

On his return, he would recount these stories to the delight of all that heard him. He soon became a popular speaker on the national lecture circuit. In 1939 he began his syndicated newspaper column "My Texas."

The University of Texas had an ongoing love-hate relationship with Frank. They loved the positive attention that he brought, yet they resented his extremely independent attitude.

For example, Frank refused to get a Ph.D., despite repeated requests from senior officials. He said, "I believe that the scholarly study of the Southwest is sufficient focus in its own right."

Other things he did were less than pleasing to the UT Board of Regents. John Henry gave me my favorite J. Frank Dobie quote. He said a reporter asked Dobie what he thought of the proposed University of Texas tower. Now with all the open land around the UT campus, Dobie saw no reason to build a skyscraper.

With his usual level of tact, Frank replied, "If the height of the UT tower is proportionate to the intellect of the Board of Regents, it will be an underground structure!"

Another time, on the same topic, Frank proposed that perhaps the UT officials could lay the tower on its side, then put courtyards and flowerbeds around it.

I doubt if it was coincidental when, shortly after completion, Frank was told that his new office was to be on the top floor of the UT tower. This was no problem for Frank. He just totally ignored every request and/or threat and stayed right where he always had been, in B Hall. Soon the UT officials gave up trying and left him alone.

On December 7, 1941, the Japanese bombed Pearl Harbor, and the United States was immediately in the middle of World War II. The English were delighted with the idea that the United States was going to be sending troops to their aid. However, they didn't have a clue about how to make them feel welcome.

England asked for some lecturers to come to England and teach the English about Americans and the American way of life. Someone put Frank's name on the list (considering the timing, one might wonder if it was a member of the Board of Regents).

Amazingly Frank was petrified. Oh, not of the war, but of teaching American history. He was quoted as having said, "I know the average length of horns on a Texas longhorn steer. I can tell you how mother rattlesnakes swallow their young. I can tell you about the duels Jim Bowie fought with his knife...but I don't know history."

"Sounds like American history to us," the English told him.

Frank's old friend Walter Prescott Webb was already in England, teaching at Oxford University. His advice was both simple and direct: "Make up your own definition of history, and come on over."

Frank often wrote to Bertha about his dread of teaching the classes. He so wanted to do well in this new environment and not be a disappointment to his class. He shouldn't have worried.

Edward R. Murrow, who, by the end of the war, became a famous newscaster, was quoted as saying about Frank, "He did more to win British respect and affection than our entire diplomatic corps and propaganda campaigns combined."

In the late fifties and early sixties, Murrow would come to the aid of Dobie's student John Henry Faulk in his eventually successful fight against McCarthyism and the blacklisting of folks.

He was barely off the boat returning from England when Frank weighed in on the side of then president of the University of Texas Homer Price Rainey, against the Board of Regents. In 1947, shortly after Rainey had resigned in disgust, it all came to a head, when then University president Theophilus Painter refused to grant Frank another leave.

Frank resigned with the administration's acquiescence. Although Frank, for the rest of his days, maintained an informal relationship with the University of Texas, his formal days as a teacher were over.

Frank Dobie was a free thinker. He didn't ever flinch from a fight, no matter what the odds or the issue. This strength of conviction is why he refused to pay a small fine that he felt was unjustified and served his time sweeping out the courthouse.

In the late forties Frank began to wonder out loud why no blacks were being allowed to attend the University of Texas. This was not a popular position at that time and place. But that didn't deter Frank for a minute.

When Herman Marion Sweatt was declined admission to the University of Texas Law School, he filed suit. The state responded by opening a one-room, all-black law school in Houston. Sweatt refused to attend the one-room school and proceeded on with his lawsuit.

Frank Dobie spoke out often in support of Mr. Sweatt and against racism in any form. Being so well known and highly quoted, Frank was a concern for the establishment. Then governor Coke Stevenson called Frank a "disturbing influence."

The U.S. War Department asked Frank to go on a tour and talk to the U.S. troops still stationed all over Europe. He was able to see the massive destruction that had taken place. He was also able to attend part of the Nuremberg war crimes trials.

While he was out of Texas he had not forgotten the way governor Stevenson had spoken of him. Upon returning he said he was going to do in-depth research into rattlesnakes. He said, "They make better company than the governor of Texas."

It should also be noted that Frank's scathing criticism was not strictly reserved for the governor and the Board of Regents. Frank once observed that journalism was the unctuous elaboration of the obvious.

J. Frank Dobie died in September of 1964. Following his death, his beloved Bertha got two more books published, based on the stacks of notes he had piled throughout their home on 26th Street.

The Texas folklore and literary triumvirate of giants consists of J. Frank Dobie, Walter Prescott Webb, and Roy Bedichek. These giants showed all the rest of us that writers could make a valuable contribution to their home state by just documenting the stories they had grown up hearing.

Bertha Dobie and friends established a most fitting memorial to Dobie in light of his contribution to Texas letters, the Dobie-Paisano Fellowship. The award provides money for writers and artists to work on their projects during a six-month stay on Dobie's Paisano ranch in the hill country outside of Austin.

I don't really know all the stories about the background of all of Mr. Dobie's many books. So, for your reading pleasure, here is a list of the books written by J. Frank Dobie, according to the University of Texas Press.

> *Apache Gold*
> *The Ben Lilly Legend*
> *Coronado's Children*
> *Cow People*
> *I'll Tell You a Tale*
> *The Longhorns*
> *The Mustangs*
> *Out of the Old Rock*
> *Prefaces*
> *Rattlesnakes*
> *Some Part of Myself*
> *Tales of Old-Time Texas*
> *A Texan in England*
> *Tongues of the Monte*
> *A Vaquero of the Brush Country*

I thought that was a definitive list of Mr Dobie's works, until I came upon the Bureau of Land Management's website for the National Wild Horse and Burro Program (www.blm.gov/whb). They have a suggested reading list that includes Ben Green's *A Thousand Miles of Mustangin'*. And, of course, the list includes Dobie's *The Mustangs*. However they also include another Dobie book entitled *Mustangs and Cow Horses*. I'll be checking with the Dobie family to get the real skinny on this.

Photo by Jim Gramon

The Black Devil

by J. Frank Dobie

I never had the privilege of knowing Mr. J. Frank Dobie. I can only imagine what I have missed. But, I was blessed by having the opportunity to hear some of Mr. Dobie's stories recalled by one of his favorite students, John Henry Faulk, and one of his friends, Ben King "Doc" Green.

Now, as far as I can tell, for John Henry and Frank, their love was for everything about Texas. Ben was a bit more focused, his biggest passion was for horses. When Ben and John Henry got together the conversation usually got around to horse stories pretty pronto. Here is one of my favorites.

As a horse lover, I had seen horses do a whole variety of cantankerous things, like kicking, rearing up, bucking, and biting. But this story scared the bejeebers out of me.

In the years preceding the Civil War the Shoshones came south into Texas, raiding for horses along the San Saba River. One night the party awoke to the sound of a commotion among their own horses. What they found was a huge black stallion gnawing on the hobbles that restrained the mares. He was releasing them and turning them into his own manada.

No matter what the Indians did, the stallion paid them no mind. They shouted, threw rocks, and shot arrows at the great stallion, but nothing deterred him from releasing more mares. One threw his riata over the stallion's neck, but he promptly turned and charged the brave, stomping him to death beneath dancing hooves.

Finally, one of the braves charged him, knife in hand. The great horse whirled on the attacker and grabbed his arm in his mouth. The horse then dashed off into the night, carrying the brave with him.

The Shoshones were shocked; they had never seen a horse that seemed so willing to attack men. They called him the Black Devil.

In the moonlight they followed the bloody trail made when Black Devil had carried off the brave. It was near dawn when they found Black Devil and the rest of his herd, standing in a circle down in a dry creek bed. The light was poor, so they couldn't make out what was going on. Quietly the braves crept closer to the herd, and then they could see that the horses were eating the flesh of the missing Indian brave.

The next night Black Devil returned and gnawed the hobbles off another sixteen of the mares in the Shoshone herd. Enraged, the Shoshones put on their war paint and went after the Black Devil to avenge the deaths of their comrades as well as reclaim their mares.

They found him in an arroyo and set upon him with arrows and knives. Nothing they did seemed to affect the Black Devil. Arrows and knives bounced right off of him. He then viciously attacked the braves, injuring several and killing another by pulling him off his horse and trampling him.

Black Devil escaped that night, apparently unharmed. To the Shoshones this proved that he was an evil spirit, and they wisely took the remnants of their dwindling herd away from the San Saba River area as quickly as they could.

Stories about Black Devil died down for a few years. Then, during Reconstruction, a troop of Negro cavalry was sent to Fort McKavett, on the San Saba. Stories of the Black Devil circulated among the black community, and the troop was told about the "Black Devil."

One morning a trooper rode out alone on a mare. Late that evening he returned on foot. He said a giant black stallion had grabbed him by the arm as he rounded a bend in the trail. The stallion had pulled him off his horse and ran off with the mare. People questioned the story, until two more troopers came back afoot the next day, telling similar stories.

Some settlers were living in a dugout dwelling along the San Saba at the time. They owned one fine stallion and had collected a pretty fine group of mares. Late one night they heard a disturbance in their corral.

When they got there, they found the Black Devil was attacking their stallion in a fight to the death. They ran back to their dugout for a gun, and the Black Devil, having knocked their horses down, took off after the men. Black Devil jumped the corral fence and charged after them. The men dove into their dugout and were shocked to see the giant horse charging down the steps of the dugout after them. Perhaps fortunately for them, the giant horse became stuck in the narrow dugout door, and this allowed them time to kill him with a knife.

The Shoshones say this wasn't the Black Devil, that he still roams the San Saba territories. The settlers that killed the black stallion say it was the Black Devil. Nobody knows for sure. But if you're traveling at night on horseback in the San Saba territory, folks 'round those parts surely do recommend that you not be a ridin' a mare.

Chapter Seventeen

Dr. J. Mason Brewer

African-American Folklorist

I knew of J. Mason Brewer's stories forty years before I knew who he was. My road to learning about Dr. Brewer's work took forty years to come full circle. Around 1960 John Henry Faulk was of a habit of droppin' in on Ben "Doc" Green at his beautiful spacious ranch just outside of scenic downtown Cumby, Texas.

When "Johnny" showed up, a round of storytellin' was sure to break out. And I would always sit in if I was in town staying with my grandparents, Kyle and Ludie Alexander. On occasion Johnny, as Ben called him, would tell stories that originated with the black folk of Texas. He seemed to have a whole passel of them—said he got a bunch from J. Frank Dobie and others from "a black folklorist from back in Austin."

Fast forward forty years and shift two hundred and fifty miles to the south. I'm chatting with my good friend Monroe Taylor at his fruit and vegetable stand in scenic downtown Manchaca. Monroe is a formidable storyteller in his own right, and hopefully someday I'll be able to share some of his stories with you. Born in Austin in 1926, Monroe has seen a lot of history come and go, and he has a lot to share.

On this cool fall day I'm chattin' with Monroe about this book, and I mention that there's going to be some stories in it about J. Frank Dobie. Monroe leans back and laughs, "Oh yea, I knew Mr. Dobie."

Not believing my good fortune, I asked, "How did ya'll come to meet?"

"Well, many years back, way back, I used to drive a cab for the Harlem Cab Company. And I had this standin' regular deal, for quite a while, with Dr. Brewer. Mostly on weekends, I'd fetch him from his home in east Austin and take him up to Mr. Dobie's place. He'd go in there for a while and then come back out and I'd take him back home. This went on pretty regular for quite sometime."

"Monroe, do you know what were they doing?"

"I don't rightly know, but Dr. Brewer normally had a bunch of books and papers. He was a teacher over at the Samuel Huston College."

This got me very curious. I knew about many of the regulars at the Dobie home. Fellow teachers at the University of Texas like Walter Prescott Webb and Roy Bedichek were regulars. Also regularly in attendance was Mr. Dobie's student John Henry Faulk.

I also had heard many stories about how Frank and Bertha Dobie's home was always an open house to all comers. Folks came in from all over the countryside to sit and chat with Frank for a while on their back porch. At least until Bertha ran them off, normally because Frank needed to come in for supper.

So who was this Dr. Brewer? Quickly I discovered that the man was folklorist J. (John) Mason Brewer. In the forward to Brewer's book *The Word on the Brazos*, Dobie tells the story of how they first met.

My interest in J. Mason Brewer and his work goes back to 1932. I was then secretary of the Texas Folklore Society and editor of its annual publications. One Sunday morning in the fall a stranger called me over the telephone, gave his name, and said he had collected a large number of Negro folk tales reflective of slavery times. I invited him to meet me in my office, which was in the old Main Building of the University of Texas, which was later demolished. It was very quiet there on Sundays, and things would come to a man's mind.

Mr. Brewer brought his manuscript in a cardboard box. I began reading at once, and by the time I had read two or three tales, knew that their author had something genuine and delightful. Getting the dialect consistent and correctly marked required an enormous amount of editorial labor, but that fall we published forty tales under the title of "Juneteenth" in the volume entitled Tone the Bell Easy (Publications X of The Texas Folklore Society).

During the twenty-one years that I acted as editor for the Texas Folklore Society hundreds of contributions came to hand, but in my estimation "Juneteenth" stands out with only three others as the freshest, most original, and most significant. The tales in "Juneteenth" and those in The Word on the Brazos complement each other, both in sociological values and in charm.

I immediately tracked down copies of several of Mr. Brewer's books. They all masterfully take you back to a different time and place. As I read on, bells began to go off in the back of my mind. I had heard some of these stories before. But where had I heard them? Then it came to me, John Henry Faulk. Things began to fall into place. The beautiful stories of J. Mason Brewer had come full circle.

John Mason Brewer (1896-1975) was arguably the premier African-American folklorist of the twentieth century. Prior to his work, African-American folklore had been dominated by the Uncle Remus animal tales for over half a century.

A native Texan, Brewer was born in Goliad, Texas, on March 24,1896. He was the son of J. H. and Minnie Tate Brewer and the grandson of slaves. When he was seven the family moved from Goliad to Austin.

He attended public schools in Austin and earned a B.A. from Wiley College in Marshall, Texas. During World War I he served as a French interpreter for the American Expeditionary Forces in 1918 (he also spoke Spanish and Italian).

After the war Mason Brewer was a teacher and principal in Fort Worth. In 1926 he got the opportunity to teach creative writing at Tillotson College. Later he taught romance languages at Samuel Huston College. During all this time he wrote poems and short stories that were published in area journals.

He first studied folklore with Dr. Stith Thompson at the University of Indiana and supplemented this training later with other nationally known folklore authorities at the Folklore Institute of America.

In 1932 he carried his now famous shoe box full of slaves' tales to J. Frank Dobie at the University of Texas. Dobie worked with Brewer to refine the raw material into the polished tales that appeared as the lead chapter of the 1932 volume of the Texas Folklore Society writings. Dobie called it "the best collection of Negro folklore since Uncle Remus."

Brewer's work was based on his extensive field work and attention to detail. Through his work, African-American folklore evolved to new levels of maturity and complexity. His boxes of collected tales, jotted down on scraps of paper, collected through years of talking with storytellers throughout the South, evolved with Dobie's help into the largest collection of African-American folk stories ever documented.

Dr. Brewer's publishing career was launched, and he never slowed down. That first prestigious publication provided Dr.

Brewer with the academic credentials to gain him cooperation in educational and social circles throughout the South. His travels allowed him the opportunity to collect thousands of songs, stories, sayings, and proverbs.

The scholarly manner in which he approached this labor of love provided the succeeding generations of folklorists with a role model. Mason Brewer used dialects unique to each region of study. This provides the reader with glimpse into the lives of those folks about whom he wrote. Their beautiful simplicity and humor can be seen in his most notable works:

> *Negrito: A Volume of Negro Dialect Verse*
> *Negro Legislators of Texas*
> *Heralding Dawn: An Anthology of Verse by Texas Negroes*
> *Little Dan From Dixieland*
> *The Life of John Wesley Anderson*
> *An Historical Outline of the Negro in Travis County*
> *Humorous Folk Tales of the South Carolina Negro*
> *Juneteenth: A Collection of Negro Slave Tales from Texas*
> *"John" Tales (a collection)*
> *Old Time Negro Proverbs (a collection)*
> *The Word on the Brazos: Negro Preacher Tales from the*
>   *Texas Brazos Bottoms (1953)*
> *Aunt Dicey's Tales: Snuff-Dipping Tales for the Texas*
>   *Negro (1956)*
> *Dog Ghosts and Other Negro Folk Tales (1958)*
> *Worser Days and Better Times: The Folklore of the North*
>   *Carolina Negro (1965)*

In 1950 Brewer received an M.A. from Indiana University. In 1951 he received an honorary doctorate from Paul Quinn College in Waco, Texas.

Dr. Brewer lectured at Yale University, the University of Toronto, the University of Arizona, the University of Colorado, the University of St. Thomas, and the University of Texas. He was a guest lecturer at the International Folk Festival in 1955.

He also served as a member of the Research Committee of the American Folklore Society and was elected their second vice president in 1954. He also served as a member of their council for several years.

In 1954 he became the first black member of the Texas Institute of Letters. This happened as a direct result of his being chosen as one of the twenty-five best Texas authors by Theta Sigma Phi, for his work *The Word on the Brazos: Negro Preacher Tales from the Brazos Bottoms of Texas*.

Dr. Brewer was the also the chairman of the Division of Languages and Literature, at Huston-Tillotson College in Austin from its inception in 1952.

Dr. Brewer spent ten years teaching at Livingston College in North Carolina. Homesick for Texas, Brewer returned to Texas and finished his teaching career at East Texas State University in Commerce, where he was Distinguished Visiting Professor from 1969 until his death.

He died on January 24, 1975, and was buried in Austin, leaving his second wife, Ruth Helen, and J. Mason Brewer Jr., his son by his first wife. Dr. Brewer's life was commemorated in a short film made in 1980 by the Texas Folklore Society in conjunction with the Texas Commission on the Arts.

Now sit back and enjoy some J. Mason Brewer folk stories about black life in Texas, as they were told to Ben Green and I by John Henry Faulk.

The Preacher and His Farmer Brother

by Dr. J. Mason Brewer
as told to Jim Gramon by John Henry Faulk

Of occasion in the Bottoms (Brazos River bottomland area), in the same family, you can find some of the best preachers that have ever graced a pulpit. And in that same family you may find a brother or sister that has never set foot in the church as long as they lived.

Once there was a Reverend Jeremiah Solomon who pastored the Baptist church in Egypt town, down on the Caney Creek. He put on the armor of the Lord when he reached fourteen; he was a deacon when he reached sixteen, and they ordained him to preach the Word when he turned just eighteen. He was surely one of the most powerful preachers to ever grace a Texas pulpit. He was even the moderator of the St. John's Association.

Yes sir, all was good with Reverend Jeremiah. Now his brother was a whole 'nother kettle of fish. He went by the name of Sid, and that man had never set foot in a church house in his life.

Everybody knew old Sid had himself a fine little spot of land, round about the falls, down on the Brazos. It had been a full twenty years since they had laid eyes on each other. So Reverend Jeremiah decided to pay Sid a how-do-you-do visit and stopped by his brother's farm.

He drove up to the house, and as soon as he was through shakin' hands with Sid's wife and the children, he said, "I want to see your farm, Sid. Let's see what kind of a farmer you are."

"Sure," said Sid. So he got on his hat and off they went, down to the corn patch, and they looked at the corn Sid had planted. The corn was pretty close to full grown and was looking good. Reverend Jeremiah said, "Sid, you've got a pretty good corn crop here, by the help of the Lord."

Then they went on down to the cotton patch and the Reverend looked at it, and said, "Sid, you've got a pretty good cotton crop here, by the help of the Lord."

Then they moseyed on down to the fine little sugar cane patch and when the Reverend saw this, he said, "Sid, you have got a pretty good sugar cane patch, by the help of the Lord."

Now when the Reverend say this, Sid eyed him kind of disgusted like and said, "Yeah, Reverend, I do truly believe that the Lord is some help, that's for sure. But he sure didn't seem to do much with this land when he had it all to Himself."

The Goliad Liars

by Dr. J. Mason Brewer
as told to Jim Gramon by John Henry Faulk

Once there were two old men that lived right around here in Goliad, Texas. Now these two do hardly a blessed thing all day, everyday, except sit on a bench in front of the grocery store, chew tobacco and spit, and tell lies.

Everyday, when the Lord looked down on these two, all they were doing was sitting there on that bench in front of the store, stoppin' everybody that came in the store to buy something, and asking them to sit a spell because they wanted to tell 'em something or another.

One of the old gentlemen was named Uncle Rufe, and the other gentleman's name was Uncle Henry. They both got their kicks out of telling stories without a lick of truth in 'em, in no shape, no form, or no fashion.

Both of them always told whoppin' big lies, but one year when election day rolled around, there was a whole heap of people in town to vote. And after they voted, most would stop by the store to buy themselves a soda pop or some cheese and crackers or something or another. On that very day Uncle Rufe and Uncle Henry went and stretched themselves way out on a tree limb with the lies they told.

They waited until the voting was done with and a big crowd of folks was a sittin' around on barrels in front of the store, eating on their cheese and crackers and sippin' their soda pop. Only then did those two start to blowin'.

They commenced to tellin' one big lie right after another, till finally Uncle Rufe turned to Uncle Henry and said, "Henry, you know what? Time was when my gran'pa had this pretty hunk of farmland. And my gran'pa didn't plant nothin' but cabbage plants on it. Well, to tell it true, only one of all those cabbages came up. And this distressed my gran'pa pretty good. But as time went on, this cabbage grew to be a giant. It grew and grew till it covered a whole acre of land."

"You know something, Rufe?" said Uncle Henry. "That there was quite a story, and it's strange that you should mention it, because it brings to mind somethin' that happened to my old gran'pa some years back. I'm sure you know that he was the best blacksmith in all the land, and one day he looked out the back of his shop and there was this big ol' pile of rustin' metal that was nothing but leftover bits and pieces of stuff he had fixed.

Well he thought and he thought, and finally he decided to make a big ol' cookin' pot out of it. So he set to workin' on this big ol' pot, and when he finished it, the pot covered almost two whole acres of land!"

Uncle Rufe rolled his eyes at Uncle Henry's story, "Why in the world would he want to build a great big ol' pot like that for?"

"To cook that damn big ol' cabbage your gran'pa raised!" said Uncle Henry, as he rocked back holding his sides from laughing so hard.

Author's Note: Earlier in this book I mentioned one of the major rules of storytelling, and this story proves it. That rule was, all together now, THE FIRST LIAR ALWAYS LOSES!

Chapter Eighteen

Critter Tales

This land of legendary people and events could not properly exist without legendary critters. Some of the critters are real, livin', snortin', and just like some of the folks, some are mythical.

A couple of young bulls mix it up.

Photo by Jim Gramon

Jackalopes

As I mentioned before, the prevailing philosophy in rural areas is "phooey on you if you can't take a joke." If you can't laugh at yourself, folks don't really trust you much. In keeping with that, it was a common practice to give someone's leg a little tug every so often, just to be sure they hadn't misplaced their sense of humor.

When I was a youngster, I'd get a leg tuggin' on a regular basis. I was a regular at D.E. Crumly's store. This rusty wonderland sat along the west side of I-35, just south of Austin. Most folks wouldn't notice this rundown two-pump filling station, except when they needed gas or at Christmastime. You see D.E. didn't seem to know how to take Christmas lights down, only how to put them up. As the years passed he just

The legendary Texas jackalope. This one is on display at
Black's Barbecue in Lockhart.

Photo by Jim Gramon

kept adding lights. Each year the place would be lit up like an oversized Christmas tree.

D.E. was big friendly guy who always had a bit of the child in him. Besides being lit up at Christmas, his old store became the collecting point for antiques/junk of every description. But what interested me more than the old tractors and car parts were the cages containing various types of critters that had been brought to him for one reason or another. At various times there were ducks, cranes, dove, raccoons, possums, rabbits, deer, fox, and many others kept in cages outside the store.

Every time you went to his store, there was something new to look at. Although I had seen all of these things in the wild, it was always neat to get a close-up look.

One day I pulled my bike into the shade of his small covered driveway. Opening the top of the icebox, I grabbed a soda out and popped the lid off in the bottle opener attached to the wall.

Then I started exploring to see what D.E. had added since my last visit. Behind the counter sat one of the strangest critters I had ever seen. It appeared to be a normal stuffed, jackrabbit, with one huge difference—this jack had horns!

D.E. explained that it was a jackalope, a cross between a jackrabbit and a small antelope! Well, this kid was amazed. Back then I spent most of my time out prowlin' the woods, and I had seen some pretty strange critters, including a solid white skunk. But I had never seen or heard anything about any jackalopes.

D.E. told me that jackalopes were one of the rarest critters on earth. He said that they only live in Texas and are so wary of people they are never seen. He said the one he had was only found because he died of old age.

In defense of myself, one, I was young and respected my elders, at least enough to not call one a liar to their face. And two, it was a pretty damn good taxidermy job! The horns from a small prong horned deer were very neatly attached to the top of the stuffed jackrabbit.

Needless to say, D.E. was right, they are very rare. They are never spotted in the wild. And they are seldom spotted far from a taxidermy shop.

Although Crumly's store is now gone, jackalopes can still be found. The jackalope pictured in this book is on display at Black's Barbecue in beautiful Lockhart, Texas. The Black family continues to carry on the leg-pullin' tradition. And I guarantee that if you search the rural areas of the southwestern United States, you will find many such critters.

Cottonheaded Rattlemouths

The South has plenty of poisonous snakes. There are rattlesnakes, cottonmouthed water moccasins, copperheads, and coral snakes, and those are just the poisonous ones. There are also dozens of breeds of other snakes that can give you a heartastroke if you stumble on them.

Kids are raised knowing that snakes are out there and that you have to keep your eyes peeled. Now, if those varieties weren't enough, pranksters over the years have come up with strange hybrids that are used to tug kids' little legs.

One of my favorites is the cottonheaded rattlemouth. The local storytellers assure the little friskers that rattlemouths are almost always skulking around in the weeds along every trail. Rattlemouths are supposed to have the ability to track young'uns down and get 'em. They can tell how big someone is by the vibrations on the ground as they walk. The rattlemouth won't go after bigger folks, 'cause they can't swallow 'em down whole.

Nope, they go after the littler young'uns that don't keep up with their parents. There's only one way for kids to avoid being caught by the rattlemouths, and it's to keep skipping till they catch up with the adults.

For many years country folk have chuckled as they watched youngsters skipping quickly along, trying to catch back up with their parents.

The legendary Texas cottonheaded rattlemouth. OK, I confess this isn't a rattlemouth; it's a rattlesnake that is on display at Austin Taxidermist. I couldn't find a rattlemouth.

Photo by Jim Gramon

The Story of Rosie

For city folk, beef is something shrink-wrapped in the grocery store. Well, there's a lot more to the process of getting meat and dairy products to your table, and most of it involves dealing with some of the most cantankerous critters in the universe. You've seen cowboys rope and throw a cow in bulldoggin' contests. Believe me, it's not easy to convince a critter the size of a Volkswagen to do what you want.

A small cow is about three times the size of the largest professional football player, and not nearly as friendly. Other times, cows can be as tame as a puppy, just following you around. The next moment, they may be trying to send you to meet your maker. It is this unpredictability that, sooner or later, causes everybody working around cattle to get caught in an awkward situation.

When I was in junior high, my good friend Mark Jones and I were sent by his mom, Polly, to move a huge old lop-horned whiteface Hereford named Rosie, from one field to another. The fields were close, only a few hundred yards apart, and Rosie was always a big sweetie, so we didn't bother getting a horse; it was normally like walking a dog. A very, very large dog.

Well, it seems that Rosie was not having a good day and decided she didn't want to go for a walk, at least not where I

A lop-horned whiteface Hereford like Rosie.

Photo by Jim Gramon

wanted to take her. I had walked up to the old girl and dropped a noose over her head. No problem. Then we headed over to the gate to the next field. While I led Rosie, Mark dropped the gap and pulled it back up after we passed through into the middle field.

As we walked, I absentmindedly looped the rope around my wrist. Things went well till we got halfway across the middle field. Suddenly, Rosie decided to slim down a bit by taking a nice long jog.

I was a wiry kid and tough as a boot. But no matter how hard I tried, Rosie towed me along over the furrows like I wasn't even there. Upon realizing I didn't have the proverbial snowball's chance at stopping the old gal, I tried to let go of the rope.

Much to my chagrin, I discovered that the lariat was knotted around my wrist, and it was time to quickly come up with Plan B. Except I didn't even have a Plan A!

Mark kept shouting for me to let go. I was finally able to convince him that I couldn't. Being pretty lean and long himself, Mark sped up and got in Rosie's way. Fortunately for him, Rosie turned instead of running him down.

Rosie continued to drag me over the black dirt rows for another twenty yards then arrived at the fence. But she headed on, running alongside the fence, still draggin' yours truly.

Pivoting around as she turned, I planted my heels in the dirt, and Rosie pulled me up to a standing position, like a water-skier being pulled up out of the water. My plan was to get up beside Rosie, then drop a quick loop over a fence post to tie her off.

Good plan, as long as you get the right knot on the post. If it didn't work, Rosie would pull the rope around the post and mangle my arm in the process.

Fortunately my knot held, and after a few minutes to calm down, Rosie very quietly followed us over to the other field.

We'll never know what excited Rosie; maybe she was just feelin' her oats. Whatever the cause, she was the sweetie that nearly mangled me.

Ballerina Bull

Now being towed along by Rosie was a pretty dangerous situation caused by a pretty friendly old cow. Imagine what can happen if you have a bull that is two thousand pounds of nothing but mean.

My aunt, Lillie Williams, was the first woman in the U.S. to own a locker plant, and for many years she was the only woman to own one in Texas. During some summers, when things were slow on James's ranch, I would work at the Hopkins County Locker Plant, in Sulphur Springs (it must have been a popular name because there are three others in Texas: in Angelina, San Saba, and Trinity Counties).

While working there I encountered a huge white bull that had no intention of cooperating. He was being off loaded from a cattle truck. Things started out OK as he headed down the chute. But seeing a bit of daylight, he dropped his head down and charged into the chute. I dropped the gate behind him and was walking down the chute behind him. Things went well for a ways, then he put it into reverse and backed up.

For the most part, cows aren't kickers. The dangerous area is up around the head. Cows will gore you, head butt you, or mash you up against anything they can find, but they aren't bad about kicking like horses, mules, and donkeys.

Normally the big danger from the backend of a cow was if she raised her tail and decided to give you a shower. So with this bull I was feeling pretty safe (famous last words). Then, without warning, he started backing up towards me. Much to my alarm, I realized the bull's first backward step was on top of my boot.

Now my momma didn't raise no fool; I always wore steel toed boots when I was working in the pens. So, I wasn't worried about getting my toes crunched, but I was concerned about getting pinned against the side of the chute or getting knocked down and having parts of me stepped on that were not protected by steel.

As I contemplated my next move, I realized that the board my foot was stuck on was bending down every time the bull rocked back and that the pressure I was feeling in the middle of my foot was a nail being pushed up from the bottom. I knew that one or two more rocks, and the nail was going to finally push through my boot and through my foot.

A very unhappy white bull that probably can't dance, yet.

Photo by Jim Gramon

I set to pushin' and hollerin' at that bull, who carefully ignored me. In desperation, I grabbed the bull's tail and twisted it up into a nice loop. When I did, he raised up, not just a little bit. His whole damn butt went up in the air.

The change in altitude of his rump roasts helped some, but not enough for me to get my foot off the nail. But I was encouraged enough to try it again, this time with an even better grip on his tail. At this point his fly swatter was looking something like the symbol for infinity (you know, like the number 8, that got drunk and fell over on its side).

Again the hindquarters began to gain altitude, and he even went up on the front of his hooves. I was amazed and amused, but I was still not loose. Seems as though this bull was willing to relocate, jiggle, and elevate every other part of his body except his left rear foot.

Personally, I think he knew exactly what he was doing and just wanted to aggravate me more. It worked. I was plenty aggravated, and I was also making plans to have him as the guest of honor at a barbecue.

Finally, grabbing that damn bull's tail with both hands (complete with a golfer's overlapping, interlaced, tight-loose, Bohemian death grip), I was able to twist the bull's tail into something like a bow tie.

It did seem to catch his attention. With a loud snort and a bunch of bawlin', that bull turned into one really ugly ballerina. Again he rose up on his toes and finally moved off of my foot, and he commenced to moving along right smartly down the chute.

I was extremely pleased that the chute was too narrow for him to hook a U-turn, because he was not pleased with me one little bit. But I guess that made us just about even.

Suffice to say, anytime you meet someone who works with farm animals, know that they have to be tough and they probably aren't gonna take much off of you, because every day they work with critters that are much bigger and badder than you, every day.

Texas Longhorned Rattletailed Crab

Legend has it there is a rare creature that inhabits the Texas Gulf Coast regions. The creature is a nightmare for the Chamber of Commerce, since it only seems to attack tourists!

I was told about the Texas longhorned rattletailed crab by my friend Dan Harris, who spent many years living down on the Texas coast. According to Dan this extremely rare critter, at first glance, looks like a large crab, complete with a pair of feisty-looking claws.

But on further examination, you will note a pair of horns protruding out of the top of the crab's shell. This is one of the types of crabs that have a small vestigial tail, on the end of which is a set of rattlers just like you find on a rattlesnake. The crab grasps the unsuspecting tourist with its claws and then inflicts a poisonous bite with a pair of fangs concealed within his mouth.

The obvious question is, How does the Texas longhorn rattletailed crab know a person is a tourist? Prevailing wisdom on the part of the experts is that it has to do with some type of pheromones or skin secretions. They believe this because if a tourist consumes large amounts of Mexican food and plenty of beer, they are never bothered by this killer crab. Amazing.

Unfortunately, I don't have a picture of this creature. If you find a picture of one, please let me know.

Chapter Nineteen

Mody Boatright
Oil Patch Storyteller

Almost any discussion of folklore in Texas eventually includes some of the participants of Texas's equivalent of the Algonquin Roundtable of New York. At the center of this group was J. Frank Dobie. His Austin home was the gathering point for several of the primogenitors of Texas folklore. Others in this group included Walter Prescott Webb, Roy Bedichek, John Henry Faulk, J. Mason Brewer, and Mody Boatright.

Mody Coggin Boatright, son of Frances Ann (McAuley) and Eldon Boatright, was the youngest of the ten children that survived infancy. He was born on their ranch in Mitchell County, Texas, on October 16, 1896. The family had a long history of ranching. He was the grandnephew of pioneer cattlemen and merchants Mody and Sam Coggin, both of Brownwood.

The Boatright family were good ranchers and did well financially. Mody was educated partly by a governess and partly in the local public schools. In 1922 he earned his bachelor's degree from West Texas State Teachers College (now West Texas A&M University). He then transferred to the University of Texas at Austin where he earned his master's degree in 1923.

From 1923 through 1926 Mody taught at Sul Ross State Teachers College. In 1925 Mody married Elizabeth Reck, with whom he had a daughter. In the fall of 1926, Mody joined the staff of the University of Texas at Austin.

In 1929 tragedy struck Mody when his beloved Elizabeth died. Following her death, while teaching at UT, Mody started work on his Ph.D.

In 1931 Mody married Elizabeth Keefer, with whom he had a son. (She was a very talented artist and illustrated his first two books.) In 1932 he received his Ph.D. and continued his teaching at the university. He eventually became the chairman of the English Department.

Mody had grown up listening to and telling stories. He had shared some of these stories with fellow UT teacher J. Frank Dobie. In 1925 Dobie asked Mody to contribute a tale, "The Devil's Grotto," to the next publication of the Texas Folklore Society, and another Texas folklorist was born.

In the following years Mody began to gather and document the cowboying and ranching stories he had heard throughout his childhood. After years of polishing, with Dobie's support and guidance, Mody published *Tall Tales from Texas Cow Camps* in 1934.

Mody's interests then turned towards another rich source of Texas folklore, the "Patch." Texans all know about the Patch. The name refers to the "patches" of oil producing areas scattered throughout the state. The oil industry in Texas was booming and in turmoil because of the incredible rate of growth. Much to the chagrin of many Texans, oil was NOT originally discovered in Texas. No, fellow Texans, it is sadly true that we weren't the first. (However, we can truly claim that we did it best.)

With his usual meticulousness, Mody wanted to make sure that the stories he documented were truly Texas oil stories. He decided that the only way to be sure was to research the folklore from the oil industry in other states like Pennsylvania and West Virginia. After years of collecting, Mody realized that the collection was a book that had never been published and should be.

So in 1945 Mody Boatright published *Gib Morgan: Minstrel of the Oil Fields*. In this book Mody presented Gilbert "Gib" Morgan as a legendary figure (which he truly had been). Mody was a stickler for accuracy, and he was careful to not embellish any of the tales, but to retell the tales exactly as they were told to him. He always emphasized putting each story within the cultural context of the time and place in which each occurred.

Despite his attention to getting the details right and being sure to not puff up stories, the stories bestowed Gib Morgan with some of the mythical characteristics of men like Paul Bunyon. At that time America was hungry for adventurous, bigger-than-life stories, and the book was well received and widely read. It earned Mody national recognition as a folklorist.

He was now getting the knack of writing books, and only four years later, in 1949, Mody published *Folk Laughter on the American Frontier*. This book was one of the earliest works to detail from what sources American humor was derived. In it he defined the true nature of the tall tale and explored many areas of folk humor. He also put forth, for the first time in print, the truism that frontier humor was not born of despair but was a manifestation of the positive "can do" attitudes and optimism of the frontiersmen.

This book also suggested that folklore may arise out of conflict between different social strata. At that time this was a very novel concept and not at all in accordance with the, then widely accepted, view that folklore only emerged as the result of the ruminations of the downtrodden and mostly illiterate "folk" of a society.

Mody Boatright's efforts were not totally focused on just teaching and writing. In 1937 he had joined Dobie in editing the annual collections published by the Texas Folklore Society. In 1943 he became secretary and editor of the society. He edited each of their annual publications until 1964. In his capacity as their principal editor, Mody edited eighteen volumes of folklore, including five that he co-edited with Dobie.

He was elected a fellow of the American Folklore Society in 1962 and was also a vice president of the society in the same year. He was chosen a fellow of the Texas Folklore Society in 1968, an honor previously accorded to only three other men. One of which was his dear friend J. Frank Dobie.

In 1958 Mody published a collection of lectures delivered by Mody, Robert B. Downs, and John T. Flanagan, entitled *The Family Saga and Other Phases of American Folklore.* In it he points out that family stories are often the starting point for most folklorists and an incredibly rich source of folklore.

In 1963 *Folklore of the Oil Industry* was published. Mody said this book contained over twenty years of research into the how, when, and where traditional character stereotypes were introduced into the oil field stories. Today it is hard to imagine that oil was ever a "new" industry. But back then it was, and Mody Boatright was among the first American folklorists to study the traditions of an emerging modern industry, to actually study the birth of folklore in a contemporary setting.

Mody's fascination with the Texas oil fields continued, and in 1970 he published *Tales From the Derrick Floor,* which he co-wrote with William A. Owens. Although focusing on tales about the Patch, this book also helped to define and refine the methodology of collecting and recounting oral histories.

In later years Mody wrote on such topics as folklore in a literate society, the relationship between popular literature and national folk heroes, and myth in the modern world—studies which attested his belief that individuals in complex, industrialized societies are not so different from "folk" or "primitive" ones as is sometimes supposed.

On August 20, 1970, Mody Boatright died in Abilene, Texas, of a heart attack. He left two children, a son and a daughter.

Three years after his death, *Mody Boatright, Folklorist,* a collection of his essays, was published.

In addition to the other honors mentioned here, Mody Boatright was a member of the Texas Institute of Letters and of the Writers Guild of America.

Mody Boatright's Oil Patch Tales

as told by John Henry Faulk and Ben King Green to Jim Gramon

Mody Boatright was a first rate storyteller and folklorist. I knew it must be so because of the respect that Ben Green and John Henry Faulk expressed for him. This was not always the case when they talked about folks who taught at institutions of higher learning. Often they would use terms like, "he's an educated idiot" or observe that, "the guy must have inhaled too much chalk dust." But that wasn't how they spoke of Mody Boatright. Their words about him were carefully chosen and respectful.

Having said that, I don't recall having heard either of them tell me any story that either attributed to Mody Boatright, but they generated enough interest on my part that I read everything I could find written by him. Just as I had found with the stories by J. Frank Dobie, Walter Prescott Webb, J. Mason Brewer, and Roy Bedichek, I recognized many of them. Some were told to me nearly verbatim from how Mody reported them in his wonderful books.

According to Mody there were three legendary oil field men who stand far above the rest. The first two, Paul Bunyan and Kemp Morgan, seem to have only existed in myth. The third was a real life, flesh and blood man named Gib Morgan. Here are some of the stories about the three. Note that some of the stories, told about different men, are quite similar.

Paul Bunyan

Many Texans never realized that the legendary woodsman had worked the Texas oil fields. Lumber has always been a big business in Texas, and the story goes that Paul was lumbering in the East Texas forests when oil was struck in Beaumont in 1901.

Being a man of great curiosity, and hearing that they were paying top dollar for healthy men, he went to work in the oil fields sometime before 1910, when the stories of his incredible feats began to circulate.

The legends tell that the scale of Bunyan's well rigs was staggering. One rig was so tall that he had to hire thirty men to be able to keep one tool dresser at the top of the rigging all the time. You see the rig was so tall that it took fourteen days to get to the top of the rig, so at any given time there was one man at the top, one man on the ground, fourteen men going up to go to work and fourteen more coming down for their day off.

Paul was famous for his gigantic hatchet. The story goes that one day he was up on the rig and became angered at a member of his crew that was slacking. Paul threw his hatchet and hit the ground beside the man, putting him into a frenzy of activity. When Paul came down to pull his hatchet out of the ground, it had stuck so deep that he struck oil.

The story continues that for bringing in this well Paul was paid a million dollars, which he promptly spent on Mail Pouch chewing tobacco and whisky. Paul's plan was to soak the tons of tobacco in the giant vat of whisky and then sell it for a fortune.

Things went quite well, and Paul's tobacco had the best flavor that had ever been produced. Stories tell of hardened oil field workers fainting plumb out at just one taste of this wonderful tobacco. Unfortunately for the tobacco chewing public, most folks never heard about Paul's tobacco blend, because it turns out that he fancied it so much that he just used all of those freight cars full of it himself.

One story goes that the drilling tool got stuck at the bottom of the hole on his cable rig well. Trying to pull it loose, Paul pulled so hard that he lifted the whole lease up out of the ground.

But Paul was not perfect. Even he hit a dry hole once in a while. When he did he would just pull up the hole and sell it to the farmers and ranchers for post holes for their fences.

On another well he had dug so deep that he hit a strike of rubber, which came gushing out of the ground, covered everything, and then cooled. When the rigger tried to descend from the top of the rig, he slipped and fell onto the rubber coated rig floor. When he hit the rubber, the man bounced high into the air and then back down again. It took Paul two days to finally catch the poor man as he bounced about.

On one well it is said that he struck a level of pure buttermilk. Drilling further he struck a layer of sweet wonderful cornbread. Drilling still further he hit a layer of fantastic turnip greens. At that point Paul quit drilling because the whole crew was so fat they weren't able to work anymore.

Kemp Morgan

According to legend, Kemp Morgan was a rotary well digger of incredible ability. Legends about his exploits began to circulate in the 1920s.

Kemp Morgan's senses were so keen that he could put in a perfectly straight well without having to use a plumb line. He could build a gigantic well rig in only half a day, not weeks like it took mere mortals.

Kemp once brought in a well when it was so cold that the oil froze as soon as it gushed out. Undaunted, Kemp just sawed it up in chunks, put it on flat cars, and sent it to market.

He put in one well that was over fifty thousand feet deep. The rig was so tall that he had to hire thirty men just so he could have one on duty at top. At all times there would be fourteen men going up, fourteen coming down, one on duty at the top, and another relaxing on the ground.

When this well came in, Kemp was paid a fortune, and he invested it in his own custom blend of chewing tobacco. He was planning on packaging it up and going into the tobacco business. But he had growed so fond of it hisself that he chewed hisself plumb out of the tobacco business.

Kemp Morgan possessed one ability that even Paul Bunyan didn't, he could smell oil. While no other person could detect anything in the air, Kemp could smell oil ten miles down. He purportedly made a good living out of charging folks for smelling out oil on their land.

Some stories even have both Paul Bunyan and Kemp Morgan working together. The story goes that Kemp had heard about Paul and had gone to the north woods to meet him. Upon his arrival at Paul's camp, he found him in great distress. Seems as though Paul's huge pocket watch had stopped, all crudded up and in desperate need of a good oiling.

Kemp then told Paul about the prettiest place on the whole earth, Texas. He also told Paul that Texas had more than enough oil to keep his watch running smoothly forever. And that's how Paul Bunyan came to be working in the Texas oil fields.

One story is that Paul and Kemp drilled a well plumb to China. At first it started spewing out a mountain of white stuff which they quickly identified as rice. Then the well started sputtering and bubbling. As they watched in amazement, the well then started spewing a fountain of chop suey, which quickly covered the mountains of rice.

On another time they brought in a well that produced nothing but Mexican blankets. And then, of course, there was their well that produced nothing but rubber.

Gib Morgan

Gib Morgan, no relation to Kemp Morgan, at first glance does not appear to belong in the same book with the likes of Paul Bunyan and Kemp Morgan. He was small in stature and never was particularly successful. And by all accounts, he was actually a pretty modest fellow. How he evolved into a folklore legend is the stuff of legends itself.

Gib was born in Clarion County, Pennsylvania, in 1842. It was a poor community, but his family did all right. Gib was bright and at an early age loved to hear the stories carried by the folks he met. At every opportunity he would start story swapping, perfecting his storytelling and learning new stories.

By the time he was seventeen he had moved to Emlenton, which is not far from Titusville, where Drake brought in the first oil well. The discovery of oil was bringing tremendous changes to the region as the oil rush began.

Gib was interested in the stories of the oil strike, but the Civil War was starting. He joined the Tenth Pennsylvania Volunteers shortly after Fort Sumter was fired upon. As a soldier, Gib was a pretty good storyteller. Although his outfit saw a good bit of action, he never rose above the rank of private. But it was duly noted by all that he was, by far, the best storyteller in the regiment, and he was often called upon to entertain the troops.

Returning home in June of 1864, he found the speculative oil boom in full swing. When he had left for the war, most of the farms in the county were barely getting by. Four years later many of the folks were rich off the land that had barely kept them fed for generations.

Gib joined in and became a driller. In 1868 he had learned his trade well and he married Mary Elizabeth Richey. But oil fields were rough places, and Mary always stayed at his father's home in Tionesta while Gib worked the rigs.

Four years later tragedy struck Gib's family when his beloved Mary died in 1872, shortly after giving birth to their third son, Warren. Gib was never the same after Mary died. He never could settle down and was constantly on the move for the next twenty years. His friends referred to him as "the gypsy driller." Mody Boatright's book about Gib is titled *The Minstrel of The Oil Fields*, a reference to the constantly wandering musical minstrels of old.

After years of roaming, Gib's health was failing. He was spending more and more time in hospitals for Civil War veterans. There are numerous stories about Gib's storytelling prowess. Often he would be found telling whoppers to groups sometimes numbering in the hundreds.

The Lie

A Gib Morgan Story

Amazingly though, Gib never lost his sense of humor and became renowned for his storytelling. One classic story was that a friend saw Gib coming down the street and said, "Gib, why don't you tell us a lie."

Gib shook his head, dabbed at his eyes, and said, "I wish I could boys, but I haven't got time to be tellin' you no lies. I just got word that my brother was killed in an accident out at the well."

The man that had stopped him was stunned. Regaining his composure, he extended his condolences to Gib. Then Gib took his leave and returned to the well.

Later that afternoon a group of folks came out from town to learn more about the accident that had killed Gib's brother and to offer any help that might be needed.

To their amazement, upon arriving at the well, they found Gib was tending the well with his brother as if nothing had happened.

Flustered by this, the town's folk demanded to know why he had said his brother was dead.

With a sly smile Gib said, "You asked me for a lie, didn't you?"

Fiji

A Gib Morgan Story

In his late years Gib had little money. To explain this, Gib told this story. He said he had been asked by the head of a large oil company to bring in a well on one of the Fiji islands. The oil company boss told Gib he would have to do a lot of politickin' with the local natives, because they weren't really fired up about having a well drilled.

Gib arrived and got the drilling started. Then the Grand Exalted Poo Bah from the local tribe asked him to come over for a party. And what a party it was. The locals had really rolled out the thatch welcome mat, and the party went on for more than a week.

Upon returning, Gib could hear the crew singing and shouting from over a mile away. Arriving at the site he found no drilling was going on, the boiler was cold, and the entire crew were falling-down-slobberin' drunk.

Gib finally got the story out of his merry band of drunks. He found that the day after he had left to visit the Grand Exalted Poo Bah, the crew had hit a gusher of champagne and had been drunk ever since.

Gib said, "We're not getting paid to pump champagne, we've got to hit oil." He then dropped casing into the well and sealed off the champagne well. After sobering up the crew, drilling began again.

Work was proceeding smoothly when word again arrived that the Grand Exalted Poo Bah wanted Gib to come to another party. The second party was even more fun than the first, and it was two weeks before he returned to the site.

Again the well rig was quiet, the boiler was cold, and all the men were sitting around fat and sleek. It seems that right after Gib left, they struck a gusher of pure rich cream and had been gulping it down ever since.

Gib pondered what he could do with a well pumping cream. The next day he left to go back to the states. He left instructions for the crew to pump the cream into the holding tanks.

Gib spent his last nickel buying an entire ice cream factory, including chillers, separators, mixers, and freezers. He was going to introduce ice cream to the Fiji Islands and make his fortune.

However, when he returned to the island, he found that his plans were ruined. The cream was no longer flowing from the well; it had gone dry. When he checked the tanks full of cream he found that they had all turned sour. So sitting somewhere on a Fiji Island, without a single cow within five hundred miles, is a rusting ice cream factory that represents every last penny of Gib Morgan's fortune.

Whickles

A Gib Morgan Story

Having lost his fortune but not his taste for liquor, Gib Morgan was always looking for someone to buy him a drink. If someone he was telling stories didn't volunteer, he would prod them into it by telling about the whickles.

Gib would explain that the whickles were oil-eating insects that were eating away the oil reserves. They were almost never seen because they are extremely quick and very shy, only coming out at night. He said that he had devoted the latter part of his life to trying to eradicate the whickles from the oil fields, for the benefit of everyone.

Gib explained that after years of experimentation, he had found that the best way to get rid of whickles was to sprinkle some form of alcohol, like whiskey or applejack, on them. The whickles would become drunk, and he would be able to catch them and kill them. He would then explain that this was the reason he was always buying liquor and was always broke.

Chapter Twenty

Some More Oil Stories

Drilling for oil is a crazy and hazardous business. It is very unpredictable, in large part because no two wells are ever the same. Geology, weather, the terrain, and often the types of equipment being used all vary from well to well.

I spent a lot of time in Calgary, Alberta, Canada, working on a computer system for a gas company. One of their drillers, Louis, commented that he planned on going over to the Medicine Hat leases and getting three wells drilled in the next week.

Stunned at the idea of putting three wells down in a week, I asked how that was possible.

Louis laughed, "Hell, boy, these ain't your deep Texas gas wells. Nope, we got gas right near the top. I tell you what, if you chase a fat woman in high heel shoes across any field in Medicine Hat, I bet you'll bring in at least three gas wells!"

Later Louis told me he had to drill many of the wells in the region during the winter months, because it was a marshy region, and winter, when the ground was frozen, was the only time they could get trucks in. They just drilled a well and ran a pipeline out to solid ground.

As we talked about the hazards of the business, he commented, "Then, of course, there are those damn bombs out on the north leases."

"Bombs? Is that an oil field term I'm not familiar with?"

"Aw hell no, I'm talking about fall-out-of-the-sky-blow-your-ass-up bombs."

"Louis, is Canada at war with somebody?"

"Not that I know of."

"Well then where in the hell are the bombs coming from?"

"Royal Canadian Air Force bombs."

"You're telling me the Royal Canadian Air Force is bombing your wells?"

"Yep."

"You're pullin' my leg."

"Nope."

"Why would they bomb your wells?"

"'Cause they can't shoot worth a damn!"

"OK, give. What's the story?"

"Well seems as though some of the geniuses in the home office approached the air force about putting some wells in on their base. The air force thought that would be OK, and it would bring in some extra money. Unfortunately, the only area that was a good producer was right next to the bombing range. So every now and again, one of them trainee flyboys blows one of our wells all to hell. A guy really has to keep his eyes peeled when he's workin' out there!"

To show just how creative these drillers have to be, here is a story from my friend Larry Lehman, a member of the gang at the Manchaca Firehall. Larry retired after many years in the oil business. He tells the story and swears that it's true.

Seems as though a well had blown out and was spewing oil all over the place. The good news was that there wasn't any fire. The bad news was that all of the conventional techniques for plugging the well had been tried, and still it spewed.

In desperation, they brought in bulldozers and dug out a ten-foot-deep, ten-foot-wide trench right next to the pipe casing at the well head. Then they brought in three eighteen-wheelers loaded with dry ice and packed it all right up against the well casing.

It worked. The dry ice cooled the casing down till it froze solid. Then, with the flow cut off, they were able to set a new valve and seal off the well. Now that is some very creative thinking!

Jim checks out some old rockin'-horses

Photo by Sally Gramon

Chapter Twenty-One

The Death of Willie Oats

As I mentioned earlier, my Aunt Lillie owned the Hopkins County Locker Plant in scenic Sulphur Springs. Some summers, when things were slow on Uncle James's ranch, I would work for her.

Willie Oats was pretty regular about droppin' in. Willie ran a smallish two-hundred-acre spread south of town. There he did a little farmin', a little ranchin', and whatever else he could do to raise a few bucks.

When he brought a few head in to be processed at the locker plant, we would often have a chance to sit and talk. Willie said he had spent most of his life rodeoin' and cowboyin' from Montana to Texas. One day, after picking up a few things out of his freezer locker, he was heading towards his old truck.

"Hey, Jim, how's it hangin'?"

"Good, Willie. You?"

"Oh it's OK I guess. By the by, did I ever tell about the time I drowned?"

"Nope, Willie, don't think you did. Frankly, Willie, I'd be pretty hard pressed to believe that one."

"Well nigh on to forty years ago, I was a herdin' about fifty head up in north Hopkins County. It was the rainy season, and the ground was already pretty soaked. And there I was a sloggin' through the mud and the muck, tryin to get that bunch of lop-horned knotheads back to pasture before it rained again.

"The water in the old river bed was still manageable low, so I started herdin' them across. Suddenly, I hears a rumblin' and then I looks up and here comes a five-foot-high wall of water tearin' down the river bed, a couple of hundred yards upstream."

"Wow, Willie, what did you do?"

"Well sir, I don't mind a tellin' ya, I was big-time worried. Yes sirree, I truly was. I turned my mare towards the highest ground I could spy, which happened to be a small island near the middle of the shallow part of the river."

"Geez, Willie, what happened?"

"Well, Jim, that wall of water swept over me, my horse, and about ten head of cattle that hadn't made it out of the river bed. Next thing I knowed, my mare and I was a tumblin' one over the other. Fight as I might, I couldn't get up to the surface. Then I passed out."

"Geez, Willie, what happened?"

"What do you mean?"

"Well what happened to you down in the water?"

"Oh that, well it was pretty sad. Yes sir, pretty damn sad. You see I just up and drowned."

"Wow, Willie, who pulled you out?"

"Nobody, I told you, I drowned."

"If you drowned Willie, you'd be dead."

"I am, but I came back."

"What do you mean you came back?" At this point I was developing some serious misgivings about Willie's mental health, a thought that had crossed my mind a time or two before.

"Well, when I died I did that heaven thing, you know, since I'm a good guy and all. And the Big Guy said he needed for me to go back down and take care of somethin for Him. Well, you know for sure that when the Big Guy asks you for a favor, you're gonna do it."

"And just what was it He asked you to do for him?"

"Strange that you ask, Jim, 'cause it had to do with you."

"It what? What do you mean it had to do with me?"

Willie rose from the fence rail where he was leaning and climbed into his old truck. He started it up and then, as he was pullin out, he leaned out the window and said, "Well, ya see, Jim, the Big Guy asked me to come back down here and teach you to not believe every story I tell ya!"

With that Willie drove off in a cloud of red Sulphur Springs dust. I could hear him laughing for a good block, as he looked in his rearview mirror to see me standing in the middle of the street, shaking a fist at him.

Chapter Twenty-Two

The Chicken Coop

his here's the story of a poor kid, done wrong by his family, 'cause of his pa's mistake. It's a sad tale, and I swear it's all kinda true.

Seems as though this young'un was not in school one day. So the next day, when he shows up, the teacher demands to know where he was (since he was a bit inclined towards playin' hooky). Well the boy presents a note from his pa, along with a plate of fried chicken. The note says he had needed the boy at home for the day, "for farm chores."

Now the teacher was gettin' a bit suspicious, 'cause it was smack dab in the middle of winter, and there really wasn't squat to do most of the time. The teacher began to suspect that the boy might have done a little forgin' on that note.

So she thanked him for the chicken and asked him, "What were you doing on the farm that took you a whole day to finish?"

"Well, ma'am, I can't really tell ya that."

"And why not."

"'Cause Pa said he'd whip my butt iffen I ever said a word about it to anybody."

Now the teacher was perplexed but more determined than ever to get to the truth of the matter.

She told the boy that she didn't believe him and that his pa was gonna hafta come in and talk to the teacher.

So the next mornin', here comes the pa and the boy. And they're both a lookin' guilty as sin, standin' there a studyin' their shoes.

Pa starts off by handin' the teacher another big plate of fried chicken. She thanks him and explains that she kinda suspicioned that the boy had done a bit of exaggeratin' on needin' the whole day off.

Pa said, "Oh no, ma'am, we truly did need the whole day, and then some."

Now she was concerned. "Was there an emergency?"

"Well, ma'am, there truly was."

"And what was it?"

"Well, you know it was frightful cold night before last. And we've been havin' a problem with a fox gettin' into the chicken coop. And you know that we've got one of the finest flocks of lay'n hens in the county."

"I do know that. But what does that have to do with your son missing school?"

"Well, t'other night I hear'd the chickens a set to cacklin', and I figured that ol' fox was out to lighten the flock by a couple of hens. And this is a fast fox. I've tried to blast him a coupla times and always get there too late."

"So, when I hear that first cackle, I jump outta bed and I grab Ol' Betsy. She's my fine ol' double-barreled twelve gauge shotgun. I cocked back both hammers, so I could get off a quick shot. And, quick like a rabbit, I headed for the chicken coop."

"Well, to tell it true, the damn fox had already skedaddled. But I didn't know that then. So I come a sneakin' up to the coop, with Ol' Betsy at the ready. And real quiet like, I open the door and poke Ol' Betsy in, whilst I'm tryin' to spot that varmint."

"Well, Teacher, I don't guess you ever had no call to know that I can't sleep with my skivvies on. So, I just sleep in the altogether. And I knew I had to move quick to get the varmint. So I just put on my boots and my hat. I'm a standin' there, a peekin' into the coop, in my hat and my boots, and here comes Ol' Blue; my fine bluetick huntin' dog has come out to investigate the goings on."

"But sir, what does all this have to do with your son missing school?"

"I'm a comin' to that. Anyhow, here comes Ol' Blue and sees me a peekin' into the coop with my shotgun at the ready. I truly did not know he was there. Anyways, I'm a peekin' and Blue walks right up, an' just big as Dallas, he goes an' sniffs me on my bare behind with that cold nose of his. Well, to tell ya true, it shocked me so bad I squeezed off both barrels of my shotgun into that chicken coop. So, the whole damn family spent the whole damn day cleanin' and pluckin' a whole damn mess of chickens!"

Pictures Too Good To Leave Out

The regular storytellers group convenes another meeting at my house. Clockwise, Jerry Heaney (back to camera), Heath Newburn, James Gramon, Jim Bartlett, Guido Bohac, and Jim

Photo by Ron Joseph

Same group, different angle, l-r, Ron Joseph, Jerry Heaney, Heath Newburn, Jim Bartlett, and John "Guido" Bohac

Al Lowman and Jim

Photo by Sally Gramon

Al Lowman's library

Photo by Jim Gramon

Caroline Dowell and Jim. She graciously allowed
me to use her beautiful ranch as a backdrop for
many of the photos.

Photo by Sally Gramon

THE END

Photo by Sally
Gramon

Storytelling and Folklore Festival Calendar

T his is a list of the events I am aware of, a bit of information about each, and some info on how to contact the organizers. If you know of an event that should be on this list, please email me at gramon@onr.com and I will spread the word. Caution: please note that this info has been collected from a wide variety of sources and specifics about these festivals do change. So please always contact them before you go.

January

EL PASO: Southwestern International Livestock Show & Rodeo

This annual event is fun for the whole family. Events include horse shows, western gala, cattle drive, team roping championship, chili cook-off; also, Junior Livestock Show and Auction, a media rodeo and a piglet roundup. Saddle up, partner! Location: El Paso County Coliseum. For information on prices and times, please call: (915) 532-1401.

February

HOUSTON: Annual World Championship Bar-B-Que Cook-Off

Come celebrate the first barbecue contest of the new millennium. Corporate and Go-Texas cook-off teams will feature the most creative in barbecue decor, with pits disguised as fire engines, covered wagons, airplanes, and waste disposal trucks, just to name a few. Live bands and other entertainment will be performing throughout the contest. Net proceeds benefit the Houston Livestock Show & Rodeo, an educational charity. This event is held in conjunction with the Houston Livestock Show & Rodeo. For more information, call (713) 791-9000, or go to www.hlsr.com.

HOUSTON: Houston Livestock Show and Rodeo

Big city, big rodeo. World's largest stock show; live country music performances by the genre's biggest stars, and top-notch PRCA rodeo action in the comfort of the famous Astrodome. Parade, carnival, and barbecue cook-off, too. For more information, call (713) 791-9000, or go to www.hlsr.com.

BROWNSVILLE: Charro Days

Celebrated with a four-day Latin Festival each year since 1938, complete with elaborate costuming, carnivals, parades, dances. A program of events is held in both Brownsville, in the Texas Gulf Coast Region, and its sister city, Matamoros, Mexico. This is a spectacular and colorful event with spectators and participants dressing up in traditional Mexican costume. Admission is free. For information call (956) 542-4245. This festival is held on the last Thursday in February.

TYLER: Squatty Pines Storytelling Festival

Retreat with us to the East Texas piney woods on the shores of beautiful Lake Tyler for three days of stories, music, workshops, hayrides, fishing, hiking, and more, all sponsored by the East Texas Storytellers. www.homestead.com/EastTexas Tellers.

MERCEDES: South Texas Music Festival

A three-day-long festival country, bluegrass, folk, western, religious, mariachi, tejano, Mexican hat dance, folkloric dancers and clogging held at the 130 acre Rio Grande Valley Show Grounds.
http://www.musicfst99.com/

ALPINE: The Annual Texas Cowboy Poetry Gathering

It will be held on the campus of Sul Ross State University in the mountains of Texas, in the Big Bend Country region. Poetry, music, storytelling, dancing, great food, and the Trappings of Texas are all a part of the second oldest cowboy gathering in the United States. As part of the gathering Trappings of Texas will open in the Museum of the Big Bend. This fine Western Art and Custom Cowboy Gear Exhibit is the oldest in the United States and features the best of the best saddle makers, braiders, silver engravers, artists, and more. Educational seminars on making gear and ranch history are all part of this exciting weekend. For more information call (915) 837-2326.
http://www.tourtexas.com/alpine.html

EL PASO: Siglo De Oro Drama Festival

Location: Chamizal National Memorial, 800 S. San Marcial, El Paso. In its 24th year, this festival celebrates the literature and linguistic ties still shared by Spain and the border region of Mexico and the United States. The festival brings the best amateur and professional groups to the Chamizal stage, presenting works of the Spanish masters, both in English and Spanish. Participants come from as far away as Puerto Rico, Spain, and Jerusalem. Call: (915) 532-7273, ext. 102.
http://www.tourtexas.com/elpaso/elpaso.html

March

DENTON: Tejas (Texas) Storytelling Festival
The festival is held in Denton's Civic Center Park.
www. tejasstorytelling.com

DALLAS: Annual North Texas Irish Festival
Location: Fair Park, Dallas, Texas. In early March this two-day festival provides top entertainers, nonstop music, and dance on multiple stages; North Texas Step Dancing Fiesta; storytellers; street performers; cultural events & exhibits; Irish food and beverages; vendors; Urchin Street Faire for the kids; parade of Celtic dogs; workshops and much more. Info: (214) 821-4174.
http://www.tourtexas.com/dallas/dallas.html

AUSTIN: Star of Texas Fair and Rodeo
Cost: $5 to park, $3 to enter gate. Rodeo tickets serve as a gate pass. Location: Travis County Exposition and Heritage Center, Austin, Texas. Region: Texas Hill Country. For info call (512) 467-9811. Held annually every March.

GLEN ROSE: North Texas Longhorn Show
Come and see Texas longhorns up close when top breeders of North Texas meet to display one of the oldest breeds of Texas cattle. Cost: free to public. Location: Expo Center, Hwy 67, Glen Rose, Texas. For more info call the Expo Center at (254) 897-4509.

GLEN ROSE: Snaketales
Learn about the myth and magic of these resplendent reptiles at a day of snake presentations by the Herp Society and other friends of snakes. Enjoy story telling, demonstrations, fun, and

facts...all for the snake's sake. Snake tales activities are included in your admission to Fossil Rim Wildlife Center. Cost: call for admission. Location: Hwy. 67, Glen Rose, Texas. Region: Texas Prairies and Lakes. For more info, call (254) 897-2960.

WINEDALE: Annual Winedale Spring Festival and Texas Crafts Exhibition

Features Texas contemporary craftspeople, as well as demonstrations of traditional crafts, music, dancing, and a barbecue. Winedale is near Round Top, Texas. Telephone (409) 278-3530.

DALLAS: Texaspride Celebration

Features recording artists, Mexican dancers, Comanche storyteller, Buffalo Soldiers, Texas Rangers, historical exhibits, and much more. Hall of State, Fair Park. (214) 426-1959 Prairies and Lakes.

FORT MCKAVETT: Annual Living History Day

Features infantry and cavalry drills by reenactors. Fort McKavett State Historic Park. (915) 396-2358 Hill Country.

CORPUS CHRISTI: Spring Round-Up Celebration of Ranching Heritage in Aransas County

Includes cowboy poetry and song, reenactments, food, and demonstrations. Also features a special ranching heritage exhibit at the Fulton Mansion. (361) 729-0386 Gulf Coast.

SAN FELIPE: Annual Colonial Texas Heritage Festival
Features reenactments, buffalo soldiers, crafts, food, and
historic tours. Stephen F. Austin State Historic Park.
(409) 885-3613 Prairies and Lakes.

GOLIAD: Annual Goliad Massacre Reenactment
Re-creation of the occupation of Fort Defiance by Col. Fannin
and the massacre, followed by a memorial service and pilgrimage to the Fannin Memorial. Presidio La Bahia. (361) 645-3563
South Texas Plains.

DENTON: Texas Storytelling Festival
Features storytellers from across the country; includes ghost
stories, bilingual, and children's concerts. Civic Center Park.
(940) 387-8336 or (972) 991-8871 Prairies and Lakes.

GLEN ROSE: Bluegrass Jamboree at Oakdale Park
Our Bluegrass Jamboree four-day program runs rain or shine.
Stage show starts at 6:15 p.m. on Thursday, with a planned program of bands, and runs until 12:15 p.m. Sunday. Informal jam
sessions are scattered throughout the park. For the early birds,
the pickin' and grinnin' starts the weekend before the show.
Come early and stay late. Cost: $11. Location: Oakdale Park,
Glen Rose, Texas. For more information, call Oakdale Park
(254) 897-2321.

April

GLEN ROSE: Larry Joe Taylor's Texas Music Festival
This year it is in Meridian, last year it was a three-day gather-
ing of 3,000 fans in Glen Rose, along the banks of the Brazos.
This collection of cookers, storytellers, and pickers featured a

chili cook-off, songwriters showcase, and lots of storytelling around the many campfires. http://www.larryjoetaylor.com/

SAN ANTONIO: Fiesta San Antonio

One of America's truly great festivals, Fiesta San Antonio is a ten-day celebration held every April to honor the memory of the heroes of the Alamo and the Battle of San Jacinto and to celebrate San Antonio's rich and diverse cultures. The Y2K Fiesta marked the 109th celebration!

One of the special parts of Fiesta is the multicultural conference. This year's conference will focus on the use of images by writers, photographers, artists, etc. to define a cultural and/or ethnic community. For more information, call 1-877-SAFIESTA (723-4378).
http://www.fiesta-sa.org/default2.asp

POTEET: Poteet Strawberry Festival

The Festival is recognized as the largest agricultural fete in Texas. The 95-acre site is located on Hwy. 16, 20 minutes south of San Antonio. The Festival includes ten areas of continuous family entertainment featuring concerts with nationally known country & western and tejano stars, dancers, gunslingers, clowns, puppets, regional bands, storytelling, various contests, and rodeo acts. Held annually during the second weekend in April. For info, call (830) 742-8144.

JOHNSON CITY: Cowboy Songs and Poetry

This annual gathering of cowboys at the Johnson Settlement presents lighter moments of the Old West. At the cabin where President Johnson's grandparents lived and ran a cattle business, modern cowboys meet to sing traditional songs, talk about the old days in poetry, and spin tales the equal of any which were told when the West was really wild. This is 1860s entertainment you can't afford to miss. Time: 1 p.m. to 4 p.m. Cost: free. Location: Lyndon B. Johnson National Historical Park, Johnson Settlement, Johnson City, Texas. Region: Texas Hill Country.

HARLINGEN: RioFest

Fair Park will host RioFest's 18th Annual Celebration of the Arts, a 21st-century Renaissance! RioFest has been voted the "Best Family Festival" in Cameron County for the past four years. RioFest is the premiere educational arts and cultural event of the Rio Grande Valley and Northern Mexico. As part of its air of festivity, the festival will provide a rich variety of performing arts, cultural arts, family and children's activities. RioFest is held in Harlingen's 40-acre Fair Park. For more information, call (956) 425-2705. Held in April, usually the second or third weekend, depending on Easter.

HUMBLE: Good Oil Days Festival 2000

Festival blending art and oil, entertainment and education, history and destiny into a three-day celebration. A 50-acre site will depict Humble's oil boomtown in the early 1900s offering a view of the oil and gas industry—its beginnings, its evolution, and its destiny in the new millennium. Educational displays, exhibits, 400+ vendors, a spectacular carnival, go-karts, live entertainment, auto shows, beer pavilion, fireworks, and fabulous food. Location: one mile east of Hwy. 59 on Will Clayton Blvd. For info, call (281) 446-2128. Held annually in April.

WAXAHACHIE: Scarborough Faire, Renaissance Festival

Scarborough Faire is one of the largest and most popular Renaissance festivals in the nation, complete with entertainment, crafts, food, drink, games, and fun! Join the festivities as hundreds of prominent entertainers perform, over 200 artisans display and demonstrate their craft, and food and beverage vendors offer a delicious variety of over 60 menu items fit for a king. For ticket information and directions refer to ScarboroughRenFest.com.

KERRVILLE: Annual Kerrville Easter Festival and Chili Classic

Saturday events include a walkathon for youth, cook-offs, 5K Easter Run, armadillo races, Easter egg hunt, chili judging, 4x4 bed post derby. Other events include washer pitching tournament and children's activities. Location: Schreiner College Campus, Hwy 27E, Kerrville, TX. For more information, call (830) 792-3535. Annual event held Easter weekend.

EULESS: Arbor Daze

For twelve years the City of Euless has sponsored this festival. Arbor Daze was selected as a White House millennium event, which receives special recognition from the president of the United States. Arbor Daze offers nightly musical entertainment from favorite oldies acts and has various opportunities during the day such as arts and crafts, business exposition, plant sale, tree giveaway, concerts, youth community stages, specialty foods, and much more. Arbor Daze was selected as the Best Festival in the Nation. Location: Bear Creek Parkway and Fuller Wiser Road. For info, call (817) 685-1821, or check out www.ci.euless.tx.us. Held annually the fourth weekend of April.

FREER: Freer Rattlesnake Round Up

Join us at the Freer Cactus Corral, Freer, Texas, for the biggest party in Texas featuring concerts with top artists. Fun for the whole family including carnival, parade, arts/crafts, stage shows, storytelling, daredevil snake show, fried rattlesnake meat, talent contest, and much more. For more info., please call (512) 394-6891. Held annually the last weekend of April.

May

KERRVILLE: Cowboy Artists of America Roundup

Annual "Art Stampede" show and sale. Cowboy Artists of America Museum. (830) 896-2553 Hill Country.

AUSTIN: Cinco de Mayo Festival: Lo Nuestro

This event is a celebration of Hispanic culture featuring live country, tejano, mariachi, and conjunto music. Food, arts and crafts, game booths, plus the Mighty Thomas Carnival will provide family fun for everyone. Event location: Fiesta Gardens, 2101 Bergman Ave., Austin, Texas, in the Texas Hill Country. For more information: (512) 867-1999.

GRANBURY: Annual Old-Fashioned Fair

Features pioneer demonstrations at the Hood County Senior Center. (817) 573-5548 (800) 950-2212 Prairies and Lakes.

LAREDO: 5th Annual Day Pow Wow Festival

Features arts and crafts, intertribal dancing, and more. Civic Center grounds. (956) 795-2080 South Texas Plains.

KERRVILLE: Kerrville Folk Festival

Since 1972 the Kerrville Folk Festival has been held annually at the Quiet Valley Ranch, 9 miles south of Kerrville on Texas Hwy 16. Starting on the Thursday before Memorial Day at the end of May, the music and good times go on for 18 days with performances by more than 100 artists such as Peter Yarrow and Butch Hancock. Interspersed between weekends are other events including workshops in songwriting and booking and management for touring artists.

The annual Kerrville New Folk songwriting competition is held on the first weekend and draws some of the best of America's emerging songwriters. Award winners are recognized at a special concert on the second weekend. Bring your tent or RV and join us for as long as you can stay. The campgrounds abound with songwriters' campfires, a favorite feature of the Kerrville Folk Festival since 1974. For information:

> The Kerrville Folk Festival
> PO Box 1466, Kerrville, TX 78029
> (830) 257-3600 Or e-mail: info@kerrville-music.com

FREDRICKSBURG: Founders Day Festival

Mark your calendar and set your sites on beautiful Fredericksburg, Texas, as the Gillespie County Historical Society presents its annual Founders Festival. This festival celebrates the founding of Fredericksburg, May 1846. Focus of the festival is on local artisans, musicians, and vendors. There will be everything from sheep shearing, stone spitting, blacksmithing, and corn grinding to children's games, lots of great music, food, beer, and wine. This event coordinates with the Indian Pow Wow also going on in Fredericksburg the same weekend. For more info, call (830) 997-2835 or e-mail gchs@ktc.com. Held annually on the second Saturday in May.

ATHENS: Uncle Fletch's Hamburger Cook-off and American Music Festival

According to research by the newspaper columnist and folk historian Frank X. Tolbert, the first hamburger was made by Fletcher Davis (known to Athenians as Uncle Fletch) at a cafe located on the square in downtown Athens. The people in

Athens are proud of their history and celebrate this great occasion the second Saturday of May with a hamburger cook-off, food vendors, exhibits, a children's area, local artists, a battle of the bands, and an antique car show for an entertaining day. For more information contact the Athens Chamber of Commerce at (903) 675-5181 or e-mail Athenscc@flash.net. Held annually the second Saturday of May.

PASADENA: Annual Pasadena Strawberry Festival
The Pasadena Strawberry Festival will celebrate its 27th annual event at the Pasadena Fairgrounds, in the Gulf Coast Region, with continuous live entertainment, strawberries, arts & crafts, children's games, carnival rides, enormous variety of foods, beauty pageants, specialty acts, commercial exhibits, barbecue cook-off, demonstrations by various craftsmen, the State Mud Volleyball Championship Tournament, the "World's Largest Strawberry Shortcake," and MUCH, MUCH, MORE!! Proceeds from the festival funds scholarships, books for college libraries, and community projects that preserve and promote the study of Texas history. For more information, visit http://www. tourtexas.com/pasadena/strawberryfest.html or call (281) 991-9500. Held the third weekend in May.

MARSHALL: Stagecoach Days Festival
Join us as we celebrate our history through home tours, parades, arts and crafts, and reenactments. For more information, call Phyllis Prince at (903) 935-7868, or visit http:// tourtexas.com/marshall/. Held annually the third weekend in May.

CEDAR PARK: Cedar Chopper Festival

The Cedar Chopper Festival is in its 24th year. The Festival is a one-day event held on the third Saturday of May. Included in this years events are: arts & crafts, three stages of music, storytelling, and performing arts from around Texas, cedar carving demonstrations, Boy Scout Jamboree, Austin Steam Train rides, many kids rides and events, classic cars and motorcycles, and a health fair. The Festival is alcohol free until 5 p.m. Beer sales begin at 5 p.m., with two bands playing blues and country until 12 midnight. For info call (512) 260-4260. Held annually the third Saturday in May.

MCKINNEY: Mayfair Art Festival

Join us on the Historic Downtown McKinney Square. Fabulous parade kicks off Mayfair, Sat. 10 a.m. Fine artists pavilion hosts artists from three states. Maypole dancing like you've never seen. ArtCars on exhibit, two stages of entertainment, storytelling festival, carnival, over 100 vendors, great food, petting zoo, train rides, ponies, great fun for the entire family centered around the fine shopping of downtown McKinney. Event details and discount lodging, (972) 562-6880. For more information (972) 562-6880. Held annually the third weekend in May.

KOUNTZE: Southern Gospel & Bluegrass Gospel Singing

Join the fun of singing the old Southern gospel songs as you remember your parents and grandparents singing. We will start at 4 p.m. and end much later. Spend Memorial Day weekend with us and let's have a great time. For more information, call (409) 246-2508.

June

SAN ANTONIO: Texas Folklife Festival

For nearly 30 years folks have gathered for the Texas Folklife Festival. The participants, who come from every corner of the state representing 43 cultural and ethnic groups, will share their traditional dances, ethnic dishes, music, stories, and handmade treasures, and exhibit products typical of the land from which their ancestors came.

The Festival is presented by the Institute of Texan Cultures as an extension of its role as a statewide educational center. For more Festival information, call (210) 458-2390. Or, check out their website at http://www.texancultures.utsa.edu/new/tff/tffpress.htm

LOCKHART: Chisholm Trail Roundup & Kiwanis Rodeo

For 28 years folks have enjoyed these four days of fun for the whole family. Activities include two nights of professional rodeo, live entertainment, dances, a Kid's Fishing Derby, interactive outdoor displays, horseshoes, washers, carnival, arts, crafts, and food. Don't miss the Old Time Fiddlers contest and the Barbecue Capital of Texas Championship Cook-Off and much more!

Info: Lockhart Chamber of Commerce at (512) 398-2818.
http://www.lockhart-tx.org/funstuff.html

ARLINGTON: Texas Scottish Festival & Highland Games

This is one of the largest ethnic festivals in North America. Featured are bagpipe bands, dining, storytelling, athletics, children's events, food and drink, vendors, and crafts. Entertainment is continuous in the largest pub tent in the U.S.A. The all-weather festival site will once again be Maverick Stadium on the University of Texas at Arlington campus. For more information, or for tickets, write to: Texas Scottish Festival & Highland Games: Post Office Box 151943, Arlington, Texas 76015 or e-mail: TxScotFest@aol.com

AMARILLO: Cowboy Roundup USA

12th annual celebration of cowboy and western heritage featuring the World Championship Chuck Wagon Roundup and the Coors Ranch Rodeo. Kicks off with a cattle drive up downtown Amarillo's main street. Location: Tri-State Fairgrounds. For more information, call the Amarillo Convention & Visitor Council at (806) 374-1497. Held annually the second week of June.

STANTON: Old Sorehead Trade Days

Located halfway between Fort Worth and El Paso on I-20, in the Texas Prairies & Lakes Region. Laid-back family atmosphere with entertainment, arts and crafts (400 vendors), antiques, historic tours, tradin' lot. Largest trade show in West Texas draws a crowd of 20,000. Free admission. For more information, call (915) 756-2006.

FORT WORTH: Juneteenth Celebration

This annual festival kicks off with a parade in downtown Fort Worth and day-long activities downtown, near the Fort Worth/Tarrant County Convention Center. For more information, call: 1-800-433-5747.

LULING: Watermelon Thump

Watermelon! It's fun. It's delicious. Some great storytellers always gather for this one. And it says, "Summer!" like nothing else. Thousands enjoy this three-day outdoor festival honoring the nutritious, auspicious watermelon. Featuring a carnival, kiddie rides, arts & crafts, champion melon judging and auction, world champion seed spitting contest, rodeo, parade, car rallye, melon eating contest, and more! Downtown Luling. For more information, call (830) 875-3214.

EL PASO/JUAREZ: International Mariachi Festival

El Paso Convention & Performing Arts Center, One Civic Center Plaza (downtown). This year, the International Mariachi Festival celebrates its fourth year in existence. The event is designed to capture the true identity of the Hispanic heritage and to promote mutual respect and understanding between cultures. The three-day event features mariachi groups, headline entertainment from Mexico, and excellent food and drink. It concludes with a Mariachi Mass. Call for times and admission: (915) 566-4066.

PECOS: Night in Old Pecos/Cantaloupe Festival

A one-day event which takes place in the late evening hours from 6 p.m. till midnight. The streets are blocked off, and there is a wide range of activities including a street dance with live music and a variety of vendors. Time: 6 p.m. to 1 a.m. Cost: FREE. Location: downtown Pecos. For more info., call (915) 445-2406. Held annually the last Saturday of June.

July

Tejas Storytellers Summer Conference
www.tejasstorytelling.com

STAMFORD: Texas Cowboy Reunion

The classic events of the rodeo, including some unique to the TCR (wild cow milking, wild mare race), get underway nightly at the beautiful SMS ranch with the West Texas sunset playing backdrop to the authentic, rustic arena.

Ranchers, cowboys, and those interested in western preservation return each year to the TCR Poetry Gathering to celebrate the history of the world's largest amateur rodeo and the unique qualities of the American cowboy.

Over the past years many of the cowboy poets who were just beginning to present their work publicly have gone on to become well known nationally for their work.

Poets, writers, and musicians from across Texas travel to Stamford each year with a new poem or song that preserves the days when cowboys rode in from the ranches to a reunion with their friends that began in 1930. During this portion of the TCR, eight to ten of the most dedicated poets and musicians in Texas leave their audiences with a sense of pride in the "cowboy way."

All of the material presented at the gathering must be authentic western verse presented by poets in authentic western attire. For information:

> Texas Cowboy Reunion
> P.O. Box 928
> Stamford, Texas 79553
> (915) 773-3614
> http://www.tcrrodeo.com/index.htm

SULPHUR SPRINGS: Independence Day Symphony on the Square

Join us on the Square in downtown Sulphur Springs for a celebration in old-fashioned style, a program of marches and patriotic favorites by the North East Texas Symphony Orchestra. When darkness falls the sky erupts in a blaze of colors as fireworks light up the sky over the historic Hopkins County Courthouse. Annual: weekend of or just prior to Independence

Day. Admission free; bring your lawn chair! For more info: (888) 300-6623.

LEVELLAND: Early Settlers Festival

Nearly 40 years old, the Early Settlers Day Festival draws some 15,000 people to celebrate country, bluegrass, and tejano music performances, old settler activities, more than 50 food booths, games, horseshoes, activities for kids, and a parade that lasts an hour or more. This year folks will "Do the Drag" on Friday evening before in cars representing our history. Sponsored by the Levelland Area Chamber of Commerce. Location: Downtown Square, Avenue H. For more info call (806) 894-3157. Held annually the Saturday after July 4th.

McDADE: McDade Watermelon Festival

This year McDade, Texas, will be celebrating its 52nd Annual McDade Watermelon Festival. The community has approximately 300 residents and is located on Hwy. 290 east, 10 miles east of Elgin, Texas, and 30 miles east of Austin, Texas, in the Texas Hill Country. Held annually every July.

EL PASO: VIVA! El Paso!

Experience four centuries of history in the picturesque outdoor McKelligan Canyon Amphitheater. In the top seven best attended outdoor dramas in the country, VIVA!'s legendary performances detail 400 years of native American, Spanish, Mexican, and Western American peoples through traditional dance, original song, brilliant costumes, and stunning special effects. "If you go for no other reason, go to enjoy the superb costumes and choreography. It's simply dazzling." *Southern Living*, March 1999. Location: McKelligan Canyon Amphitheater, El Paso. Region: Texas Big Bend Country. For more information, call (915) 565-6900. Outdoor musical performed annually from first weekend in June through August.

CLUTE: Great Texas Mosquito Festival

Held the last weekend in July, this festival pays tribute to the Texas mosquito! Features include a mosquito legs lookalike contest, a mosquito calling contest, sharing of Texas mosquito stories, and any number of excuses for a good time. (409) 265-8392. http://www.brazosport.cc.tx.us/~sbcvcb/Festivals.html

UVALDE: Sahawe Indian Dancer's Summer Ceremonials

The Sahawe Indian Dancers, members of Boy Scout Troop and Venture Crew 181 from Uvalde, annually present their summer ceremonials the last part of July. The fast moving colorful dances of the Plains and Southwest Pueblo Indians are set against a backdrop of teepees to set the mood for the performance. The 90-minute performances feature 16 to 18 different dances that have thrilled audiences for almost 50 years. Location: Sahawe Outdoor Theater, 1 block S. US 90. For more information, call (830) 278-2016. Held annually last weekend of July.

MEDINA: Texas International Apple Festival

Texas International Apple Festival in Medina, the Apple Capital of Texas, on Highway 16 on the banks of the Medina River in a pecan orchard. Great entertainment, arts & crafts, food booths, clowns, children's area with a petting zoo. We will have the San Antonio Chorale Society to sing, Jubilee Banjo Band, Gospel Stage, Fiddlers Contest, Story Telling Stage, Children's Stage called the Johnny Appleseed Stage. For more info. call (830) 589-7224 or e-mail mtdc@indian-creek.net. Held annually the last weekend in July.

August

DALHART: **XIT Rodeo and Reunion, Rita Blanca Park**
A PRCA rodeo and a reunion for cowboys, most from the XIT
Ranch, which at one time was the largest ranch in Texas. Activities also include storytelling, dances, pony-express races, and
parades. http://www.dalhart.org/xitrodeo.html

ROANOKE: **Hawkwood Medieval Fantasy Faire**
Re-creation of a fictitious medieval village based around the
turn of the first millennium (1000 AD). 100+ permanent shops;
ten stages with continuous entertainment; hundreds of village
characters and entertainers. Real stunt show! storytelling,
music, dance, combat, comedy, drama, horse shows, games. We
have both bawdy shows for the adults and play areas for the
kids! All in the shade of a beautiful, old-growth oak woods, with
nearly 100% coverage. Location: Southeast corner of I-35W &
SH 114, 20 miles north of Ft. Worth. For more information, call
1-800-782-3629. Held annually, weekends mid-August through
the end of September.

August-September

WEST: **Westfest**
A Czech folk festival with traditional storytelling, street dances,
costumes, and foods. http://www.westfest.com/westfest.html

September

ARANSAS PASS: **Official Shrimporee of Texas**
Great food (shrimp cooked in over 15 ways), continuous live
entertainment (tejano, country & western, rock, and more).
Over 150 arts and crafts booths, shrimp eating contest,

carnival, parade, men's sexy legs contest, culinary tent including cooking demonstrations, children's entertainment, and much more. Location: Aransas Pass Community Park, Highway 361 and Johnson Ave. Region: Texas Gulf Coast. For more information, call 1-800-633-3028. Annual event generally held the second weekend in September.

ANAHUAC: Texas Gatorfest

Held in Anahuac, the alligator capital of Texas, this truly unique festival combines the alligator, family, and good old-fashioned Texas two-stepping fun. A celebration of the alligator and its wetlands habitat, this festival has something for everyone. From the Great Texas Alligator Roundup, where alligator hunters from all over the state bring in their harvest to adult carnival and kiddie rides, arts and crafts, Texas artisans, and even airboat rides. Two stages of continuous entertainment along with street performers combined with over 25 food and drink booths serving a variety of fare including alligator prepared in an assortment of ways make for a bargain in family entertainment. Texas GATORFEST is located 45 miles east of Houston and 45 miles west of Beaumont, exit #810 off I-10 and travel 8 miles south on FM 563 to Fort Anahuac Park. For more information, call (409) 267-4190. Held annually the weekend following the opening of alligator season on September 10.

DALLAS: State Fair of Texas

Started in 1886, this event has something for everyone, fair, football game, exhibits, livestock show, and a great glimpse at Texas. Enjoy 24 days of nonstop food, fun, and entertainment. The State Fair is located in Fair Park, Dallas (about 2 miles east of downtown). For more information, call (214) 565-9931, or visit the State Fair of Texas homepage: www.bigtex.com or http://www.texfair.com/

BANDERA: **All American Cowboy Get-Together**

Come to Bandera—the Cowboy Capital of the World—and relive the Old West. Cowboy entertainers, poets, storytellers, chuck wagon cooks, and western vendors come together to create a true Old West experience. West Quest millennium trail ride and parade on Saturday morning. Cowboy Holy Eucharist on Sunday. Rodeo on Saturday evening. Location: Mansfield Park (3 miles north of Bandera on Hwy. 16). For more information call (830) 796-3045 or (800) 364-3833. Held annually Saturday and Sunday of Labor Day weekend.

October

FREDERICKSBURG: **Oktoberfest**

Three big musical stages, 22 great German bands, 55 unique craft booths, and 18 tempting food vendors will greet visitors to the famous Oktoberfest this fall in Fredericksburg. Traditionally held the first weekend in October, this year's event gets underway on Marktplatz in downtown Fredericksburg. Music, food, and fun are the heart of this irresistible festival that celebrates Fredericksburg's German heritage. Oktoberfest is one event where the food and drink command center stage. Pureyors on the grounds will offer German pretzels, Opa's sausage on-a-stick, fajitas, burgers, shiskabobs, nachos, kraut, and the largest variety of beer (domestic and imported) of any festival in the area. Location: Downtown Market Square, Fredericksburg. For more info, call (830) 997-4810. Held annually the first weekend in October.

TEMPLE: **Early Day Tractor and Engine Association Annual Show**

The festival takes place on a 48-acre fairground near IH-35 in Temple. Watch as hundreds of antique tractors, engines, and farming implements demonstrate early day farming activities—from grain threshing to corn shelling, rope making, and water pumping. Enjoy delicious homemade ice cream, barbecue, and beans. Become a member and enjoy swapping parts or yarns and restore a piece of your heritage. Bring the whole family! Location: Exit 302 west on Nugent, right on Eberhardt. For more info, call (254) 774-9988 or (254) 298-5720. Held annually the first full weekend in October.

REFUGIO: Refugio's Festival of the Flags

Join us for a two-day festival celebrating our Native American culture on the downtown streets of Refugio. Enjoy a Native American pow wow, storytelling, demonstrations, art and craft booths, food booths, children's area, musical entertainment, volleyball and horseshoe tournament, and historic homes tour (Sunday only for tour). No carnival or alcohol. Located in the Texas Gulf Coast Region. For more info call (512) 526-2835.

ATHENS: Black-Eyed Pea Fall Harvest

Events from the cook-off to the Miss Black-Eyed Pea Pageant, Miss Athens Pageant, and Little Miss Black-Eyed Pea Pageant. Gospel music, arts and crafts, square dancing, games for young and old, horseshoe tournament, a carnival, lots of food everywhere. Participation sports include a jaunt, bass tournament, terrapin races, pea eatin', pea shellin', watermelon eatin', a pet show, and entertainment at the bandstand. Plus a lot more coming. Region: Texas Prairies and Lakes. For more information, contact the Athens Chamber of Commerce at (903) 675-5181 or 1-800-755-7878.

KERRVILLE: Kerr County Fair

Activities include chili and barbecue cook-off teams, stage entertainment featuring storytellers, bands, and performers, various contests including ugly hat and lovely legs, shoebox parade, pig scramble and goat milking, bull and barrel fest, team roping, petting zoo, carnival and midway, cowboy church, 5-K run, talent contest, judged exhibits of crafts and skills, 75+ vendors selling wares and providing demonstrations, good food and plenty of beverages, judged livestock, scholarship pageant, classic car show, and a country auction. Located at the Hill Country Youth Exhibit Center on Hwy. 27 East adjoining the Guadalupe River, 60 miles northwest of San Antonio on IH-10. For more info, call (830) 257-6833. Held annually the second weekend in October.

MARSHALL: Fire Ant Festival

Our Fire Ant Festival is on the wild and wacky side, with its rubber chicken chunking contest, fire ant calling (are you getting the feel for this one?), and other zany activities. Region: Texas Piney Woods. For information, call Phyllis Prince at (903) 935-7868, or visit http://tourtexas.com/marshall. Held annually the second weekend in October.

GREENVILLE: Cotton Jubilee

This annual festival salutes cotton, the fiber that weaves together our local history, and is a great weekend getaway filled with a variety of exciting events and activities for the entire family. Enjoy the arts & crafts show, business expo, health fair, Civil War encampment, cotton exhibits, children activities and entertainment, bike rally, bed races, bingo, static displays, kids product show, 42 domino tournament, and live entertainment. Saturday's special events include a German Fest hosted by Knights of Columbus. Food and drink concessions will be available all weekend. Free admission. Location: American Cotton Museum, located on the north frontage road, off I-30, between exits 94 and 95. For more information contact The Greenville

Chamber at (903) 455-1510, visit http://www.greenville-chamber.org, or e-mail: jubilee@greenville-chamber.org. Held annually the third weekend in October.

PALESTINE: Hot Pepper Festival

It's the hottest little festival in Texas. Starts the day off with a parade and ends with a street dance. In between enjoy arts and crafts and food booths, children's activities, classic car show, entertainment on three stages, quilt show, Macho Man pepper eating contest, chili cook-off, salsa contest, Tour de Pepper bike tour, and a whole lot more. For more information, 1-800-659-3484. Held annually on the fourth Saturday in October.

FREDERICKSBURG: Fredericksburg Food & Wine Fest

A celebration of Texas food and wine. The Fredericksburg Food & Wine Fest is in its 9th year. A full-course celebration of Texas food, wine, music, arts & crafts, food court, and fun is expected. Musical entertainment includes polka, jazz, blues, ethnic, and German oompah! Don't miss the grape stomping, cork tossing, and other games that are also on the agenda, including the great grape toss and a fabulous auction. Location: Downtown Fredericksburg, on Market Square. For more information, call (830) 997-8515.

NEW BRAUNFELS: Wurstfest

Bring the entire family to Wurstfest because there's food and entertainment to suit every taste! Enjoy sausage and strudel, pretzels and potato pancakes served up by fun loving folks; polka and waltz to good ol'-fashioned oompah music performed by Myron Floren, Jimmy Sturr, Alpenfest, The Seven Dutchmen, and more entertainment groups. See native attire like lederhosen and dirndls worn by friendly Texans who are proud of their German heritage. Region: Texas Hill Country. Admission $6. For more information, call 1-800-221-4369.

November

GEORGE WEST: George West Storyfest

The Storytelling Capital of Texas. This festival features cowboy poetry/music/storytelling. It is held at the Live Oak County Fairgrounds. www.georgewest.org/storyfest.htm

Tellabration

An annual event where storytelling takes place the world over at the same time. Tellabration is traditionally held on the Saturday night before Thanksgiving. (Some events may be at an alternate time during the same weekend.) This last year there were nine Texas events in Austin, Houston, Burnet, Frankston, San Antonio, and Grapevine. To learn more about the whens and wheres, check out members.aol.com/tellabrate.

National Storytelling Week

(NSW) is a long-range plan under development by the Program Committee of the National Storytelling Network (NSN) Board of Directors. Their goal is to promote NSW, which became part of the USA's official calendar last year, in conjunction with Tellabration.

TERLINGUA: Terlingua Annual Championship Chili Cook-off

Held the first Saturday in November, the history is a little complicated. It started out as one festival in the late sixties and has broken up into several festivals. You can get the whole story by looking up http://www.bigbendquarterly.com/terlingua.htm. Whichever one you attend, you will have plenty of good chili and fun listening to some of Texas's best storytellers and chili cooks.

> http://www.chili.org/terlingua.html
> http://www.chili.org/chili.html
> http://www.iitexas.com/gpages/terlinga.htm

(Author's Caution: Good advice for any Texas chili cook-off; Never, never, ever try any of the chili without having a cool drink handy, no matter how much the cook assures you it's not hot!!! Most are wonderful, but I guarantee, no matter how tough your mouth is, some of them will light you up!)

CRYSTAL CITY: Spinach Festival

This South Texas Plains town provides free live music all three days. Parade on Saturday. Carnival all three days. All kinds of food booths, variety booths. Softball tournament, car show, 5K run, walk-a-thon, basketball tournament. For more information call (830) 374-3161 ask for Mary. Cost: free. Location: downtown Crystal City. Held annually the second week in November.

HENDERSON: Heritage Syrup Festival

Held in the Texas Piney Woods region, this festival features ribbon cane syrup making, folk artist demonstrations, arts and crafts, music, food, and lots of fun. Location: syrup making & folk artists at Depot Museum, arts/crafts fair downtown Henderson. For more information, call (903) 657-4303. Held annually on the second Saturday in November.

December

STONEWALL: Christmas Tree Lighting and Evening Tours of the LBJ Ranch

Join members of the Johnson family and enjoy festive choir music and light a beautiful tree to usher in the Christmas season. Then hop on a tour bus to see the Sauer-Beckman Farm, all decked out for a German Christmas, circa 1915. The tour continues through the LBJ Ranch for lighting displays around the historic buildings where Lyndon Johnson was born, attended school, and had his Texas White House. Location: event begins at LBJ State Historical Park, one mile east of Stonewall. For more information, call (830) 644-2420.

Hill Country Regional Christmas Lighting Trail, thru January 1—Blanco, Bulverde, Burnet, Dripping Springs, Fredericksburg, Goldthwaite, Johnson City, Llano, Marble Falls, Mason, Round Mountain

Beginning Thanksgiving weekend, millions of lights will make miles of memories for families who follow the Hill Country's elaborate Regional Christmas Lighting Trail this holiday season. Eleven towns are set to dazzle visitors with breathtaking holiday extravaganzas between Thanksgiving and New Year's. Each of these charming and unique communities extends a heartfelt invitation to everyone to come view their wonderful seasonal displays. Santa parades, Christmas tree lightings, carriage rides, shopping, festivals, worship services, food, dances, and chorus concerts. Each community has something special to offer. For a free brochure with a complete listing of each of the eleven communities events, write or call: Regional Christmas Headquarters, 703 N Llano, Fredericksburg, TX 78624: (830) 997-8515. Most activities are free to the pubic. For more information, call (830) 997-8515.

Storytelling Groups and Websites

I've never heard of a webliography, but I needed a word that describes what this section is.

Austin Writers' League. This web site hosts a wide variety of activities that can help aspiring or experienced storytellers improve their skills and meet others with common interests. http://www.eden.com/~awl/

Bureau of Land Management, Wild Horse and Burro Program. This web site contains a number of references to publications dealing with horses and burros in the west. www.blm.gov/whb

Dyanne Fry Cortez. *Hot Jams & Cold Showers*, Scenes from the Kerrville Folk Festival. A neat book by a neat lady I just recently had the pleasure of meeting. It's about what it's like to attend this wonderful festival over the years. Printed by Dos Puertas Publishing, 2000. http://www.dospuertas.com/

Cultural Crossroads, Regional & Historical Perspectives. This is an interesting web site that provides short stories and links into a variety of interesting directions. www.geocities.com/~lostdutchman/roads.html

Dallas Storytelling Guild. The home page of the Dallas Storytelling Guild, telling web users about storytelling in general and about their guild, members, and activities in particular. http://www.geocities.com/SoHo/Study/1578/

The Digital Storytelling Festival. Held in September, in Crested Butte, Colorado, to encourage thought, exchange ideas, and to ignite sparks for the creative application of digital technology and the internet to the art of storytelling with a focus on art and innovation, education, and marketing and branding opportunities. It is an intimate gathering in a scenic remote location that inspires our audience to leave with new connections and a better understanding of how the oldest art form of storytelling is moving into the new millennium. www.dstory.com/dsf5/home.html

East Texas Storytellers. A group of storytellers and listeners who meet monthly for story sharing. We are an affiliate guild of Tejas Storytelling Association. We strive to provide a supportive network for tellers in our area. We help produce the Squatty Pines Storytelling Festival, a very special three days held on the shores of Lake Tyler, near Tyler, Texas. www.homestead.com/EastTexasTellers

Folklife Sourcebook. A Directory of Folklife Resources in the United States. lcweb.loc.gov/folklife/source/sourcebk.html

The Handbook Of Texas Online. Provided as a joint effort of the Texas State Historical Society and the University of Texas. I heartily recommend it as an excellent resource on many aspects of Texas. www.tsha.utexas.edu/handbook/online/articles/view/

Houston Storytellers Guild. Box 131644, Houston, Texas 77219-1644

Houston Storytelling Circles :

Northeast Circle, Second Tuesday Storytelling Circle
http://users.aol.com/drroff/SecondTuesday/html
Meeting dates: second Tuesday of each month
Time: 7:00 P.M.
Site: Jacinto City Library, Jacinto City, Texas
For more info contact James H. Ford Jr. at
11811 I-10 East, Suite 185A, Houston, Texas 77029,
or call (713) 455-1707 or e-mail drroff@aol.com

1960 Area Storytelling Circle. Box 131644, Houston, Texas
77219-1644, (713) 523-3289 Maryanne Miller (contact)

Bay Area Storytelling Circle. Box 131644, Houston, Texas
77219-1644, (713) 523-3289 Charlotte Byrn (contact)

Ft. Bend Storytelling Circle. Box 131644, Houston, Texas
77219-1644, (713) 523-3289 Tom Burger (contact)

The Institute of Texan Cultures at the University of Texas at
San Antonio. http://www.utsa.edu/

International Folk Culture Center. San Antonio, Texas, has
information and links dealing with folklore, folk dances,
and folk music. http://www.n-link.com/~ifccsa/

Kinky Friedman's Websites. Get the real skinny about what
Kinky is up to. Find out all the latest about where he will
be appearing, new books and CDs.
http://www.kinkyfriedman.com/
http://www.kinkajourecords.com/

La Pena, Latino Arts in Austin. La Peña is a community-based
organization dedicated to the preservation, development,
and promotion of Latino artistic expression in all its forms.
The board of directors and staff of La Peña believe that
cultural expression and knowledge is crucial to the sur-
vival of the community. www.hyperweb.com/LaPena

Lone Star Spirits. A web site devoted to things related to the
supernatural and paranormal in Texas. This includes a section on tales relating to those topics.
http://www.lonestarspirits.org/

Main (The Metropolitan Austin Interactive Network). This
interesting site regularly has folklore and storytelling
related events on it's calendar. MAIN is a nonprofit organization whose mission is to establish and operate efficiently
a community-access computer network. The purpose of
this network is information sharing and communication
among the people and governmental, educational, commercial, cultural, religious, and civic organizations, in order to
enhance lives and make the best use of community
resources. If you are a noncommercial organization, MAIN
will! www.main.org

The National Storytellers Network (NSN). Also known as
StoryNet is the web site for the National Storytelling
Association, described below.
www.storynet.org/index2.htm

The National Storytelling Association. The largest organization
of its kind in the United States, it has been probably the
greatest single influence on the revival of storytelling as a
professional art form. It offers a great many benefits for
members and nonmembers interested in storytelling.
www.storynet.org/index2.htm

The Rio Grande Folklore Archive. Situated in the University of
Texas-Pan American Library, is one of the largest collections of Mexican American folklore. It is the major
depository for the folklore of the Lower Rio Grande Valley
of Texas and Northern Tamaulipas, Mexico. This archive's
holdings include over 99,000 items that represent the
major genres of folklore. Data for the Rio Grande Folklore

Archive is collected on the basis of genre-specific collection forms. For example, "The Folktale Collection Form" is specifically designed to collect folktales. Demographic and contextual information is also collected for all genres of folklore. www.panam.edu/dept/folklore/

StoryNet. Also known as the National Storytellers Network (NSN), is the web site for the National Storytelling Association, described above. www.storynet.org/index2.htm

Storytell. An information source sponsored by the School of Library and Information Studies at Texas Woman's University in Denton, Texas, is a forum for discussion about storytelling. All persons interested in storytelling are invited to participate: It can serve as a source for information on conferences, workshops, and events or a place to ask (and answer) questions about derivations of stories, intellectual freedom concerns, or organization of storytelling events.

The Storytelling Ring. A series of web sites that include a wide variety of storytelling areas. www.tiac.net/users/papajoe/ring.htm

The Storytelling Round Table. Sponsored by the Texas Library Association to promote an appreciation of the art and tradition of storytelling, particularly its uses in the library setting; exposes TLA members to storytelling through education and performance; and encourages TLA members to share stories and storytelling. www.txla.org/groups/story/storyrt.html

Tejas Storytellers Association. Their mission is to foster the appreciation of storytelling as an oral tradition and a performing art. Their goal is to influence the values of the citizens of our region by promoting and supporting the art,

craft, and history of storytelling so as to ensure the contin-
uation of the tradition. www.tejasstorytelling.com

Texas Folklife Resources website. This site maintains links to
a variety of folklore links. www.main.org/tfr/links.htm

Texas State Government Information website. This is another
official state site. Information here focuses on doing business, traveling, and which government agencies perform
which functions, and how to contact them. There is also
info about all of the state symbols.
http://www.texas.gov/TEXAS_homepage.html

Texas State Official website. This site is the central site for
the state. One area of particular interest is the Texas Information, including a Texas History area, as well as
information on the Census, courthouses, state symbols,
legends, and landmarks. http://www.state.tx.us/

Texas Travel - @Texas. This is a great web site, offering valuable information about a wide variety of destinations and
attractions taking place in the Lone Star State. This site is
jointly sponsored by the Texas Festivals & Events Association, Texas Travel Industry Association, and @ction
Travel Group. http://www.tourtexas.com/

@round Texas—Clicking on this icon will take you to a section of this site that is quite handy for locating upcoming
events. It offers three different ways to search their data-
base of events. You can search by date, by geographic
region, or by the type of event.
http://www.tourtexas.com/@roundtexas.html

Texas State Historical Association. Organized on March 2,
1897, the Texas State Historical Association is the oldest
learned society in the state. Its mission is to foster the
appreciation, understanding, and teaching of the rich and

unique history of Texas and by example and through programs and activities encourage and promote research,
preservation, and publication of historical material affecting
the state of Texas. www.tsha.utexas.edu/

University of Texas Friends of the Library Calendar of Events.
This site lists a number of events throughout Texas, many
of which relate to folklore and storytelling.
www.lib.utexas.edu/About/friends/friends.calendar.html

Utopia Animal Rescue Ranch. Founded by a group headed by
Kinky Friedman, this organization cares for neglected and
deserted animals. Annually Kinky and his friends put on a
"Boneifit" to help fund the ranch's activities (normally in
March). Be sure and watch this site to see who will be
appearing. And be sure to donate to this very worthy
group. www.utopiarescue.com

VirtualTexan.com. This is a site devoted to the state of Texas.
It is sponsored by the *Fort Worth Star-Telegram* and occasionally has Texas storytelling related items.
www.virtualtexan.com

George West Storyfest. Held in the Storytelling Capital of
Texas. http://www.georgewest.org/storyfest.htm

Bibliography

Adams, Florene Chapman. *Hopkins County and Our Heritage.* Sulphur Springs, Texas: 1974.

Abernethy, Francis Edward. *J. Frank Dobie* (Vol. I of the Southwest Writers Series). Austin: Steck Vaughan Company.

Austin American-Statesman, April 10, 1990. Michael C. Burton, *John Henry Faulk: The Making of a Liberated Mind.* Austin: Eakin Press, 1993.

Bedicek, Roy. *Adventures with a Texas Naturalist.* Austin: University of Texas Press, 1947.

Boatright, Mody. *Folk Laughter on the American Frontier.* New York, The Macmillan Company, 1949.

_____. *Folklore of the Oil Industry.* Dallas: Southern Methodist University Press, 1963.

Bode, Winston. *J. Frank Dobie: A Portrait of Pancho.* Austin: Pemberton Press, 1965.

Brewer, J. Mason. *The Word on the Brazos: Negro Preacher Tales from the Brazos Bottoms of Texas.* University of Texas Press, Austin, 1953.

_____. *Aunt Dicy Tales: Snuff Dipping Tales of the Texas Negro.* University of Texas Press, Austin, 1956.

_____. *Dog Ghosts and Other Negro Tales.* University of Texas Press, Austin, 1958.

_____. *Worser Days and Better Times: The Folklore of the North Carolina Negro.* Quadrangle Books, Chicago, 1965.

Byrd, James W. *J. Mason Brewer: Negro Folklorist*. Austin: Steck-Vaugh, 1967. Who's Who in America, 39th ed.

Cannon, Bill. *A Treasury of Texas Humor*. Plano: Republic of Texas Press, 2000.

_____. *A Treasury of Texas Trivia*. Plano: Republic of Texas Press, 1999.

_____. *A Treasury of Texas Trivia II*. Plano: Republic of Texas Press, 2000.

Caro, Robert. *Path to Power*. New York: Vintage Books, 1983.

Carpenter, Liz. *Getting Better All The Time*. Texas A&M University Press, 1993.

Chariton, Wallace O. *Texas Wit & Wisdom*. Plano: Republic of Texas Press, 1990.

Cortez, Dyanne Fry. *Hot Jams & Cold Showers: Scenes from the Kerrville Folk Festival*. Dos Puertas Publishing, 2000. http://www.dospuertas.com/

Dobie, J. Frank. *Apache Gold and Yaqui Silver*. Boston: Little, Brown, 1939.

_____. *Coronado's Children*. Austin: The University of Texas Press, 1978.

_____. *The Longhorns*. Boston: Little, Brown, 1941.

_____. *The Mustangs*. Boston: Little, Brown, 1952.

_____. *Rattlesnakes*. Boston: Little, Brown, 1965.

_____. *Some Part of Myself*. Edited by Bertha McKee Dobie. Boston: Little, Brown, 1980.

_____. *Tales of Old Time Texas*. Boston: Little, Brown, 1955.

_____. *A Texan in England*. Boston: Little, Brown. 1945.

_____. *Tongues of the Monte.* Garden City, New York: Doubleday, Doran, 1935.

_____. *Some Part of Myself.* Boston: Little, Brown & Co., 1967.

Dugger, Ronnie (editor). *Three Men in Texas.* Austin: University of Texas Press, 1967.

_____. "Dobie, Bedichek, Webb: Workers in the Culture," *The Texas Observer* 19 Aug. 1983: 18.

John Henry Faulk Papers, Barker Texas History Center, University of Texas at Austin. Andie Tucher, ed.

Fehrenbach, T. R. *Lone Star: A History of Texas and Texans.* New York: American Legacy Press, 1983.

Frantz, Joe. "The Forty Acre Follies." *The Third Coast*, Dec. 1983: 100.

Friedman, Richard "Kinky." *Greenwich Killing Time.* (hardcover, Beech Publishing, 1986), (paperback, Berkley Press, 1987).

_____. *A Case of Lone Star.* (hardcover, Beech Publishing, 1987), (paperback, Berkley Press, 1988).

_____. *When the Cat's Away.* (hardcover, Beech Publishing, 1988), (paperback, Berkley Press, 1989).

_____. *Frequent Flyer.* (hardcover, William Morrow Publishing, 1989), (paperback, Berkley Press, 1990).

_____. *Musical Chairs.* (hardcover, William Morrow Publishing, 1991).

_____. *The Kinky Friedman Crime Club* (a compilation). (hardcover, Faber and Faber Publishing, 1993).

_____. *Elvis, Jesus and Coca-Cola.* (hardcover, Simon and Schuster Publishing, 1993), (paperback, Bantam Books, 1996).

_____. *Three Complete Mysteries.* (a compilation). (hardcover, Wings Books, 1993).

_____. *More Kinky Friedman.* (a compilation). (hardcover, Faber and Faber, 1993).

_____. *Armadillos & Old Lace.* (hardcover, Simon and Schuster Publishing, 1994), (paperback, Bantam Books, 1995).

_____. *God Bless John Wayne.* (hardcover, Faber and Faber, 1995), (paperback, Bantam Books, 1996).

_____. *The Love Song of J. Edgar Hoover.* (hardcover, Simon and Schuster Publishing, 1996), (paperback, Ballantine Books, 1997).

_____. *Road Kill.* (hardcover, Simon and Schuster Publishing, 1997), (paperback, Ballantine Books, 1998).

_____. *Blast From the Past.* (hardcover, Simon and Schuster Publishing, 1998).

_____. *Spanking Watson.* (hardcover, Simon and Schuster Publishing, 1998).

Germann, John J. and Myron Janzen. *Texas Post Offices by County* (1986).

Green, Ben King Papers, Jenkins Garrett Collection, University of Texas at Arlington.

Green, Ben King. *Horse Tradin'.* New York: Alfred A. Knopf, Inc., 1967.

_____. *Wild Cow Tales.* New York: Alfred A. Knopf, Inc., 1969.

_____. *The Village Horse Doctor.* New York: Alfred A. Knopf, Inc., 1971.

_____. *Some More Horse Tradin'.* New York: Alfred A. Knopf, Inc., 1972.

Handbook of Texas: A Supplement. Vol. 3. Austin: Texas State Historical Association, 1976.

The Handbook of Texas Online. I heartily recommend it as an excellent resource on many aspects of Texas.

Henderson, Tim. *Sweeping Up Dreams, Lyrics As Poetry.* Sun Country Publications, 1996.

McLeRoy, Sherrie S. *First in the Lone Star State, a Texas Brag Book.* Plano: Republic of Texas Press, 1997.

McMurtry, Larry. *In a Narrow Grave.* (The chapter "Southwestern Literature?") Austin: Encino Press, 1968.

Miller, Doris L. *At Least 1836 Things You Ought To Know About Texas, But Probably Don't.* Plano: Republic of Texas Press, 1995.

Mitchell, Mark. *The Mustang Professor.* Austin: Eakin Press, 1993.

Moyers, Bill. *A World of Ideas II: Public Opinions from Private Citizens.* New York: Doubleday, 1990.

Orren, C. G. *The History of Hopkins County* (M.A. thesis, East Texas State Teachers College, 1938). *Texas Magazine*, February 1911.

Patman, Wright. *History of Post Offices-First Congressional District of Texas* (Texarkana, TX, 1946?).

Porterfield, Billy. "Dobie's Roots Helped Texas Writers Blossom," *The Austin American-Statesman*, Sep. 1990: B1.

Posey, Ellis. *The Funny Side of Texas.* Plano: Republic of Texas Press, 1995.

Powell, Lawrence. *Books in My Baggage.* (The chapter "Mr. Southwest.") Cleveland: World, 1960.

Pryor, Richard "Cactus." *Playback*. Austin: University of Texas Press, 1995.

_____. *Cactus Pryor: Inside Texas*. Austin: Shoal Creek Publishing, 1982.

Ragsdale, Kenneth B. *Quicksilver: Terlingua and the Chisos Mining Company*. College Station: Texas A&M University Press, 1976.

Sederwall, Steve. *Puncher Pie and Cowboy Lies*. Plano: Republic of Texas Press, 1999.

Texas Almanac, Millennium Edition. The Dallas Morning News, 1999.

Tinkle, Lonnie. *An American Original: The Life of J. Frank Dobie*. Boston: Little, Brown, 1978.

Vertical Files, Barker Texas History Center, University of Texas at Austin.

Woolley, Bryan. *Mythic Texas*. Plano: Republic of Texas Press, 2000.

Author

Jim lives at Rancho Gramon, in the Village of San Leanna, Texas, with his wife Sally, their son James, and a couple of head of wild critters.

Previously published works have included songs, poetry, articles, and a book on computer fraud and some really boring stuff about down and dirty, bits and bytes computer programming. (He says everyone should have one, as a sleep aid!)

Volume II of *Famous Texas Folklorists and Their Stories* is already in the works, because there was just too much good material to distill down into one book. It will include great stories by and about legendary storytellers Walter Prescott Webb and Roy Bedichek.

Jim is currently completing the manuscript on a techno-thriller, complete with computer fraud, murders, espionage, terrorists, and a good old Texas boy trying to solve the mysteries.

Jim hosts a weekly Internet/radio show called "The Liar's Table" on www.TexasChannel.com. He also reviews books about Texas for *Roadhouse Magazine* and TexasChannel.com.

Index